PREVIOUS PRAISE
FOR KAREN DUDLEY

THE RED HERON

Karen Dudley's first mystery with an ecological twist, Hoot
to Kill, *got her nominated for [an] Arthur Ellis Award.
This one ... is better.*
—Globe and Mail

MACAWS OF DEATH

*Her story strides along at a brisk pace and she injects a
healthy dollop of sauce in her humour.*
—Winnipeg Free Press

OTHER
ROBYN DEVARA MYSTERIES

THE RED HERON

Devara's adventures continue in *The Red Heron,* this
time in the small town of Holbrook, where a
contiminated industrial site, a fragile wetland,
sabotage and snipers complicate an already diffucult
job. But fears over poisons in the ground and hints
of long-buried secrets in town take a bizarre turn
when a missing garden gnome shows up alongside
a brutally murdered man—an environmentalist
with family connections to the site.

MACAWS OF DEATH

Tropical birds in a smuggled suitcase. Expensive.
Beautiful. Dead. But for field biologist Robyn
Devara, this latest grim reminder of the illegal trade
in endangered species includes an unexpected
surprise—one of the birds is unknown to science. Hot
on the train of the mysterious Macaw, Robyn finds
herself stationed at an isolated field camp in the Costa
Rican jungle. It's certainly an exciting change from
routine paperwork. Exciting, that is, until
communication with the outside world is cut off,
deadly snakes start slithering into cabins, and
members of the field team begin to die . . .

HOOT TO KILL

A Robyn Devara Mystery
by Karen Dudley

Karen Dudley

RaveN
STONE

Hoot to Kill
copyright © Karen Dudley 1998

Ravenstone
an imprint of Turnstone Press
607-100 Arthur Street
Artspace Building
Winnipeg, MB
R3B 1H3 Canada
www.TurnstonePress.com

Turnstone Press gratefully acknowledges the assistance of the Canada
Council for the Arts, the Manitoba Arts Council and the Government of
Canada through the Book Publishing Industry Development Program
and the Government of Manitoba through the Department of Culture,
Heritage and Tourism, Arts Branch, for our publishing activities.

  Canada

Cover design: Doowah Design
Interior design: Sharon Caseburg
Printed and bound in Canada by Kromar Printing Ltd.
for Turnstone Press.
First edition: 1998
First mass market edition: 2003

National Library of Canada Cataloguing in Publication Data
Dudley, Karen.

Hoot to kill : a Robyn Devara mystery / by Karen Dudley.
ISBN 0-88801-291-8

I. Title.
PS8557.U279H66 2003   C813'.54   C2003-910843-0
PR9199.3.D8315H66 2003

For Michael
in memory of The Turb

ACKNOWLEDGEMENTS

For help in researching this book, many thanks go to John McLaughlin and John Henigman, who were invaluable sources of information about forest health and silviculture practices; biologist Susan Holroyd for information about environmental consulting; and the staff at the Calgary Public Library for information about almost everything else. Any errors are mine alone. A big thank you and a box of doughnuts for Manuela Dias and Patrick Gunter at Turnstone Press; also my great copyeditor, Marilyn Morton, who saved me from an overabundance of adverbs and a couple of real howlers. Thanks to Kaye Due, Janice Parker, Janet Wells, and Alanna Vernon for their helpful comments and suggestions; Gael Blackhall for making my zoo work possible; and Carolyn Walton for "promising." Thanks must also go to my parents: my mom, who has plugged my book so often to family, friends, business associates, and total strangers that it seems as if she has embarked on a second career in marketing; and my dad, who let me abuse his photocopying budget most horribly and to whom I probably owe my first-born royalty check.

I am also grateful to my writing buddies (a.k.a. cats) for keeping me company when the words did not come and reminding me to get up and stretch once in a while when they did. And finally, heartfelt thanks and a big smooch to my husband Michael who believed in me, read and reread the manuscript *ad nauseum*, and corrected all my misplaced, commas.

HOOT TO KILL

CHAPTER 1

A wise man once observed that a field biologist's greatest danger lies not in encountering fierce animals or treacherous terrain, but in finding comfort and being reduced by it. Quite frankly, at this particular moment, I was willing to take that chance.

I was in the remote forest of Marten Valley, British Columbia, on what bird-watchers call an owl prowl. Except I wasn't prowling for just any owls, I was looking for one kind in particular—spotted owls. Chocolate-colored, dotted all over with white splotches, they were smallish, unassuming little birds. They were also endangered.

So far, my recent spate of luck was holding steady. I had a head cold as thick as a coastal fog, and I hadn't laid eyes on a single owl—spotted or otherwise. The ungrateful birds hadn't even uttered so much as a hoot all night long. It was a nice clear night too: moon shining, no wind—perfect for owling. Or so you'd think.

I'd soaked my jeans slithering across sodden, moss-shrouded logs. I'd pushed through close clusters of young hemlocks, which had promptly dumped the heavy, wet contents of their branches on my head. I'd stood patiently, feet sinking slowly in icy, black mud, playing and replaying spotted owl calls.

Nothing.

I'd even run through the whole tape, playing all the different owl calls. Saw-whet, pygmy, spotted, barred, great horned—I'd played them all. Still nothing.

Stupid owls. Didn't they know they were being surveyed? Not even the great horneds were calling tonight.

"Okay, you guys," I wheezed, "you've got one more chance. I'm going over to the next clearing...." My voice crackled and broke. I coughed cautiously, afraid I'd bring up my lungs.

"C'mon, give me a break," I pleaded. "Tell me I didn't come out here for nothing."

Silence rang in my ears. Or maybe it was the two Aspirin I'd taken an hour ago.

My head was pounding out an enthusiastic polka by the time I'd struggled and huffed my way to the next clearing. I've always hated polka music. Despite the smoldering warmth of my fever, I felt chilled through. The salesman had told me my new parka would keep me warm in minus forty degrees. It wasn't even minus ten. Stupid parka salesman.

Then it happened. A flicker of movement over to my right. I swung my head around just in time to catch a glimpse of a small, pale form sailing between the trees and disappearing into the brush.

"All right!" I exclaimed softly to myself, chills and stuffed head momentarily forgotten. It *must* be an owl. No other bird would be moving around at this hour. And the last call I'd played had been a spotted owl. Maybe a spotted owl heard the call. Maybe it had come to check it out. My heart started revving with excitement.

Just another example of my luck that the bird had flushed into the densest part of the forest. I was going to need both hands to get through that brush. I dumped the tape deck on a rotting stump and hustled off in pursuit.

A short while later, I was wishing for three or four hands. Not to mention infrared vision. My eyes were feeling the strain of trying to burn through the darkness, while trees with sharp twigs seemed to be going out of their way to smack me in the face.

I had stopped to untangle my scarf from a snag when I saw it again. A ghostly form against the inky feathers of a cedar. An owl?

I crept a little closer. As the pale blob came into focus, I blew out my breath in a sigh. No such luck. Just a clump of snow caught on a bough. Trying not to feel too disappointed, I tightened my scarf under my chin, took another careful look around, and pushed my way deeper into the forest.

A few more snow-clump owls later, I was starting to get a little cross about the whole thing. As my excitement ebbed, my flu symptoms began to frolic. What the hell was I doing out here anyhow? The way I was feeling, I wouldn't see an owl if it flew over and pooped on my head, and besides . . .

Whump!

Stunned, I lay on the patch of ice that had tripped me up, gasping and trying to catch my breath. I knew exactly what to do with it once I caught it. . . .

"Shit!" I managed to croak. I'd fallen on my back and knocked the wind right out of myself. To make matters worse, a sharp stick was doing its best to save me eighty dollars at a body-piercing boutique. I rolled onto my side away from the stick and heard a tearing noise. Coming from my new parka, of course. I waited for a few seconds, certain the owl would fly over and poop on me now, but the gods must have had their fun for the day or else they'd gone off to screw up some other sucker.

By the time I'd finished going through my repertoire of R-rated words, I'd hauled myself up and had a look around the forest. Dark, damp, and nary a hint of movement. I shook my head in disgust, though whether at myself, the slippery terrain, the elusive owl, or the fun-loving gods even I couldn't say for sure. Maybe I hadn't seen an owl after all. Maybe I'd imagined the whole thing. I definitely had a fever brewing, and didn't people with fevers sometimes hallucinate?

Go back to the motel, my little voice of reason piped up. Have a bath. Go to bed.

It was a persuasive little bugger, I thought. Fine time for it to make an appearance, though. I should never have come out tonight in the first place. I looked again at the empty forest. "Better late than never," I mumbled to myself before turning and retracing my footprints back to the tape deck.

Where I promptly discovered that when I'd set it down on the stump, I'd accidentally pressed the record button.

"Ah, hell!" I exploded. "Damn it all anyway!" I had erased quite a bit of the tape. Of course, it was the part with the spotted owl calls.

"Okay, owls," I snarled, shaking my mittened fist at empty, indifferent trees. "That's it! I've had enough! We'll try this another night. You guys better come through for me next time. You hear me? You owe me big!" The word "big" came out in a cracked squeak several octaves higher than my usual tone. Now I was starting to lose my voice. Great.

The outburst only made my headache feel worse and the rest of me feel childish. Comfort—with all its attendant dangers—was looking better all the time.

I'd parked the car by a sign marked "Seidlin Lumber Mill." In this remote area, the large, yellow sign was one of the few man-made landmarks around. It was also a good half-hour's walk away—back through thick bushes, wet trees, and cold, slippery moss. I heaved a deep sigh, wallowing for a moment in self-pity, then tucked the player under my arm and trudged wearily back to the car.

Forty minutes later, I tossed my tape deck and the ruined tape into the back seat. The drab, brown rental car was cold and uninviting, but at least it wasn't damp. Even more appealing, however, was the thermos of tea I'd had the foresight to leave in it.

Ahhh, hot tea. Spicy and fragrant, it burbled cheerfully as I poured it into the plastic cup. The honeyed drink flooded my mouth, trickling down to caress my raw throat. Truly, it was the elixir of life. And had I . . . ? Yes, there was my old, plaid blanket under the back seat. I'd thrown it into the car as an afterthought. Complimenting myself on my prudence (maybe my luck was finally changing), I dragged its comforting woolliness to the front seat and enveloped myself in soft warmth.

I tried telling myself that it really wasn't that cold. I should have saved my breath; I didn't listen to myself. In my home province of Alberta, winter temperatures routinely plummeted to minus thirty or below. So cold that even teenagers put on hats. Logically I *knew* the climate in this coastal province was milder, but in reality, it was so damp here the cold seemed to seep right into one's bones, settling in like an unwanted guest.

Maybe those owls weren't so bad after all, I reflected from the snug shelter of my plaid cocoon. If they'd been calling tonight, I wouldn't have been finished for hours yet. Now, at least, I could listen to my voice of reason, go back to my tiny room at the Rest EZ Inn, take a hot bath, and go to bed. The survey could wait till tomorrow. I yawned and slurped down the rest of my tea. Yeah, good old owls.

As I drove off, visions of steaming water and plump feather pillows danced seductively before my reddened eyes. Distracted by their performance, I hardly registered the battered blue pickup truck parked about fifty yards away. It was off the road, tilted at an angle and partially hidden by drooping bushes. When I did finally remember the truck, it was far too late.

CHAPTER 2

I woke Friday morning, headachy, crusty-eyed, and confused. I lay in bed for a long time, face mashed into the pillow, as questions drifted in and out of my mind. Where exactly was I? Why wasn't Guido the cat snuggled up to my back? Why did I feel so horrible? Were civilian construction crews really on the second Death Star when the rebel forces blew it up?

As consciousness imposed itself more insistently on my brain, it all started coming back to me. I was in Marten Valley to look for spotted owls. Guido the cat was back home in Calgary under the excellent (in his feline opinion, barely adequate) care of my brother Jack. And I felt like an old rat turd because I had a cold. A nasty one. I waited a moment longer, but there were no divine revelations on the Death Star question. I guess you can't have everything.

Oriented now, I cracked my eyes open and squinted around the room. Judging from the light that peeped through the weave in the curtains, the day was gray and overcast. A good day to snooze away the hours. I rolled over and burrowed under the covers.

Unfortunately, my brain didn't agree with my assessment of the day. Clouded and confused though they were, my thoughts refused to nod off. Instead they were nodding in the direction of Marten Valley.

Nestled amongst British Columbia's luxurious forests, Marten Valley was a logging town—an old-growth logging town, which in the minds of some environmentalists was the same as Sodom and Gomorrah all rolled into one. I wasn't that extreme; in my line of work you couldn't afford to be quite so judgmental, and, after all, people had to survive. But when greed wins out over survival and respect for other life forms gives way to the idea that you have the god-given right to domination over the "lesser" creatures, well, that's when I start to have problems.

This was not to say that Marten Valley's loggers were greedy pillagers. I hadn't been in town long enough to form an opinion one way or another, but I strongly suspected they would simply turn out to be regular people, trying to make a living in a difficult world. Unfortunately, the cold, hard truth of the matter was, although I liked most of the loggers I'd met over the years, when threatened, they could be like any cornered creature. And surveying for endangered species in the Marten Valley forest certainly had all the earmarks of a threat. I planned on being in and out before any whisper of my activities reached the general populace.

Restlessly I rolled over again and tried thumping my pillow into submission. It didn't help.

I was supposed to have a guide and contact in town, one Jaime Cardinal. Apparently, he'd sighted a spotted owl here last month. He was the only person in Marten Valley who knew about it—a fact for which I was exceedingly grateful. I did not want to be involved in a situation like Washington State again.

I muttered to myself and kicked the blankets off, then

snatched them up again as the cool motel air brought goosebumps jumping to attention. But I couldn't put off the inevitable forever. I needed to contact Jaime Cardinal, and I should also touch base with the office. I spoke severely to my goosebumps and threw the blankets off.

Creaking and groaning, I heaved myself out of bed, staggered into the bathroom, and flicked on the light. The fluorescent glare was excruciating.

Scrunching my face up, I caught sight of myself in the mirror. "Ahhh!" I croaked, appalled. "The real reason I'm still single."

The image staring back at me had hair and eyes the deep coppery color of fine sherry—a fact that had, at first, greatly puzzled my dark-haired, blue-eyed parents. A helpful neighbor pointed out that the mailman was a handsome redhead with warm brown eyes, but my parents simply laughed at the suggestion and explained away my unusual coloring as an aberration of nature. Regardless of the reasons, it was normally an attractive combination—one that had earned me many compliments. Right now, I wouldn't win a beauty contest against a warthog.

In the overly bright (and extremely unkind) light, my face looked puffy and splotched. Like some weird, poisonous fungi, I finally decided. My Bristol Cream eyes were bright with fever, and, sometime during the night, auburn curls had decided to pull a Medusa. I shuddered.

Never a sucker for punishment, I turned out the light, and washed my face in the dark.

"Good morning. Woodrow Consultants."

"Hi, it's Robyn. Could I speak to Kaye, please?"

"Robitt?" The voice on the phone was slow and confused. I must sound worse than I'd thought.

"No, Robyn," I repeated. "My name's Robyn Devara. I work there."

"Robitt Deva . . . Oh! Robyn!" the voice exclaimed with divine revelation, then giggled.

I winced. Another temp.

"Just a moment please and I'll get Kaye."

"Thanks."

I played idly with the phone cord, wondering how many people named Robitt ever phoned.

"Kaye speaking."

"Hey, Kaye, who's the new temp?"

There was a shocked pause, and then, "Is that you, Robyn? You sound terrible, dear! Is everything all right?"

"I'm fine," I assured her. "I got here safe and relatively sound. But I caught a stinker of a cold somewhere along the way."

Stinker indeed. I hadn't been this sick since fourth grade when I'd done a Harry Bailey into the not-quite-frozen pond behind our house. I could have lived without the reminder.

"I'm afraid this is going to delay things for a day or two," I continued. As if on cue, I was wracked with a fit of coughing that left me gasping.

Kaye seemed torn between concern and amusement. Concern won. Now I knew I sounded worse than I'd thought.

"Don't even *think* about going out like that," she ordered. "A day or two isn't going to make any difference. You need to take care of yourself—you know, chicken soup, plenty of fluids, that kind of thing."

I chuckled weakly. "Yes, mom."

"Don't you 'yes mom' me either. Do you need anything? Have you managed to get in touch with Jaime yet?"

"No and no. I'm okay for supplies, but Jaime's not answering his phone. He didn't skip town, did he?"

"No, no, he's there, but I'm afraid he's had an accident. Dave called just after you left. It seems Jaime's broken his leg rather badly."

I grimaced. Things were not shaping up well. "What happened?" I asked.

"Just a stupid accident, really. He slipped on a patch of black ice and fell the wrong way. Not that there's a *right* way to fall, but you know what I mean. I'm afraid he won't be up to surveying anytime soon."

"Okay," I said finally, trying not to sound too disappointed. "I guess tromping through the forest on crutches is above and beyond the call of duty. Can he at least tell me where he saw the owl?"

"Oh yes, apparently he's got some detailed maps of the area and he can show you exactly where he was. I'd give him a couple of days before you phone him, though. His leg was broken in three places and he sprained his opposite ankle."

I winced in sympathy. "Ouch."

"Yes, indeed. Hmmm.... Hang on a minute, Robyn."

She was back quickly. "Listen, dear," she said with the air of someone who has solved a knotty problem. "Kelt's in BC for his sister's wedding. He's due back to work on Monday, but I could send him up to give you a hand—"

"Uh, that's not really necessary, Kaye," I broke in hastily. "I'm sure I'll be up and about by then."

"Yes, I know, dear, but we do need to get this survey done quickly. Ben's still wrestling with the final recommendations for that Mitsui development plan—I'll be so glad when he's finally done. Honestly, I can't remember the last time he was this grouchy!"

I grinned. "You always say that."

Benjamin Woodrow was normally a gentle bear of a man, kind-hearted and soft-spoken. But whenever he worked on a development plan, he was more like a bear fresh from a long winter's nap and far from a berry patch. Professionally, he knew that sustainable development meant a compromise between business and wilderness. Personally, he felt the planet would be a lot better off if the entire human race were quietly obliterated.

"I know, I know," Kaye was saying. "I just wish he wouldn't take everything so damn personally. Ah, don't get me started on that now! Where was I? Oh yes, Kelt finished up his part of the report before he left. I don't know if he's much on birds, but I'm sure he'd be a fast learner. To tell you the truth, I haven't anything pressing for him to do right now. And you sound like you could use all the help you can get."

"You're right." I admitted defeat gracefully. Kaye always got her way eventually; I might as well save myself the argument. Besides, with Jaime now out of the picture, I really could use some help. I had a fairly large area to cover. "It would be nice to have another pair of feet," I told her.

"Good, we're settled then. I'll call him right away and make the arrangements. You take care, and phone if you need anything."

After Kaye rang off, I collapsed against the pillows. I felt like Indiana Jones confronted with a pit of snakes. "Kelt," I groaned. "Why does it have to be *Kelt?*"

Kaye and Ben were great bosses and good friends too. But ever since I'd moved to Calgary to join their team, they had been oh-so-discreetly introducing me to nice, single young men.

I'd always been a bit of a loner, even as a kid. While other girls played with Barbies, I caught tadpoles in the woods behind our house. While those same girls were giggling and dreaming of *Teen Beat* idols, I had been collecting species for my bird list. My parents didn't quite know what to do with such an odd daughter, but fortunately for me, Mr. Vickers, my sixth-grade science teacher, had been both understanding and encouraging. He often took our class out on long, rambling nature walks, slogging through field and forest in his bell-bottom jeans and platform shoes. I remember thinking his drooping ginger mustache looked exactly like the furry caterpillars we collected to bring back to the class for study. It was Mr. Vickers who really nourished my love of nature and who taught me that science skates the edge of the unknown.

My parents tried to fit me into the mold of ideal daughter. I was enrolled in piano and flute lessons; I took tennis and gymnastics, but, the fact of the matter was, I was happier mucking about in woods and creeks than I was doing anything else.

But identifying fungi and naming all the bones in the human body are not considered appropriate topics of conversation at cocktail parties, and pulling the guts out of dead frogs doesn't really prepare you for the intricacies of romantic entanglements. At thirty-three, I'd had a few relationships, but with one exception they'd all been short-lived and quickly and thankfully forgotten.

I appreciated Kaye and Ben's kindness in introducing me to their male friends, they never pushed anything, and I had developed some lasting friendships. Just nobody *special*. At least, not until Kelt Roberson had joined the firm two months ago. Trouble was, he didn't seem to have a clue about my attraction to him (let alone any similar sentiments). And, as a fellow biologist, he'd pulled enough guts out of his own share of dead frogs, so I couldn't impress him with that. It was just my luck that Kaye would decide to send him to Marten Valley—especially when I looked like a toxic saprophyte.

Probably another one of Kaye's attempts at matchmaking, I mused, then instantly dismissed the thought. No, in all fairness, I knew the British Columbia Wilderness Association was in a hurry for my results.

The Marten Valley Timber Supply Area, or TSA, was part of a huge section of land leased to the logging giant Seidlin Lumber. The Wilderness Association had already had a few nasty run-ins with Seidlin over clear-cutting and forest preservation. Until recently, the association's legal position had been about as stable as a muddy bluff. Concepts like "intrinsic value" and "stewardship of the land" always seemed to take a back seat to jobs and economic growth.

But the winds of change had blown in a month ago when a member of the BCWA, Jaime Cardinal, saw a spotted owl in the Marten Valley old-growth forest. The association's board members had immediately decided to hire outside expertise to verify the claim and strengthen their legal position. That's why I was here. If I could prove that endangered owls were living in the Marten Valley TSA, then the Wilderness Association would have the means to get at least some of the forest protected.

And that, in itself, I decided, was worth dealing with Kelt. I crawled back into bed and pulled the covers over my head. My last conscious thought was a sincere prayer that Kelt's family lived a long, long way from Marten Valley.

After a lengthy nap followed by a scalding shower, I decided to venture out into the town in search of Aspirin, chicken soup, and a bag that I could put over my head in case Kelt showed up anytime soon.

The Rest EZ Inn was just off Main Street, a few blocks away from the local drugstore which was, in turn, a few blocks from the grocery store. In fact, everything in Marten Valley seemed to be just a few blocks away from everything else. A nice, cozy town—quite different from the sprawling suburbs of Calgary.

There were two main roads, built extra wide to accommodate the logging trucks. Neat rows of Sitka spruce decorated the narrower residential streets. Lawns were heavily manicured, boasting blushing, snow-covered flamingoes and miniature scarlet-roofed windmills. Chubby garden gnomes chewed their plastic pipes and smiled knowingly among the bushes. In a different frame of mind, I might have described the town as quaint. In a different frame of mind.

I blinked painfully in the weak sunshine and made my way down Main Street. The largest structure was Seidlin Lumber's head office. Dwarfing even the town's administration building, Seidlin's offices stretched over two blocks and towered five floors above the community. Tasteful woodwork graced the exterior, imparting a rustic look to the building. A large, woodcut sign hung above massive oak doors:

Seidlin Lumber
Since 1956

A line of minivans and pickup trucks was parked along the road. I squinted sore eyes to read the cheerfully colored bumper stickers and then wished I hadn't.

"Loggers Are An Endangered Species"

"Save a Logger, Shoot an Owl"

Was this a show of solidarity with the loggers further south? Or did they already know about the owls here?

Inside the drugstore, the young clerk sported a shirt declaring "I Like Spotted Owls—for Breakfast." Wordlessly I paid for my purchases. I was suddenly glad that I'd rented a car for this job. My own car, plastered with wildlife stickers and messages urging people to save the planet, would not have gone over well here.

There were more anti-owl bumper stickers on cars parked by the grocery store, and similar shirts adorned the store's staff. Business was pretty slow.

A glass ashtray piled high with cigarette butts was perched on top of the till. The cashier lounged against the counter. Flame-red lipstick bled into the lines around her mouth; her steel-gray hair had been permed to within an inch of its thin life. She gave me the once-over a good two or three times and took a long drag on her cigarette before ringing through my groceries.

"Long winter," she observed. The classic Canadian ice-breaker.

I smiled my agreement.

"Haven't seen you around here before," she remarked with a pop of her gum. "You here for the demonstrations?"

"No, just visiting for a few days," I replied automatically as I rummaged through my knapsack for my wallet. It was a moment before the meaning of the question struck me. I snapped my attention back to the cashier. "Demonstrations? What demonstrations?"

"Ah, those damned environmentalists are tryin' to hassle the company. Some big-shot jerk from Natural Defence, or somethin', has been gettin' people worked up 'bout some stupid owls." The woman pursed her lips. "I don't hold with killin' owls like some folks in this town, but I say keep loggin'. Families gotta live, y'know. Damn owls can just move along if they don't like it."

"Nature Defence is here? Now?" My rotten luck was holding steady.

"Oh yeah." The woman settled more comfortably against the counter, delighted to have an audience. "Their leader, you know, the one that's always on the tube gettin' himself arrested? He's been here for 'bout a week now. Climbin' trees, chainin' himself to the equipment, organizin' demonstrations just 'bout every day. They been busin' in the tree-huggers all the way from Downtown. Can you believe it? If he keeps this up, the TV stations are gonna be here soon and we'll all be famous."

She lowered her voice conspiratorially. "That is, if somebody don't wring his neck first." With an unpleasant laugh, the cashier reached again for her cigarette. "He's not exactly winnin' friends and influencin' people around here, y'know."

"Uh, yeah, I can imagine." I gathered up my bags quickly.

"Say, who're you visitin' here anyways?" the woman asked.

"I'm doing some work in the forest," I replied cautiously. I didn't want to mention Jaime Cardinal yet. I'd never met the man and I wasn't sure how popular he was in town.

"Work, eh?" The woman's eyes hardened and she ground her cigarette in the ashtray. "For who?" She didn't wait for a response. "You're not with the company an' the government guy was out last month. Must be working for the environmentalists," she concluded before sniffing

19

critically. "Well, you just tell them what I said. If it's a question of jobs or owls, people oughta come first."

Deep in thought, I watched my feet retrace my steps back to the motel. Judging from the gossipy cashier, both my presence and my environmental leanings would be common knowledge throughout Marten Valley by tomorrow—at the very latest. I blew out my breath. So much for my tidy little plan for anonymity. Especially now that Nature Defence was involved.

The group was one of the most militant environmental organizations in the world. For the most part, I agreed with their sentiments, but not their actions. Wild places had to be protected—and now. In many regions we had already passed the point of no return. I understood Nature Defence's frustration all too well. But sabotaging expensive equipment only angered logging companies past any hope of negotiation, and driving metal spikes through trees was just plain criminal.

I'd heard about a mill worker in Ontario who had narrowly missed death when the giant saw he'd been operating had hit one of those spikes. The man had survived, but he'd paid for it with his left eye. With Nature Defence already in Marten Valley, the situation here promised to be much worse than I'd imagined.

Sunk in unpleasant thoughts, I only gradually became aware of voices raised in anger. Looking up, I spied a group of people across the street surrounding the entrance to Seidlin Lumber's office building. The crowd was tense, angry voices buzzing and blending into a kind of low-pitched, growling mass. As I drew closer, the hairs on the back of my neck developed a sudden aversion to my skin.

Loggers and environmentalists were squared off in

front of the building. A bright orange school bus was parked to one side. One man seemed to be the focal point of the disturbance. Unsurprised, I recognized the familiar figure of Jurgen Clark, founder and leader of Nature Defence.

Jurgen certainly looked the part of a rabid environmentalist, I noted wryly. His clothes were baggy and wrinkled, and hung loosely on his compact frame. His brushy black hair and piercing blue eyes made him seem fanatical—an impression undiminished by the purpling black eye he sported. I wondered who had given him that, or perhaps the real question was, who wouldn't have?

"Save the spotted owls!"

"No more clear-cutting!"

As I drew nearer, the voices became increasingly hostile.

"Owls were here first!"

"Tree killers!"

The loggers responded with shouted obscenities. Eyes flashed and faces reddened in anger as abuse from both sides grew more strident.

I didn't see who actually started the scuffle, but suddenly the demonstration took on a darker, more violent edge. Men began pushing, jostling both friend and enemy. In the center, bristling with aggression, Jurgen and another man started shoving at each other.

"Anytime you feel strong enough, asshole!" Jurgen's voice was raw and distorted.

"Oh yeah? You want a taste of this, jerk?" The man punctuated each sentence with a fierce jab. "I'll teach ya not to cause trouble around here!"

Jurgen's reponse rang out defiantly. "Think you're man enough, asshole?"

Unable to tear my eyes away from the scene, I watched helplessly as other men shoved and screamed at each other. I saw one kick out viciously at another.

"C'mere, asshole! You wanna say that to my face?"

"Anytime!"

Across the street, I held my breath as violence threatened to engulf the crowd. One man staggered and fell to the ground, rolling up to protect himself. A foot came down hard on his hand, and he shrieked in pain. With an inarticulate roar, his friends jumped to his defense, fists flailing. Just as it seemed the situation would explode into a full-fledged brawl, I saw a detachment of RCMP officers sprint towards the troublemakers.

Slowly I let out my breath, unaware until now that I had been holding it. As police broke up the angry demonstration, I fled back to my motel room, chilled and shaken by much more than my fever.

CHAPTER 3

By Saturday morning, I felt that I might possibly live. By lunchtime I was feeling well enough to start getting restless. The motel "suite" was claustrophobic and had been decorated in what some designer had probably labeled ecru or fawn, but was, in reality, plain old beige. It really didn't have much to recommend it—except, of course, the dial telephones.

"DIAL TELEPHONES IN EACH ROOM!" the dilapidated sign outside proudly proclaimed. How could I resist?

But the bright day beckoned and I decided to go for a walk outside. The question was, where? After what I'd seen yesterday, I didn't really fancy a leisurely stroll through town. The forest? A good possibility. I could walk around the first block of my survey area again.

I had decided to give Jaime Cardinal another day or so to recover before I called him. I'd brought my own set of maps, and even if I didn't see an owl today, there were other things to watch for. A stray downy feather, the whitewash of droppings, or a furry regurgitated pellet could tell me a lot about the inhabitants of the forest. Decision made, I gathered my gear and headed out to the car.

The forest was considerably lighter than it had been

the other night. Still damp, though. With binoculars and a camera slung around my neck, I concentrated on walking soundlessly through the trees. I looked for anything unusual: a hole in a tree, a stick nest, or a solid form lurking amidst lacy branches. I stopped periodically, scanning tangles of branches and snags for the telltale cakey blobs of whitewash.

Most of the trees in this stand were cedars, their rich green foliage drooping down like so many giant ostrich plumes. For a while, black-capped chickadees accompanied me through the forest. Swooping and diving, they danced on the mild breeze before perching on feathery branches and whistling their name merrily. *Chickadee-dee-dee. Chickadee-dee-dee.*

Enk. Enk.

I turned my head at the high, nasal note and smiled as I spied a red-breasted nuthatch scurrying headfirst down the scaly brown trunk of a mature Sitka spruce. It doesn't get much better than this, I thought, looking around me. The birds were singing, the wind was warm, and mosses were draped in gay festoons from tree limbs and shrubs. I breathed in the tangy air; it was sharp, clean, and fragrant with the spicy scent of spruce and cedar. Maybe my luck was changing. In the distance, I could hear the rat-a-tat-tat of a dining woodpecker. Probably a downy or a hairy woodpecker, I guessed. Although it could be a three-toed, or maybe even a pileated. . . .

"Stick to the program, Robyn," I reminded myself. "You're here for owls, not woodpeckers."

Forty minutes later, my search was rewarded when I caught a flash of white a short distance away. Through my binoculars I could see the accumulation of whitewash dripping down like candle wax through the boughs of a lodgepole pine. I scanned the thick tangle of twigs and branches. There! A shape by the trunk!

Heart pounding with excitement, I crept toward the tangle, keeping my eyes on that solid form. Slowly I raised my binoculars again and focused.

It was an owl. Dark, liquid eyes regarded me sleepily. Its head was chocolate brown; its undersides, coppery. But the bird's earthy coloring was enlivened by numerous small, white markings. A spotted owl.

I inched closer to the tangle, sinking down on my knees to avoid scaring the bird. Spotted owls were usually pretty tame, often allowing people to approach within a few feet. But I didn't want to take any chances with this one. It was much farther north than it was supposed to be; it was essential for my report; and it had probably been laughing at me the other night while I'd been playing my tape. He was beautiful, though.

I eased my camera from its case and snapped a few pictures. He blinked a few times, then thoughtfully fluffed his feathers out and began preening. Obviously an owl who knew a photo op when he saw one. When I had taken five photos, I pulled out my notebook and scribbled down the location, distinguishing features of the bird, and other pertinent information about the sighting. I couldn't wait to tell Kaye and Ben.

As I stood to put away my notebook, I turned and froze. While searching for owls I'd been watching out for anything unusual. Now I had found it.

The moss in this part of the forest was as thick as a wolf's winter coat. Blanketing the ground and trailing over branches from tree to tree, it resembled the tattered rigging of some moldering pirate ship. But in this particular area the moss had been shredded and slashed from its ancient masts, the ground buckled and torn. On the other side of the tangle over a tall hummock, there was a man.

He lay motionless, arms outflung, one leg bent beneath him, a pale figure against the bright green moss. From contorted features, glassy blue eyes stared, unseeing, at the emerald canopy above. Reddish-brown stains soiled his hands and soaked his tan-colored parka. As my knees began to buckle, I saw the long metal shaft protruding from his chest. A tree spike had been driven through his heart.

CHAPTER 4

"Here you go; try this."

The dark-haired RCMP sergeant handed me a mug that was battered and chipped. With shaking hands I brought it to my mouth and gulped convulsively. The coffee's stale, bitter flavor bespoke its office-brewed origins. But at least it was hot.

"Thanks. That's good."

"Good?" His tone was surprised. "You must've had some shock. I'm renowned for my terrible coffee. It's quite possible you've ruined my reputation with that remark."

He waited until I smiled shakily before continuing. "I'm Sergeant McIntyre, and there'll be some questions that we need to have answered soon." He squinted at my face. "But I think we'll wait till you feel a bit better. Just sit there, drink your coffee, and let me know when you're up to it."

I nodded and looked around the detachment office. It was a small, brown square of a building, nestled between four, huge Douglas fir trees at the north end of town. Inside, the main room had been painted a soft yellow; ancient-looking venetian blinds covered the windows with their dusty slats. The desks had seen more than their fair share of years but were neat and clean, with papers piled tidily in black metal in-baskets. There were two tiny rooms just off the main one, offices or interrogation rooms, I supposed. A faded, silver-framed picture of the Queen graced the far wall.

I hadn't even noticed the office before, when I'd burst in with the news about the body in the forest. I'd had to go out again to show the officers where I had found the man. Shivering with horror and shock, I had been careful to keep the tangle of bushes between myself and the gory sight. But there was nothing I could use to block my memory.

I finished the coffee in silence before bringing my attention back to the sergeant sitting patiently at his desk. "Thanks. I feel better now," I said.

McIntyre regarded me somewhat doubtfully. "You sure about that? You still look a little green around the edges."

"No, really, I'm better now," I assured him. At least my hands had stopped trembling.

McIntyre flipped open his notebook. "All right then. I need to get some general information about you first, and then you can tell me about what happened. Sound okay to you?"

"Yeah."

"Good. Now, I need your full name and occupation."

"Robyn Devara. I'm a biologist with Woodrow Consultants in Calgary. It's an environmental consulting agency."

"Calgary, eh? What are you doing in Marten Valley, Ms Devara?" McIntyre glanced up from his notes. "Or do you prefer Robyn?"

I smiled wanly at him; my face felt very pale. "Robyn's

fine. I'm here to do a preliminary environmental impact assessment of the Marten Valley TSA for the British Columbia Wilderness Association."

"I see. Why would the BCWA hire an Albertan company to do an impact assessment?"

"Their president, Dave Stubbings, is an old friend of my boss, Kaye Woodrow," I explained. "I think Dave wanted someone from outside the province to gather the data. Just to be a little more objective. Woodrow's a good firm, and with his connection to Kaye, I guess it was a logical choice."

"Exactly what kind of assessment are we talking about here?"

"Well, it's sort of a quick, general survey of the birds in the area."

"Birds."

I crooked my mouth up in a half-smile. "I know it sounds a little strange," I told him. "But owls winter here along with a few other kinds of birds. Right now most of the owls are starting to set up their territories and build nests. It's really the best time of year to go owling."

My voice became more animated as I warmed to my topic. Owls had always been one of my favorite birds. "Last month a member of the BCWA reported a spotted owl in the vicinity. It was pretty foggy that evening so viewing conditions weren't ideal. He may have mistaken a barred owl for a spotted owl—it's easy enough to do; the two are quite similar in appearance. Anyway, he only got a brief look at it before it took off. I've been asked to verify his report and see if there're any others around—spotted owls, that is.

"You see, in terms of spotted owls, Marten Valley is too far north—about 180 miles too far. There aren't supposed to *be* any spotted owls around here. At least that's what all the bird books say. Now, the one that was sighted may have just been a rare stray—which is pretty interesting, but not really scientifically significant. A population, on the other hand, is an entirely different thing. If there *is* a population of spotted owls around here, it'll cause quite a stir." Understatement of the year. Once such a report was verified, quiet little Marten Valley was going to explode.

McIntyre nodded slightly. "And are there? Any spotted owls, I mean."

"Yes, I found one just before I saw—" I broke off. While talking about my work, I had been able to ignore the memory of the body on the moss. Now the image rose again: the emerald moss, the reddish-brown stains, and the horrible blue-tinged face twisted in death. I closed my eyes to block out the sight. It didn't help.

I took a deep breath and opened my eyes. Sergeant McIntyre regarded me sympathetically.

"Before I saw the body," I finished quickly. "Who was he?"

"Name was Bill Reddecop. He was a foreman with Seidlin Lumber."

Gods. A logger killed with a tree spike. I felt sick. I stared down at the scratched and pitted surface of the desk. Over the years, its antique finish had darkened to a deep mahogany that was almost black. At some point in its history someone had carved the name *Peter* into the wood.

"Can you tell me about finding the body now?" McIntyre asked gently.

I dragged my eyes back up to his face. "I think so." Even to my ears, my voice sounded toneless. As if describing the scene impassively would somehow lessen its impact. "I went out to do a walk-around. Just a quick daytime survey. I didn't really expect to find any owls; mostly I was looking for signs. Droppings, pellets, a perching tree, that kind of thing. I'd been walking for about a half-hour when I noticed some whitewash on one of the spruce trees."

"Whitewash?"

"Owl droppings. Most owls like to perch in the same tree, and, after a while, their droppings accumulate. It sort of looks like whitewash dripping down the branches. Anyway, I saw the whitewash and went over to the tree and found a spotted owl sitting there. I took its picture and wrote some notes. When I stood up to leave, I saw the body."

"Any idea what time that would've been?"

"Yes, it was 2:37."

McIntyre raised one eyebrow quizzically.

"I'd just written down the time in my notebook," I explained. "It's standard procedure with a rare bird sighting."

McIntyre scribbled some words and waved me to continue my story.

"Uh, I turned around, ran back to the car, and came here."

"You didn't get any closer or touch the body?"

"No. I guess I should've checked for a pulse or something," I said miserably.

Somehow it seemed that I should have done more, although I didn't know what. I suppose I could have covered his face. It would have been the decent thing to do.

Tears stung my eyes. I tried unsuccessfully to blink them away. "But he . . . he was so obviously dead, and . . . well, I guess I just panicked," I finished lamely.

"A perfectly understandable response," McIntyre said kindly. "And better for us to have the scene undisturbed. Don't worry, Robyn, you did exactly the right thing."

I shrugged, weary and long past comforting. My head had begun to pound again. The shaky feeling inside had spread once more to my hands. I hoped that Sergeant McIntyre was almost finished with me.

"Was this the first day of your survey?"

"Sort of. I got here Thursday night and drove out to the site for a while. Just to see if any owls were calling."

"Same part of the forest?" McIntyre was intent.

I nodded. "Yeah, I think so. Pretty close anyway. I parked in the same spot. Just by that lumber mill sign."

"Did you see anything unusual that night?"

"No, not at all. The owls weren't even calling." I lifted one shoulder in a shrug. "It was pretty quiet."

McIntyre jotted a few more notes, then snapped his book shut. "All right, I think that's all we need for now. You'll be in town for a few more days?"

I nodded.

"Good. We'll probably have a few more questions to ask you later, but, for now, why don't you go get yourself something to eat? It's way past suppertime and you've had a nasty shock. You're staying at the Rest EZ?" It wasn't so much a question as a statement. The Rest EZ was the only motel in town.

I nodded again.

"Well, if you're looking for a home-cooked meal, try Irene's Diner. It's just a few blocks away. Normally I'd recommend the Italian restaurant, but the owner's gone down to Florida to get away from the winter. There's a Burger World, but unless you've got the stomach of a goat or a teenager, I wouldn't recommend it. At the moment, Irene's is the only decent restaurant in town."

Irene's Diner was your typical small-town café, complete with red Formica tabletops and chrome-accented chairs. A long counter stretched the length of the room, a line of faded red stools on one side and the kitchen on the other. The walls appeared to be a pale blue, although through the haze of cigarette smoke it was hard to tell for sure. An old jukebox stood forgotten in one corner, a curling, yellowed "out of order" sign slung haphazardly across its front. A heavy, greasy smell hung, unmoving, in the thick air.

The diner was packed and noisy that night. When I came through the door, all eyes turned towards me. Voices quietened in curiosity, then rose again in speculation. I almost turned and walked out, but I was drained and hungry, and I didn't feel like facing another bowl of chicken broth in my lonely, beige motel room. I found a stool at the far end of the counter, as far away from the curious crowd as I could get.

A thin man sat by himself at the opposite end of the counter, seemingly oblivious to his surroundings. As he hunched over the scratched Formica, his sunken eyes stared sightlessly down at the plate in front of him. He looked exactly like I felt.

"Evenin'. You want some coffee to start?"

The waitress stood over me, coffee pot poised to dispense its black, oily contents.

"Uh, can I have tea instead?" I knew that I'd have enough trouble sleeping tonight without pouring more coffee into myself.

"Sure thing," she said with a cheerful smile. "Have a

look at the menu while I go get your tea. The special tonight is meatloaf with gravy, fries, and veggies."

"Thanks."

I scanned the menu. Hamburgers, beef stew, meatloaf, liver and onions, roast beef, and a variety of steaks that came in small, medium, large, and logger size. Good thing my younger brother wasn't here. With his vegetarian sensibilities, he'd take one look at the menu and run screaming into the night. Despite Jack's persistent influence, I wasn't a vegetarian yet....

"I'll have the small steak, please," I told the waitress when she returned with a steaming metal teapot and a friendly grin.

Predictably, the teapot leaked, dribbling its contents merrily over the counter, the saucer, the serviette—everywhere, it seemed, except in my cup. I did manage to get some in the cup, and the hot drink warmed the cold pit in my stomach. As I waited for my dinner, I closed my eyes and let the noise of the diner flow over me.

In my thirty-three years, the closest I had ever come to violent death was driving by a traffic fatality moments after it had happened. Even then, it had been an accident; the driver's brakes had failed. But this? A consciously brutal act, the sole purpose of which was to deprive someone of his life. I shivered. I had never come close to anything like this before.

In a bid to distance myself from such dark thoughts, I concentrated on the conversation around me. I should have saved myself the effort. Like the meatloaf, murder was the special tonight, and everyone had heard the news.

"I can't believe it, I just can't believe it."

"Who woulda thought that somethin' like this would happen in Marten Valley?"

"An' a *tree spike*, fer Chrissake!"

"When Carol told me, you coulda knocked me over with a feather."

Despite the general feeling of shock, speculation was running rampant. From what I could hear, environmentalists were the favored suspects—and not only because of the manner of Bill Reddecop's death. Environmentalists were universally despised in Marten Valley. It appeared Nature Defence had been busy.

After intercepting a couple of inquisitive and less-than-friendly glances, I slumped down on the stool, trying to detract attention from myself. I felt like the word "environmentalist" was emblazoned across my forehead.

At a nearby table two couples sat discussing the crime over coffee and thick wedges of pie.

"Well, with all those goddamned environmentalists here makin' trouble, what'd you expect?"

"Ya think it was them?"

"'Course. Someone got him with a goddamn tree spike! I mean, who else would be sick enough to do that? They come bargin' in here tryin' to ruin our lives. Christ Almighty! Old trees an' owls! It makes me wanna puke!" The man's voice was bitter with disgust. "An' after that fight the other night in the bar, I guess they didn't feel like waitin' any longer to ruin Bill's life."

"Yeah, makes you kinda think twice 'fore goin' out now."

"Huh! Just let them assholes try to pull somethin' on me!"

"Fold your faces up," a woman's voice ordered. "That kinda talk isn't gonna do anyone any good. 'Sides, I already saw them bringin' in that environmental guy. The one Bill punched out. If he did it, they'll throw the book at him."

"Janey's right," another woman's voice twittered. "We should be thinkin' about the family now. Little Todd's gonna need a lot of support, and Lori'll be a wreck."

"Hmph! If she even notices he's gone. You know, Beth Tremblay told me that—"

"One steak dinner with all the fixins." The waitress slapped the plate down on the counter and whisked away. I looked down at my dinner, appalled.

The "small" steak was at least two inches thick and fully three-quarters the size of the plate. A large baked potato oozed butter and sour cream, while a few wizened carrots tried gamely to add a bit of fiber to the meal. I could feel my arteries hardening just looking at it. But breakfast and lunch had been meager, and despite the shock of the afternoon, my stomach growled hungrily. I picked my jaw up off the floor, tucked my eyeballs back into my head, and bravely set to.

I wished Guido the cat were here. With everything that had happened, I missed his purring, comforting presence. And besides, he always loved a good feed of steak.

A lot of people think Guido is an odd name for a cat, but the truth of the matter is, he reminded me of someone I used to date, namely my one and only relationship that lasted longer than a couple of months. Before I got him fixed, Guido the cat fancied himself quite the ladies' cat—very much like the original Guido, except, of course, *he* preferred women (a little something I'd been too naïve at the time to recognize), and I don't think he would've taken kindly to being fixed (although, after he'd stood me up on my birthday for dinner with a dainty blond, the thought had been tempting). My friend Megan always maintained I had named the cat after

Guido so I could have the satisfaction of getting him neutered. I was willing to concede that possibility.

But there were no generous genies or kind fairy godmothers lurking around Marten Valley that night, and despite my wishing, Guido the cat remained in Calgary and I was left to finish the monstrous steak by myself. It was a measure of my current spate of bad luck (or perhaps the presence of an ill-tempered sprite) that Kelt arrived just as I was wresting a piece of gristle from between my teeth.

"Flosses Are Us," a voice behind me remarked.

I whirled around and lost myself in a sea-green gaze. He was tall and fit-looking, lean without being scrawny. His faded jeans, while not tight, hugged him in ways that should be declared illegal. His hair, black as a raven, was thick with just a hint of curl. And those eyes. . . . I blinked, recalling myself. Ye gods, I was beginning to sound like a bodice-ripper.

"Kelt!" With all that had happened, I'd completely forgotten he was coming.

"Robyn!" he mimicked. "Mind if I sit down?"

I waved him to the stool beside me. "You'd better. Have you heard what happened?"

"Uh . . . apart from the Oilers winning the hockey game, no." He looked at me expectantly. "You don't look so good, though. Are you still sick?"

"No, no. Kelt, a logging foreman was murdered. I found his body this afternoon."

"*What?!*" Kelt froze in the act of sitting down and stared at me in shocked horror.

"I was out at the site and I damn near tripped over him. He was just lying there on the ground. Somebody stabbed him with a tree spike. I've been over at the RCMP office for hours."

Slowly Kelt lowered himself to the stool and rubbed his temples. "Are you okay?"

"A little shaken."

"But you're not hurt or anything? You didn't see it happen?" His green gaze, still a bit shocked, was warm and concerned.

"No. No, I just found him. That was bad enough!" Despite my best efforts, my hands began shaking again. I buried them in my lap and squeezed them into fists. It helped a little.

Kelt laid a sympathetic hand on my shoulder. "Have they found whoever did it?" he asked gently.

I struggled to get my emotions under control. "Well, they've brought some people in for questioning. I don't think they've arrested anyone yet." I took a deep breath and spat out the rest of the bad news. "But Kelt, Nature Defence is here."

Kelt whistled in disbelief. "Oh shit." He enunciated each word clearly, slowly. "I suppose Jurgen's here too, getting everybody worked up?"

I nodded morosely. "Oh yeah, I've already seen him right in the middle of a nasty little confrontation with the loggers. It was about as ugly as they come."

"That doesn't surprise me. He was pretty inflammatory at the Mitsui hearings. Is ND here about the old-growth or"—he lowered his voice—"about the you-know-whats?"

I shook my head. "Don't ask me how, but they know about the you-know-whats. The whole bloody town knows." I paused. "And, they also know that *we're* here about them."

Kelt blew out his breath in a heavy sigh.

I couldn't have agreed with him more.

CHAPTER 5

Despite my exhaustion, I slept poorly. Not surprising, given my gruesome discovery. I'd expected to dream of corpses and blood, but instead I spent the night fleeing from gigantic spotted owls that swooped down to slash my face and arms. I woke thankfully the next morning to a polite but insistent knocking on the door.

I poked my head out from under the tangle of covers and looked at the clock. Ten-twenty! I cursed and rolled out of bed. I never slept this late! Kelt had probably been up for hours.

We'd agreed to meet for breakfast at eight-thirty, then check with the RCMP and head out to the site. Kelt was eager to see a spotted owl, and in spite of the murder, we still had a job to finish—one that was now more important than ever.

The crime had been an unusual one; even I knew that. The fact of Bill Reddecop's murder was bad enough by itself, but the tree spike provided the sort of grisly element of which reporters are so fond. I suspected that the sensational story, combined with Nature Defence's demonstrations, would soon bring Marten Valley its fifteen minutes of fame. I wanted our survey to be well on its way before the circus rolled into town.

"Okay, I'm coming, I'm coming." I pulled on my robe and shoved my feet into slippers. "I'm sorry I'm late, I must've . . ." I opened the door; the motel room's warmth escaped in a cloud of icy condensation. An RCMP constable stood on the mat.

He was a big, burly man—probably a football player in his younger days—bald as an egg, with thick, snowy eyebrows. He was bundled in a sturdy RCMP-issue parka. His face and head were pink with cold. With the navy-black coat and his rosy bald head, he looked like a turkey vulture—a bird normally associated with carrion. It was not a reassuring thought.

"Ms Devara?" His voice was deep and gravelly.

I nodded dumbly.

"We'd like you to come down to the detachment office and answer a few more questions. Nothin' serious, ma'am," he hastened to reassure me. "We just need some clarification on parts of your statement."

"Um . . . okay. I have to get dressed first."

"Of course. Take your time, and I'll wait for you in the truck."

As the constable strolled back to the parking lot, Kelt opened his door and peered out. He was wearing a faded navy sweatsuit; his dark hair fell fetchingly in his eyes. His face, creased and lined from the pillow, brightened when he saw me, then crinkled in amusement when he noticed my attire. So much for making an impression—at least a good one.

At some point in its now faded life, my old robe had fallen prey to Guido the cat. I kept meaning to get a new one, but somehow never seemed to have the time. The once cheerful yellow terrycloth was now covered in long, pulled threads, courtesy of Guido's sharp claws. Together with my fuzzy orange slippers (a present from the fun-loving Jack), it made me look like Big Bird. Great.

Kelt was too polite to say anything about it, but I detected an odd glint in his eye. "Robyn! Thank god you slept in too. I couldn't believe it when I saw the time. I never sleep in this much!"

"That's okay, Kelt. I, uh . . . I have to go back to the RCMP office to answer some more questions."

"More questions?" Kelt's eyes took in the RCMP constable waiting by his truck. He didn't even hesitate. "Okay, I'll be ready in a flash," he called, zipping back into his room.

I pulled on jeans and a dark green sweater and yanked a brush through my curls. Stubbornly I refused to wonder why the police wanted to talk to me. I had nothing to do with the crime. I'd just found the body. I didn't even know the man. Thank the gods Kaye had decided to send Kelt out here. At least I wasn't facing this alone.

When we arrived at the detachment office, a young blond constable informed us politely that Inspector Danson had just arrived. Whoever this Inspector Danson was, he would, apparently, see me shortly. We were motioned over to a sturdy oak bench that squatted directly across from the two tiny offices. Peter had been here too; his name was scratched deeply into the wood. Kelt sat close to me, offering silent support. His arm rested easily along the back of the bench.

One of the office doors stood ajar; inside I could see two RCMP officers sipping coffee at the desk. I recognized one of the officers from the day before—a local middle-aged constable with the uncomfortable air of one who had never dealt with anything worse than disorderly drunks or petty theft. I could see the other only in profile. He was well built, with pale skin and a wide, dark mustache that pointed down at the sides.

I could hear the constable recounting details of the demonstration I had witnessed on Friday morning. The other man had obviously heard nothing about the incident until now. Not part of the local detachment then.

I wasn't surprised that word of the conflict had not yet spread beyond local news. In recent years, both the media and the public had become blasé about demonstrations—angry or otherwise. Though with this tree-spike murder, I thought cynically, that was bound to change in a big hurry.

Suddenly the outside door banged open, bringing with it a blast of damp, icy air. A parka-clad Sergeant McIntyre escorted in a pretty, blond woman. She was tiny, barely coming up to the sergeant's shoulders. He had slowed his pace to match her dainty steps, his expression unreadable.

The woman's hair had been softly permed and fluffed, her face artfully made up. The young constable sprang up eagerly to take her coat. Glossy fur slipped from her shoulders to reveal a slim figure clad in black slacks and a jade silk blouse. She had gold rings on every finger, and diamonds dripped like sparkling tears from her earlobes. She was an exotic quetzal in a town filled with drab house sparrows.

It was a few seconds before I realized that I recognized her.

"Lori?!" I exclaimed in surprise.

Sun-kissed curls spun around, flinging out wafts of spicy perfume.

42

"Oh my god! Robyn?!" Lori's violet blue eyes showed surprise and something else I couldn't identify. Fear?

"What are you doing here?" I asked. "How've you been?"

"I . . . I'm sorry, I really can't talk right now. . . ." Her bottom lip began to quiver becomingly; sapphire eyes filled with tears.

"Are you okay?" I blurted out.

She took a deep breath. "It's just . . . I . . . I'm not doing very well at all, I'm afraid," she said with a soft catch in her voice. "Something terrible has happened!" She paused and lowered her voice. "My . . . my husband was just found murdered! Out in the forest."

I was stunned. "*You're* married to Bill Reddecop!?"

Her eyes fixed on my face. "Yes, but how . . . did you know him?" she asked, her voice trembling.

"I heard about it," I said, unwilling to reveal my part in the tragedy. Lori certainly didn't need to hear a description of how I'd discovered his body. "I'm sorry."

"We've been married for almost nine years now. We have a son. Todd." Lori allowed a single crystal tear to gather on her mascara-coated lashes before blotting it away carefully with a Kleenex. "I can't believe this is happening. Bill's lived here all his life. The people here love him. *Everybody* loved Bill!"

What could I say to that?

"Excuse me, Ms Devara." A firm, deep voice cut through the awkward conversation. "We're ready for you now."

I glanced up. The lean RCMP officer stood at the door to the adjacent room. His dark eyes flicked from me to Lori and back again.

A few years ago, I had done some work at a peregrine

falcon breeding facility. The first day I'd been there, one
of the falcons had taught me a lesson in respect with a
well-timed swipe of her talons. I still bore the vertical scar
across the center of my bottom lip. I'd quickly learned to
be more careful around the birds, but that one falcon
always seemed to be watching, just waiting for me to give
her another opening. With his black, pointed mustache
and those sharp, dark eyes, the lean RCMP officer reminded
me of that particular peregrine.

I nodded to him before turning back to Lori. "Look,
I've got to go, but if there's anything I can do, just let me
know. I'll be in town for at least a few more days. Over at
the motel."

"Thank you, Robyn, I will." With studied grace, Lori
collapsed wearily onto my vacated spot on the bench.

The Falcon gestured me toward one of the interrogation rooms. Briefly, I glanced back at the main office.
Kelt smiled and gave me the thumbs-up signal. The
young constable had brought Lori a cup of coffee. She
was touching his hand as if in thanks.

The tiny interrogation room was cold and uninviting. It
was painted an unwholesome green, and its white venetian blinds were closed, shutting out even the negligible
warmth of the weak winter sunshine.

Sergeant McIntyre had introduced the Falcon as
Inspector Danson from the General Investigative
Services branch in Vancouver. We sat at a wooden table,
dented and splintery with age. As far as I could see,
Peter hadn't been here, or, if he had, someone had been
watching to make sure he hadn't graced this piece of furniture with his name.

McIntyre and Danson sat across from me, a manila folder and a pad of yellow legal paper in front of them. As they began going over the statement I'd made yesterday, a part of me waited for them to play good cop, bad cop. I glanced around surreptitiously for the bright desk lamp. I guess I'd been watching too much television.

Finally, the inspector leaned forward and tapped the folder. "Ms Devara," he began, "you said in your statement that you were out in the forest on Thursday evening. Exactly what time would that have been?"

"It was just after seven o'clock when I headed out to the site. I got back to the motel around ten-thirty, I think. I'm afraid I didn't really look at the time."

Frowning, he jotted some notes on the yellow paper. "Hmmm. And how long did it take you to drive out to the site?"

"About twenty minutes, give or take a few." I fidgeted nervously. "Am I a *suspect* in this?" The thought was startling and more than a little disturbing.

"We're just trying to find out what happened." His tone was not reassuring. "You see, Bill Reddecop was killed sometime early Thursday night."

In the quiet room, my indrawn breath was audible.

The inspector continued. "You saw the body, Ms Devara. It was a savage murder. Someone pierced his heart with that spike. It ripped through his aorta, causing massive hemorrhaging in his chest cavity."

I wished he would stop talking about it. Black eyes bore into mine. Not likely.

"But there were other wounds on the body," he said. "Bruising and scrapes. There was obviously a struggle; the ground was torn up, and his coat was ripped in several places. Now, I'm told that the deceased was a man given

45

to loud outbursts. I find it hard to believe this struggle was a quiet one. You were there that night; did you hear anything unusual?"

I shook my head apologetically. "I'm sorry, I didn't hear a thing. Not even any owls. I wish I could tell you more." Although it was the truth, it felt inadequate. From the look on his face, I suspected that Inspector Danson thought so too.

Sergeant McIntyre entered the questioning. "How do you know Lori Reddecop?" Up till this point, he'd been sitting quietly to one side. Even now his manner was unthreatening—merely curious, as if chatting with an old friend over tea. Maybe he remembered how upset I'd been the day before. Or maybe they were playing good cop, bad cop.

Fortunately, I was prepared for the question. I'd noticed the sharp look Inspector Danson had given Lori and me. "We were in university together," I answered. "As undergrads. Until this morning, I hadn't seen her for, let me see . . . probably over ten years."

"Did you know that she was married to Bill Reddecop?"

"Not until she told me this morning. That must've happened after second year. I changed schools for my third."

"But you knew she was living here?"

"No, I didn't. We didn't stay in touch after school."

"Do you know Jurgen Clark?" The inspector rapped out the question.

Startled, I replied, "Uh, only superficially. I've met him a few times during the course of my work. I'm not involved with Nature Defence if that's what you want to know." Pausing for a second, I thought back to the conversation I'd overheard in the diner—the one about how Jurgen got his black eye. "Is Jurgen under arrest?"

"Mr. Clark is awaiting his lawyer." The answer was clipped. Something told me Jurgen had refused to talk to the police without his lawyer present. Something else told me the predatory inspector hated waiting.

Danson leaned back and stretched his lips into a smile that was bright and even and failed miserably to reach his eyes. "Thank you for coming in today, Ms Devara. I understand that you'll be staying here for a few days?"

I nodded.

"Fine. If we have any more questions, we'll contact you. Please let us know when you're leaving town."

"Why?" I asked bluntly. "Am I a suspect?"

"We're just trying to find out what happened."

Which wasn't really an answer. Or maybe it was.

"I wasn't able to tell him anything else," I confided to Kelt afterwards as we drove out to the site. I stared out the window dejectedly. The winter sun had made its brief appearance while I had been in the RCMP office. Now, the ever-present clouds had closed ranks once again, muffling the countryside in soft, gray mist. Even the tips of the trees were lost in that ghostly shroud.

The inspector had given us permission to continue our survey as long as we stayed away from the cordoned-off crime scene. I didn't think *that* would be much of a problem. Spotted owl notwithstanding, I wasn't likely to want to go back anytime soon.

"I think he was suspicious," I told Kelt. "But, in retrospect, I felt so sick that night, I'm not sure I would've noticed a whole troop of spotted owls, let alone a murderer sneaking around. But," I added glumly, "I'm supposed to let them know if I leave town, though."

"A parliament."

"What?"

"It's a parliament of owls, a troop of gorillas, and . . . ah, never mind. So, you're not supposed to leave town? Why? Are you a suspect?"

"I don't know. They seemed pretty curious about how I knew Lori Reddecop."

"How *do* you know her?"

"I met her at university during my undergrad. We were lab partners in first-year biology. To tell you the truth, I didn't like her much."

"Oh?" he prompted.

I slanted a quick look at him. His bland tone indicated a somewhat less than favorable impression of Lori Reddecop. I was surprised; most men thought she was marvelous.

"She was pretty self-absorbed," I explained. "Sure didn't give a rat's ass about biology—at least not the kind we were studying."

"Meow, meow."

I grinned. "Sorry, I guess that *was* sort of catty. But seriously, she was a terrible flirt, and always in a snit about her makeup and clothes. It was years ago, but I still remember how she used to come to eight a.m. labs dressed to the teeth—"

"Nines."

I waved my hand. "Teeth, nines, whatever. Her hair was always pouffed up to here, her makeup was always perfect, and she always wore freshly pressed blouses. I don't think I even *owned* an iron when I was in university! Jeans and a sweatshirt were more my speed. I felt like a total bum next to her. But," I added smugly, "I bet I got a lot more sleep!"

Kelt let out a bark of laughter. "Always an important concern for hard-working university students."

"Damn right!" I chuckled. "Now that I look back on it, I guess I was just a teeny bit envious of how well put-together she always seemed. But it wasn't just that, though. You see, if Lori was in the mood, she could be warm and friendly—the most charming person you'd ever met. But if you caught her at a bad time, she was a stainless-steel bitch. Unless, of course, you happened to be male. It sounds harsh, but at the time, I thought she was just a self-centered tease."

"I'm surprised that you remembered her after all these years."

"Well, I couldn't tell you her maiden name if you paid me, but as for remembering her?" I paused, recalling images of a younger Lori.

People had always been attracted to her beauty and vivacity, like moths blindly fluttering and flocking to a porch light that burns very brightly. It was only after you'd joined the crowd that you realized the light was a bug zapper. Ostensibly, Lori had been the reason that Guido and I had broken up. To her it had been just another one-night fling; she didn't even know that I'd been seeing him. To me, left alone on my birthday, it had spelled the end of what I'd believed was a loving relationship. Although, I reflected with the 20/20 vision of hindsight, perhaps now I should thank her.

"I'd never really met anyone quite like her before," I said. "She had the ability to make you feel like the most interesting person in the world, or a loser ten times over. It's funny, but since my undergrad years I've met a few women like Lori—even one that looked like her. In my mind, I've always thought of them as having a 'Lori' personality." I laughed a little self-consciously. "It's sort of weird, I guess."

Kelt smiled warmly at me. "I don't think so."

"I wonder why she ever came to Marten Valley," I mused aloud. "As I recall, she was seeing some medical student. Or maybe he was in law? Grant? Gary? Something like that. He was the campus Adonis, of course. You know the sort: handsome, charming, active on Student Council, made sure he knew all the deans. A real Mr. Popularity. I wonder what happened to him. I sure wouldn't have pegged her as a logger's wife."

I paused for a moment, watching absently as the forest zipped by in a blur of emerald and jade. "On the other hand, loggers make very good money; it's one of the highest-paying careers in BC. But stuck in a little town like Marten Valley? I'd've thought that would be anathema to Lori."

"Perhaps she married for love."

"I guess so. . . . I hope so."

"Though if that's true," Kelt reflected, "you'd think her behavior as a grieving widow would be more convincing. While you were in the interrogation room, she was all over that young constable."

"Yeah, I noticed that just before I went in." I shrugged distastefully. "It's hard to say. . . . People grieve in different ways, and I don't think I ever really knew her well."

I fell silent then, uncomfortable with the turn the conversation had taken. Just because Lori had slept with my boyfriend years ago was no excuse for me to slander her now. I thought of Bill Reddecop's lifeless body lying on a gurney under cold, fluorescent lights. I thought of Lori having to go in and identify it. Nobody deserved that.

Chapter 6

Nobody, that is, except perhaps whoever was responsible for what we saw next.

I had pored over my maps the night before, selecting as our next survey block part of an area known as Wolf Creek. I'd picked five-mile block, heavily forested, with a couple of large ponds and, of course, the creek. Like most other living things, owls like to be fairly close to a water source. But although the section may very well have had a number of ponds and a creek running through it, it didn't have much in the way of forest, at least not anymore.

We stood at the side of the road, at the side of what was supposed to be the beginning of our survey block. To our right, the forest towered in waves of uncountable shades of green. To the left as far as the eye could see, gray soil lay exposed, parched and barren. Sun-bleached stumps poked up amidst scattered mounds of tangled, broken branches, smashed as if by some colossal hand.

"Gods," I breathed. "I thought cutblocks were supposed to be smaller than this!"

The midday light was softened by cloud cover, but the air was crisp with winter's chill. Brisk winds had scoured the denuded land and piled the snow up along the edges of the clear-cut. Whirling dust devils cavorted across the ruined landscape; a lone raven soared high above them, barely visible in the clouds, its metallic *tok tok* a desolate echo in the wind.

"I thought so too," Kelt answered finally, his eyes still bugged out a bit in shock. "Although, in all fairness, I'm out of touch with BC's current forestry legislation."

"Same here," I said. "But, even so, I sure wasn't expecting to see clear-cutting on this kind of scale—even in such an isolated area. They must have cut *hundreds* of acres."

Kelt nodded sober agreement. "I think there may be some exceptions with regard to cutblock size . . . you know, in case of disease or something." He shrugged. "I don't know any of the details, though."

I stared doubtfully at the trees along the edge of the block. The foliage was green and healthy-looking, without a spot of telltale yellow or red that would indicate disease or infection. "Do you see any signs of disease?"

We stamped into our Sorels and hiked a little way around the perimeter of the cutblock, but even upon closer inspection, the lodgepole pines looked healthy and unblemished. Puzzled, we headed back to the car to get our birding gear. Our plans had obviously changed, but I had maps for the entire area, and we could survey the block adjacent to the slash. The creek even meandered through part of it.

"You know," I remarked, as we dragged out backpacks and maps, "I've got a good friend in Calgary who's articling right now. She's concentrating on environmental law. I bet she'd know about this." I waved my hand in the direction of the clear-cut.

"She'd know about BC laws?"

I laughed. Megan was a self-confessed child of the forests. The bald prairies of southern Alberta held little appeal for her beyond the promise of a respected law degree. "I think she's been studying up on BC legislation since elementary school," I told Kelt. "Her fondest dream is to relocate to the Pacific coast as soon as humanly possible." I looked around again at the vast expanse of shattered forest. "I'll give her a call tonight. This just doesn't seem right."

We bundled up, shrugged on our packs, draped binoculars around our necks, and resolutely turned our backs on the slash. Lush trees beckoned with whispered promises of spotted owls.

Along the boundary, the snow lay heavy and slushy. Covered as it was by the loose soil blowing across the cutblock, it looked more like banks of ashy mud than snow. We slopped through the filthy mess, trudging through mud-choked weeds and brush on our way deeper into the forest, each step taking us further from the slash and deeper into untouched wilderness.

I took a deep breath of the forest-scented air and felt the tension drain off my neck and shoulders like water flowing off the feathers of a diving duck. The ubiquitous moss covered both tree and rock, carpeting the ground in forty-ounce green broadloom. Captured by myriad branches high in the canopy, the snow was barely visible here, a mere dusting of silvery flakes fading the moss to a pale green and lending a fairy-like quality to the surroundings.

We walked quietly, heads constantly turning this way or that, eyes scanning trees and shrubs for signs of owls. Conversation was non-existent. Kelt seemed to be in a quiet, thoughtful sort of mood, and, as for myself, I wasn't exactly Ms Exuberance.

On a rocky outcrop at the top of a ravine, we stood for a moment in silence, gazing across the narrow valley. The sky had cleared, and bright sun shone down on the virgin forest. The trees protected us from any breeze, but it must have been windy higher up. Puffy clouds scooted across the sky like so many tardy white rabbits. We could have been the only people on earth.

The breathtaking view seemed to revive Kelt from his pensive mood. As we started down the slope, he asked about owling.

"I've been bird-watching before," he assured me. "Just never specifically for owls."

"Well, I guess the most important thing to know about owl prowls is that for every ten times you go out, you'll be lucky if you see an owl once. And you'll probably pass right by a dozen of them and never even know they're there. They're masters—and mistresses—of camouflage. Have you ever seen one in the wild?"

"Just once." Kelt's eyes sparkled. "I was checking an old barn for rodents when these two glowing eyes swooped down on me. I just hit the dirt—almost had to change my shorts. It was a great horned owl. What a beauty too! Her talons sliced right through the back of my leather jacket, though, and I've been very careful around barns ever since."

"The great horneds are spectacular, aren't they?" I chuckled. "Aggressive too. I'd bet you anything she had a nest in that barn."

"Maybe, but I was too rattled to go back in and check."

I laughed and shook my head. "Most of the time, you don't get quite as close as that," I assured him. "Owls usually hear you long before you're in sight, and they flush away silently before you even know to raise your binoculars. It's sort of frustrating sometimes."

"Sounds like it."

"Daytime owling is a little different from at dawn or dusk. Owls like to go deeper into the woods in the day. We'll just be looking around for owl signs—a perching tree, the odd feather, pellets are good. Spotted owls nest in tree cavities so we can check those out too. If we find some signs, then we come out again really early tomorrow morning and maybe find us an owl or two."

"*Really* early? That sounds ominous."

"I'm afraid so. You mammals biologists have it easy. The best owling time is about four a.m."

Kelt groaned, and I smiled sympathetically. "I've got a permit to play spotted owl calls," I continued. "So even if we don't see them, we might be able to get one calling to us. Not that I had much luck with that the other night. Although with what was going on in the forest at the time . . ."

Kelt clapped an understanding hand on my shoulder. "C'mon, let's see what kind of owls are hanging around."

We moved as quietly as possible through the forest, following faint wildlife trails across the ravine. Wherever the canopy opened up, snow had accumulated in wet piles, leaving the moss beneath slick and icy. We peered through tangles of branches, and scanned trunks and ground. We found trees that sported promising holes and rapped politely on their deeply grooved trunks. Nobody was home. The sky grew darker, the chill more pronounced. It was a long and fruitless afternoon.

Damp, discouraged, and owlless, we arrived back at the Rest EZ just before dinnertime. The motel's previously deserted parking lot was now jammed full with cars, news trucks, and people darting back and forth between rooms and vehicles. The circus had come to town.

A few reporters and camera people lounged on the sagging olive sofas in the motel's lobby, equipment and notebooks spilling out across the floor. They gestured and talked excitedly, like so many killdeer in distraction displays.

Watching as they sipped coffee from snowy Styrofoam cups, I spared a fleeting moment of pity for them. I'd made the mistake of having some of the motel's coffee just after I'd checked in. One of my favorite coffee shops back home offered something called "Black as Hell" coffee. The Rest EZ's coffee made "Black as Hell" seem like a latte.

Kelt eyed the activity with dismay. "So much for a quiet evening."

"As long as I don't have to talk to them," I yawned. I loved being outdoors all day—as far as I was concerned, it was the best part of being a biologist—but it always wore me out. "I'm all for a long soak in the tub, dinner at Irene's, and an early bedtime."

"No complaints here," Kelt replied. "Do you want to call Kaye and Ben or shall I?"

"No, thanks anyways, I'll do it. If I know Kaye, she'll fuss until I personally assure her I'm all right. I'll meet you in, say, an hour?"

As I ran my bath, I dialed the Woodrows' home number. Ben picked it up after the first ring.

"Robyn!" His voice was harsh with an odd combination of irritation and relief. "What the devil is going on there? Are you all right?"

I was taken aback. "Uh, what? You know about what happened?"

"Of course we know what happened! It's been all over the news. Don't you pick up your messages?"

"Sorry, Ben," I apologized guiltily. He hadn't been this worked up since the Mitsui deal had gone through. I really should have phoned them before now. "Kelt and I were out surveying all day; I haven't had a chance to get the messages."

Kaye picked up the extension. "Robyn, is that you?"

"Hi, Kaye. Yes, it's me, and I'm sorry I didn't call earlier. I'd no idea that you would hear about this so soon. I'm fine, and Kelt arrived safe and sound on Saturday."

"We were so worried about you, dear. They're saying that Nature Defence is there and that people are being murdered."

"Well, yes, Nature Defence is here, but, jeez, it's hardly a bloodbath! Somebody was killed, but they don't even know if it's related to the demonstrations."

"Demonstrations?" Ben asked.

"Yeah, someone squealed about the owls, and the whole town's up in arms. Jurgen Clark's here too, so I'm sure you can fill in the blanks."

Ben let out a disgusted snort. "That asshole! I knew we wouldn't be able to keep this owl thing hushed up for long, but I thought we'd have a *little* more time. So what's the deal with the dead guy, then?"

"I don't know. He's a logger, and he had a fight with Jurgen; that's about the extent of my knowledge." I took a deep breath. "I uh . . . I actually found the body. Yesterday before Kelt arrived."

Kaye and Ben were aghast. It took a while to reassure them, both of my safety and my emotional well-being.

"Maybe we should postpone the survey," Ben suggested. "Dave never let on that this could be a dangerous job." He sounded like he was barely holding on to his temper, and I wondered if he was thinking about obliterating people again.

I was surprised when Kaye agreed with him. "A few weeks or a month won't make that much difference."

"Look, you guys." I was firm. "It was pretty upsetting but I'm okay now. I think we should just finish up the survey. It's more important than ever now. You should see the motel; the media are here in force. Seidlin's harvesting practices are bound to come into it. It's a perfect opportunity. And"—I played my trump card—"I found a spotted owl."

"Did you!?" Kaye was delighted. "Dave will be ecstatic!"

"I hope so, and you can tell him he owes me dinner and a bottle of wine, but we need to get a better idea of the numbers and distribution before we can even *think* of establishing the Marten Valley TSA as an active owl site. So far, I've only seen the one."

"But you think there might be more?" Ben asked.

"Yeah, I do. The forest is pretty far north, but from what I can see, it's prime spotted-owl habitat. It's possible I saw the same owl that Jaime Cardinal reported, but it's been a month since he saw that bird. If it was just a stray, it likely would've moved on by now. So either I saw the same owl and it's a permanent resident, or I saw a different one, which means a possible population. Either way, it looks promising. I think there's a good possibility that more are skulking about."

I paused for a moment. "I'd like to find them," I continued slowly. "The clear-cutting here is beyond belief. I've never seen anything this bad before. If I can find more owls, then maybe Dave and his bunch can put the brakes on it."

It took a little more fast talking, but they finally agreed with me.

"Well, if *you're* okay with staying and finishing the survey, I guess it's all right," Kaye concluded reluctantly. "At least there are two of you now. If anything else happens, though, you call us immediately."

"And be careful!" Ben added. "Don't go into that forest alone."

"I promise."

Refreshed and revitalized from a long, bubbly bath, I decided to give my brother a quick call before dinner. Jack didn't normally watch the news, but with the way my luck was running, today would be the one day he turned it on.

Jack and I had not always been close. In fact, I hadn't been close to either of my brothers while we were growing up. Of the 2.3 children that people were said to have back then, I was the .3 in my parents' eyes—a fact that had caused a lot of hurt and resentment to my younger self. The sun rose and set on my elder brother Neil, and on Jack too until he became both a musician and a vegetarian—two strikes against him, according to my father. My parents hadn't yet clued in to the fact that Neil, despite being a successful dentist, was also gay. I didn't have a problem with it, but I often wondered what they would do once they discovered their golden boy was flesh and blood just like the rest of us. It wasn't any of my business—I assumed he'd tell them when he was ready to—but it was a little tough to listen to my mother complain about Neil's lack of wife and (perhaps more importantly) offspring. I would have talked to Neil about it, but he had a superior attitude that was hard to take, and, if there had been any love lost between us, I sure didn't know where it was hiding.

It took me until six years ago—when Jack and I had gone for pizza and ended up getting drunk together on a bottle of red wine—to realize that Jack felt just as hurt and left out and resentful as I did. Since then, we'd formed a united front against the favoritism shown to Neil and, in the process, become good friends too.

The call was just ringing through when Kelt tapped at the door.

"C'mon in!" I smiled at him. "I'm just calling my brother. It won't take a minute."

Kelt nodded and leaned easily against the heavy door frame.

"Hey Jack, it's Turd."

"Turd!" My brother's voice was warm. "How's be-ooo-tiful BC?"

"Turd?" Kelt echoed.

Embarrassed, I shrugged and covered the receiver with my hand. "I'll explain later," I mouthed. Damn. I wasn't thinking.

"Well, BC's great, but there's been a little trouble."

"What do you mean?" Jack's bantering tone sobered abruptly. "Are you okay? What's wrong?"

"I'm okay, but one of the loggers was murdered."

"What?!"

Quickly I filled him in, up to and including the conflict in Marten Valley. Jack was shocked.

"Are you going to be okay?"

"Yeah, I'll be fine. Kelt's here to help out and—"

"Kelt? As in Small Mammals Biologist Kelt? *the* Kelt?"

I glanced at Kelt and flushed. Turning away, I pressed the phone more tightly against my ear. Trust Jack to tease me now. "Yes, Jack, Kelt came up yesterday, we've just finished our walk-around, and we're about to head out for dinner."

"Wow, talk about your silver linings!"

"Um, right. How's Guido the cat?" I asked quickly.

"Ah, you know him, he wants to be fed ten times a day! If I don't lay out the crunchies, he sucks in his stripy little stomach and pretends he's wasting away."

I smiled. Guido the cat's antics were legendary. The first time I'd gone away on fieldwork, he'd carried on so insistently that the gullible Jack had fed him a twenty-pound bag of food in just two weeks. I'd come home to discover my cat masquerading as a Christmas butterball. "Just make sure the food's closed up tightly when you go out. He once ate the better part of a bag when I forgot."

"No sweat."

"I might have to get you to look after him for a little longer," I said carefully. "The RCMP don't want me leaving town just yet and I'm sort of behind on this survey now."

"Not a problem. Are you *sure* you're all right, though?" Jack was serious again. "What do you mean, the cops don't want you to leave town?"

"It's just because I found the body, that's all. It's nothing serious. I need to finish the survey anyway."

Jack wasn't fooled. "Uh huh. Look, Turd, don't go trying to pull the big, strong mountain-woman thing on me. That must've been a terrible thing for you to see. Do the police think you had something to do with it?"

"I don't know what they think, Jack. And yeah, it was a terrible thing to see. Truthfully, I'm trying very hard not to think about it right now, but I promise we'll talk when I get back."

I hung up the phone then and turned to scoop up my coat. "I'm starved," I told Kelt. "I might even eat a logger-sized steak!"

Kelt didn't budge from the door frame. His arms were folded across his chest and he looked at me expectantly.

"Turd?" he prompted.

I blushed. "I was hoping you'd forgotten that."

"No such luck."

I sighed. "I've loved watching birds ever since I was a kid," I explained. "So, naturally, my brothers used to tease me about having a bird name. Then Jack, my younger brother, discovered the Latin name for robin is *turdus migratorius*. I'm sure you can guess the rest. It really isn't a pleasant story. Jack and Neil were the bane of my junior high school years. Unfortunately, the name sort of stuck. Even my parents slip up and call me Turd every now and then."

Manfully, Kelt tried to smother his laughter. He was not successful.

"Look." I shook my finger at him threateningly. "I'd appreciate it if you didn't tell anyone at the office about this. Nobody there knows and it's not really what you would call professional. I *don't* want to be known as 'Turd' at the office!"

Kelt's eyes danced with merriment. "Oh, I wouldn't dream of it," he assured me with false sincerity.

I eyed him suspiciously. "Uh huh. If you do I'll—" I broke off, unable for a moment to think of a suitable punishment.

"What?"

"I'll get Guido the cat to deal with you!"

"Oh no!" Kelt threw his hands up in front of his face.

"Not the dreaded Guido the cat! What is he? A member of the Meowfia? Are you going to send him to claw my kneecaps?"

Laughing at his clowning in spite of myself, I grabbed his arm and propelled him out the door. "Come with me! You're obviously delirious with hunger."

CHAPTER 7

"So, who do you think did it?"

Kelt and I sat at a large table in Irene's Diner. The restaurant was almost empty tonight, its regulars sitting down to Sunday dinner at home. The thin man I had noticed the night before occupied the same place at the counter. Alone again, sitting with his shoulders bowed forward like a weary Atlas, he single-mindedly shoveled his food into his mouth.

The clouds of cigarette smoke had dissipated along with the crowds, but the greasy scent of fried foods still permeated the air. Two waitresses, garbed in apricot-colored uniforms, sat at a corner table, chatting quietly as they stuffed stacks of paper serviettes into shining aluminum dispensers.

Our table groaned under the weight of two, massive (size small) platters of the Sunday roast beef and Yorkshire pudding special. It wasn't any more appealing than the steak of the previous night. The beef lounged insolently against the edge of my platter, its pale pink flesh marbled with fat and gristle. A few gravy-soaked green beans poked out timorously from under a pale, doughy mass of pudding.

I finished my mouthful, chewing endlessly on a piece

of gristle before swallowing it down. By unspoken agreement we had, up until now, avoided any discussion of the murder. I, myself, had been trying hard not to think about it. It's not that I wasn't curious about who had killed the logging foreman and why, but the shock of discovering his body was still a little fresh, and besides, I was a biologist, not some trench-coated detective. Best to leave any such investigations to the RCMP. Still, speculation was unavoidable, and now Kelt had finally voiced the question.

"Well," I answered finally, "there's the obvious suspect."

"Jurgen Clark?"

I nodded. "The only problem is, I can't for the life of me figure out why he would do it. For one thing, he'd be the first person they would suspect, and for another, it would hurt the organization. I mean, can you imagine the headlines? 'Nature Defence Leader Arrested for Murder.' The whole organization would go down the toilet. I know they're militant but they do have a certain credibility—and a definite code of right and wrong. Besides, he's spent years building up Nature Defence. It's his family. It means everything to him."

"Sounds like you know the guy personally."

"Actually, I do."

Kelt groaned and rolled his eyes. "Don't tell me, *another* old school chum?! No wonder the RCMP don't want you leaving town."

"No, no, nothing like that." I shrugged the question away impatiently. "We met down in Ford, Washington, during the spotted owl controversy down there. I had dinner with him. He's really quite a fascinating person—very well read, some interesting insights—but he tends to see the world in black and white." The first time I'd met with him, the man had ranted at me for an hour before I'd managed to tell him he was preaching to the converted.

"I can believe that."

"Yeah, but we need people like him too. You know, extremists on both ends to achieve moderation and all of that. Anyway, in spite of his, ah, somewhat overzealous beliefs, Nature Defence is his baby. I don't think he'd do anything to jeopardize it."

Kelt agreed. "It seems a little pat, doesn't it? Still, ND is well known for spiking trees, so Jurgen would have had access to the spikes. You can't just waltz into your local hardware store and ask for a set of tree spikes."

"Well, what about the other environmentalists? They're not all from Nature Defence. Some of them could be from other militant groups."

Kelt took another huge bite of Yorkshire pudding. The greasy gravy ran down his chin. "Oops, sorry." He wiped his face off. "It's possible," he conceded, "but I don't think we can rule out Jurgen. Yeah, it would have been stupid for him to do something like this, but maybe he got carried away."

"What, a crime of passion?"

"It happens all the time," Kelt assured me. "Just take a look at the newspapers. From what I've heard, Jurgen is your classic example of a hothead. It wouldn't take much to push his buttons, and someone like Bill Reddecop was probably real good at pushing."

"How do you figure that?"

"All the stuff his wife was saying in the RCMP office. She kept going on and on about how much everybody loved Bill."

"You think the lady doth protest too much?" I asked.

"Well," Kelt began pedantically, "it's like the cheese slices."

I paused, fork raised halfway to my mouth. "Um, I think you lost me there. Cheese slices?"

"Yeah, you know, those individually wrapped, bright orange things. They call them 'process cheese food slices.' Why do they do that? Why do they have to assure us that these little neon squares are food?"

I looked at him, bemused. "Uh, I don't know. I guess they don't look like food?" I suggested uncertainly.

"Exactly!" Kelt punctuated his remark by spearing another piece of roast. "And really, they're processed so much as to barely rate the description of food. In other words, they're not really food even though the label says that they are."

"So Bill Reddecop . . ."

"Was, in fact, *un*loved by everyone." Kelt grinned boyishly. "According to the cheese-slice theory, anyhow."

I laughed and shook my head. "Don't give up your day job," I advised.

Kelt leaned back and studied me. "Why are you so eager to defend Jurgen, anyway?" he asked.

I shrugged uncomfortably. "I'm not sure. . . . It's not like I know him very well. It's just that everybody—the police, the people who were in here the other night— they're all so certain that he's the one who did it. Maybe he did; I'm not denying the possibility. But if he wasn't a militant environmentalist, I wonder if people would be so eager to pin it on him."

"What about that fight with Bill Reddecop?"

"I know, I know. But a lot of people fight, Kelt, and a lot of people belong to militant environmental groups. It doesn't mean they're capable of murder. And, if the cheese-slice theory holds up and Bill *was* so unlovable, what about the rest of the people in Marten Valley? He was a foreman; maybe one of his workers had something against him. Maybe he was rude to the bartender. At this point, I don't think anybody can be discounted—or convicted."

I'd just about finished my dinner when the little bell above the front door tinkled the arrival of another customer. I glanced over and saw the RCMP officer who had escorted me to the station that morning. He caught my look and smiled and nodded. I tried to smile back in a friendly sort of way, but it came out a bit wobbly. It was hard to look at police officers in the same way when you might be a murder suspect.

The constable strode up to the counter and clapped the thin man on the back.

"Hey, Lem, how's it hangin'? Those sandwiches ready, Jennie?"

The thin man must have been worlds away. At the friendly clap on his shoulder, he jumped like a startled jackrabbit. Though we sat a few tables away, I could see the blood drain from his face. He managed a sickly smile after a moment, but the constable, intent on his sandwiches, hadn't noticed the man's nervousness or his attempt to cover it. I thought it odd, but as the waitress packaged up the constable's dinner the bell tinkled another arrival, and I forgot all about the strange, thin man.

"Robyn Devara! Whatever the hell are you doing here?"

I turned. Of course. Speak of the devil, and he will

come. I could have wished that he'd waited to greet me until after the constable had left.

"Hey, Jurgen." I managed a tight smile.

Jurgen Clark still sported the black eye given to him by the murdered man. The mottled, purple bruise had begun to fade to greenish yellow around the edges. The eye was pretty bloodshot, though, lending a weirdly demonic cast to his features. Frankly, it didn't do much for his appearance.

Bonnie came up just as I finished my inspection; I smiled a warm greeting. His significant other for some years now, Bonnie was, in many ways, the antithesis of Jurgen. Though she was a card-carrying member of Nature Defence, you would never peg her as a militant.

Pale skin, short white-blond hair, and washed-out gray eyes—her personality often seemed as colorless as her appearance. I'd never seen her exhibit much in the way of emotion. In fact, although I'd seen her at many demonstrations, I'd never even heard her raise her voice. Privately I thought she served as a kind of sink, siphoning off Jurgen's excess energy (of which there was a great deal). The few times I had met her by herself, she had seemed even paler and less substantial. It was almost as if she needed his energy for the basic functions of living.

"Robyn," Jurgen was saying pleasantly, "I don't think I've seen you in over a year, and now you turn up here. Have you come for the demonstrations?"

I shook my head and smiled. "No, you should know me better than that. I'm doing a survey for the BCWA."

At that point, the constable and his sandwiches sauntered out the door with a long, last, curious look at our little party. Great. One murder suspect consorting with another. I wondered what the falcon-like Inspector Danson would have to say about it.

With an effort, I shook off that line of thought. "Jurgen, Bonnie, this is my colleague, Kelt Roberson. We both work for Woodrow Consultants in Calgary."

"Kelt." Jurgen's handshake was brief. I guess he'd figured out that Kelt wasn't here for the demonstrations either. Bonnie just smiled vaguely.

Kelt smiled. "Hi, Bonnie. Jurgen. I hear you've been busy," he said mildly.

I gave Kelt a long look. Jurgen was touchy at the best of times, and I wanted to talk to him before he went ballistic about something. You never knew what was going to set him off. Fortunately, he seemed pretty calm tonight.

"Those bastards! Tearing up the land like there's no tomorrow. Too stupid to understand they're killing themselves! I don't know what the hell they think they're going to do when it's all gone. Unbelievable! Well, Nature Defence will be here in full force in a couple of days. Just because this place is remote, those assholes at Seidlin think they can get away with anything! I think we've got them scared, though; they're trying to pin some goddamned murder on me. On *me*!" His tone was one of righteous outrage.

At Jurgen's mention of the murder, Bonnie started. I flicked a glance at her and caught her stricken look before she lowered her eyes. Strange. What was up with her?

"Yeah, we heard," I said sympathetically.

"Heard you had a fight with the guy too," Kelt said. I aimed a swift kick his way. He was about as subtle as a bulldozer in virgin forest.

Jurgen's face darkened. "That Bill Reddecop was the worst of all of them, and he wasn't even on the goddamn board. Son of a bitch hauled off and punched me in the bar. No provocation whatsoever. If he hadn't been killed, I would've slapped him with a lawsuit faster than—"

"He would've won too," Bonnie piped up. "I was there and I saw the whole thing." She was speaking a little too quickly and her fingers kept plucking at the zipper of her jacket. At a stern glance from Jurgen, she lapsed into silence.

"But you've got an alibi, don't you?" I asked Jurgen. "I heard the RCMP were holding you...."

Jurgen laughed humorlessly. "Oh yeah, they were holding me all right. Had to let me go as soon as my lawyer got here too. They haven't got anything on me, and they know it. Bonnie was with me that night. So what kind of a survey are you doing here?"

"Looking for spotted owls. It was supposed to be a quick and quiet job, but somebody squealed. How long have you been in town?"

"About three weeks now. I heard the BCWA was going to try to fight Seidlin again. When I arrived, I tell you, I took one look at the clear-cutting around here and decided to stay for a while."

"So who let on about the owls?"

Jurgen snorted. "Take a guess. Those sons of bitches weren't about to stop ripping up the forest for any other reason."

"But Jurgen, we're not even certain that this is an active owl site yet. Why get people worked up about something like this if it may not be true?" My voice held a note of reproof that was completely lost on Jurgen, though Bonnie shot me an odd look.

"Of course there're spotted owls around here. No question. But even if there weren't, Seidlin Lumber's board of directors should be strung up by the balls for what they're doing to this land. Have you seen the clear-cutting? It has to be stopped! You know as well as I do that owls just give the public something to focus on."

"I know, but what if there aren't any?" I insisted. "I don't like the clear-cutting either, but it's unethical to lie to people to try to stop it. All it does is get a lot of nervous people very upset."

Jurgen looked at me pityingly. "You sure haven't changed much since Washington, have you? Still trying to play upfront and honest. Well, what about the logging companies? Surely you're not naïve enough to believe *they're* telling the truth." His voice became deeper. "'We have teams of dedicated workers replanting with painstaking effort every single tree we cut. In a few years, the forest is completely regenerated.'"

His voice returned to normal. "Give me a break. Even if they do bother to replant, they hire a few students who don't give two shits about it and end up dumping all their seedlings in a pit when nobody's looking. And what about the forests that *do* get planted? Acre after acre of monoculture. What happens to all the diversity of a natural forest? You think *they* care? The forest is replanted, that's all that matters. I tell you, Robyn, if you want to have a hope in hell of winning this fight, you're going to have to learn to play by their rules."

"Jurgen." I was trying to be patient. "I've heard all this before. I'm not disputing the fact that there are problems with the whole process, but you'll never convince me that I need to lie to people to further my own agenda."

"My *own* agenda?!" His eyebrows shot up and his voice went up an octave. The waitresses were watching us curiously. "Listen, I'm just trying to do my bit to make sure there'll be a world left for my kids, if I ever have any. There's no personal glory in this."

Now Kelt was kicking me. I sighed. This wasn't going very well. "Look, Jurgen, I never thought you guys were doing this for some kind of personal glorification. But in Washington, at least we knew the spotted owls were there. Here, we don't, and you running around getting everybody worked up about them isn't going to make my job any easier. And if it turns out that Marten Valley isn't an active owl site, you run the risk of discrediting the whole campaign!"

"Well, I guess you'll just have to find some owls then, won't you?" Jurgen snarled before spinning on his heels and stalking out the door. With a last nervous look at us, Bonnie scurried to catch up with him.

Kelt mopped his brow dramatically. "Whew! Does he always jump down people's throats like that?"

I nodded glumly. "Jumps down and burrows in; it's part of his charm. I'd sort of forgotten how excitable he was." I let out my breath in a sigh. "Well, now we know how Marten Valley found out about the owls."

"Do you think Jurgen's guilty of murder too?"

I shrugged uncomfortably. "I don't know. He sure changed the subject in an awful hurry, didn't he?"

"Mmmm," Kelt agreed. "But I got the distinct impression he would have rather hit Bill with an assault charge and a lawsuit."

"Yeah, I got the same feeling. But, gods, I'd forgotten how angry he can get! If ever there was a candidate to commit a crime of passion, it would be him. Somehow, I have a hard time believing that Bill Reddecop slugged him without provocation."

I didn't think the murder was any of my business to investigate, but the massive clear-cut that Kelt and I had discovered was an entirely different matter. And before I did any sort of snooping around, I had to find out if it was legal.

It was pretty late by the time I got a chance to phone Megan. I wouldn't normally have called anybody at that hour, but Megan was an articling lawyer. Out of necessity, she functioned on a few hours' sleep a night, a couple of pots of coffee, and numerous chocolate-dipped biscotti from Lina's Italian Market where, incidentally, we'd met four years ago. I knew she'd be awake.

"Hey Meggie, it's me."

"Robyn! I was just talking to Jack. I hear you're in the middle of a bloodbath."

I sighed and brought Megan up to speed on the events in Marten Valley. When I got to the part about the overly large cutblock, she latched onto it like a burr.

"There's no way they're allowed to clear-cut such a large area," she assured me. "At least, not without special permission. Just a sec, I've got the latest forestry legislation around here somewhere."

I smiled. Of course she did. The trick would be to find it. With stacks of legislation, policies, law books, and scribbled notes, Megan's apartment looked like it was on the woodland caribou's migration path.

I heard the sounds of rummaging, books falling on the floor, and a few heartfelt curses. Then Megan's voice, low and cajoling, followed by the disgruntled *maou* of The Bob, her immense orange tabby.

The quintessential immovable object, The Bob had the disquieting ability to be perched directly on top of whatever Megan needed to find at the time. I grinned and waited.

"Sorry that took so long," Megan said a little breathlessly when she finally got back on the line. "The Bob was on them and he didn't want to move."

Big surprise. I often wondered why Megan even bothered looking for anything anywhere *except* under The Bob.

"Okay . . . let me see what it says here. . . . Yes, that's right, cutblocks in the Interior cannot be in excess of sixty hectares without a special exception. Now, special exceptions are . . . if the timber is in imminent danger of being lost or destroyed. For an area the size of what you're describing, it looks like bark beetles are the bad guys."

"Bark beetles?"

"Yeah, hang on a minute." Megan paused while she scanned through her documents. "Okay, from the sounds of it, if you've got a bad bark beetle infestation, you pretty much have to cut down all infested trees—either that or burn them if the access infrastructure isn't there for logging. Whatever you do, it has to be done before the little beggars can fly off to make merry in other trees.

"In the case of an infestation, the Regional Manager can authorize the holder of the Timber Supply License to harvest the timber, even if it exceeds the cut control limit. It's called sanitation harvesting. If I had to hazard a guess, I'd say your Marten Valley had itself a bark-beetle infestation."

"So a clear-cut that large is definitely legal." It was hard to swallow.

"Yeah, it looks that way. . . . Sanitation harvesting includes all harvesting methods: selective cuts, clear-cutting, you name it. From what I can tell by this, it's the only way to control an epidemic. Why? What's up? Did you think you had another case of the Big Bad Logging Company?"

I laughed. "I must admit, the thought had crossed my mind. I guess I go a little funny when I see clear-cuts half the size of Calgary."

"I can relate. Why do you think I'm studying to become a blood-sucking lawyer?"

I chuckled. "And you'll drain many dry, I'm sure. Thanks a bunch, Meggie. I appreciate you looking that up for me."

"The sweat was minimal," she assured me. "Now, what's this about Kelt Roberson....?"

CHAPTER 8

The next morning, my alarm clock went off at three a.m. Fortunately I had purchased a clock with a snooze button.

CHAPTER 9

At 4:10 I managed to roll out of bed with a minimum of grumbling and groaning.

"Tomorrow, we'll go out before dawn," I had told Kelt the previous night. "We'll play the tape of owl calls and see what answers." It had seemed like a sound approach.

At this time of the year, owls usually spend their days high in the forest canopy where they can warm themselves in the winter sunshine. That might explain why we hadn't had any luck in finding any during our daytime walk-around. As well, spotted owls are strictly nocturnal, so logically we had a better chance of finding one at night. The owls would be more active, and, hopefully, they'd be closer to the ground, nearer to their food source—and our binoculars. This sort of reasoning, I reflected sleepily, always sounded great until you actually had to get out of bed.

Under the flickering fluorescent lights of the bathroom, I washed my face with warm water, following it up with an icy splash of cold water to wake myself. Then I dialed Kelt's room number.

"Grzphltz?"

"Rise and shine!" I said brightly.

There was a long pause, then a groan. "Sshlurguska!"

Not a promising sound.

"Tired?" I asked.

"Jluugmmh." Another pause, longer this time, then, "You sure i's time to geddup?"

"I'm afraid so."

"Fiv' more minutes?" Kelt asked hopefully.

I had been expecting that. "Sorry, we've slept in as it is."

"Three more minutes? Jus' three? Two? One and a half?"

"Don't be pathetic. I'll meet you outside in fifteen."

When Kelt finally emerged twenty minutes later, he looked as rough as he'd sounded. His face was pink from a vigorous scrubbing, but his hair had been combed half-heartedly, and wasn't his sweatshirt . . . ? I looked at him more closely. Yes, it was inside out. Wordlessly, I handed him the thermos of coffee.

It was just instant coffee, and not very good at that (I am notoriously bad in the kitchen), but he pounced on it with eager desperation. A brief look at his face, and I gestured him to the passenger's side of the car. I wasn't about to trust my life to a refugee from *Dawn of the Dead*.

We were out of town and halfway to the site before Kelt recovered enough to start looking around. At last, I ventured to speak.

"I thought all you mammal biologists were early risers."

"We are. I am. I don't know what's wrong today." He looked at me and smiled disarmingly. "Sorry I was grumpy. Thanks for the coffee."

My heart almost skipped a beat. He had the nicest smile, and those eyes. . . . "Hey, don't mention it," I managed to say. "If I'd had a syringe, I would have pumped it directly into your veins."

"Not a bad idea." He cleared his throat and began in a businesslike tone, "So, do we have everything together for this?"

"Yep, all we need is a tape recorder, a tape of owl calls, a flashlight, binoculars, maps, and a compass. We'll also take the thermos of coffee, which, incidentally, you better not have drained or I might be forced to commit a crime upon your person." In my dreams, I already had. Well, okay, maybe it wasn't a *crime*.

"Don't worry." He made a show of peering into the thermos. "I think I see a few dregs left. Where are the tapes?"

"I've got a fresh one in the glove compartment. It should be labeled. Why don't you dig it out?"

Kelt opened the glove compartment and began to rummage through. He held up a tape. "Here we go, 'Owl Calls—Pacific Coast, general.'"

"Good, we're all set then. We'll try playing the tape along the roadside first. During the night, owls usually move to the edges of open areas. Better for hunting."

I eased the car off the road and coasted to a stop just at the beginning of our section. The sky was a velvety purple, rosy dawn still hours away. Despite a carpet of fresh snow, the air was mild. As I got out of the car, a soft breeze ruffled my hair. I inhaled deeply and let my breath out in a soft sigh. I loved this quiet time when the whole world seemed to lie deep in slumber, promises of the day were yet to be realized, and field biologists waxed poetic.

Unconsciously, we lowered our voices in keeping with the early morning hush. With any luck, the owls would be out.

"It's beautiful out here," Kelt murmured.

"Mmmm, yes. Definitely worth getting out of bed for," I agreed. "Feeling more awake now?"

"Awake, sharp-eyed, and ready for action." He stood grinning with his hands on his hips. "Yep. Mr. Alert. That's what they call me."

"I see," I said gravely. "Perhaps Mr. Alert would care to turn his sweatshirt right side out before we get started?"

Hoo! hu-hu-hu Hoo! Hoo!

The resonant call of a great horned owl reverberated down the empty logging road. That was close! Kelt started in surprise. Immediately I raised my flashlight and scanned the trees nearest us. Two great golden eyes stared down at me.

The owl's ear tufts were raised in alarm, its feathers fluffed out threateningly. I moved the flashlight beam off to one side so as not to impair the bird's night vision. The call seemed to set off a chain reaction down the edge of the shadowed treeline as other great horned owls, roused by the hoot of a possible intruder, called out to announce their presence and proclaim their territory.

We stood spellbound. I thought I could distinguish four, maybe five owls, their songs echoing distantly through the hushed forest. As the serenade gradually faded, I sighed happily and nudged Kelt to continue on.

"Let's go further in. Even if any of the smaller owls are around, they won't call now."

"Why not?" Kelt asked absently, still captivated by owl song.

"The great horneds are pretty formidable predators. If they get the chance, they'll even eat other owls."

"You're kidding!" He turned to look at me in surprise. "I never knew that."

"Oh, yes. They've been known to take the small saw-whets, and occasionally one of the bigger ones like a barred or a spotted owl. Now that the little guys know the great horneds are around, they won't let out a peep. That's why the tape is arranged with the smaller owl calls first and the great horned call last."

"So what you're saying is the tape is something along the lines of a dinner bell."

"A what?"

"A dinner bell. When we play the tape, all the little guys answer, then the big ones can pick 'em off more easily."

I rolled my eyes. "It's not like *that*," I said. "The little owls would have to be flying or otherwise exposed in order for the big guys to get them. Besides—" I stopped short, belatedly catching the twinkle in Kelt's eyes. "Great. All of a sudden, he's a comedian. C'mon, Mr. Comic, into the woods with you."

Dawn had long since brightened the sky by the time I called a rest break. We had seen innumerable chickadees, a few white-breasted nuthatches, and one rather bedraggled-looking crow. But not a single owl, besides the ones that had greeted us by the road. Dejected, we sat on a fallen log and divided the remaining coffee into two plastic cups. I unfolded the map between us.

"What now, Kemo Sabe?" Kelt asked as he rummaged around in his pockets. Pulling out a rather disreputable-looking granola bar, he solemnly broke it in half and offered a piece to me.

I accepted the offering gratefully. I wasn't much of a breakfast person, but two hours of slogging through wet forest was enough to get anyone's stomach growling. I munched on sweetened oatmeal and nuts, and pensively examined the map.

"There's a pretty big ravine a little ways ahead," I answered finally. "Maybe we should check it out. Spotted owls like protected ravines. They can sun themselves to their heart's content and stay out of the wind at the same time."

We slurped down the last of the coffee in companionable silence. The morning had warmed, and snow had begun to fall from the branches in wet plops. As I refolded the map, Kelt pushed himself to his feet, brushed granola crumbs from his coat, and offered me a hand up.

"Onward and downward we go," he said jauntily.

The ravine turned out to be more of a canyon, with precipitous sides and a narrow stream at its base. It was also thigh-deep in fresh, heavy, wet snow. Huffing and puffing our way down, we were soon drenched to the skin. But, at our first sight of the owl pair perched sleepily on a snag, clammy clothes and soggy socks were completely forgotten.

As with most raptors, the female was slightly larger than her male partner. Their facial discs were pale buff against the white-spotted red-brown of their heads and bodies. Their bills were pale and yellowish, their eyes dark and dreamy. The two spotted owls drowsed in the winter sunshine, completely unconcerned with such inconsequential creatures as field biologists.

Breathless with elation, Kelt whipped out his camera and snapped away. "There's no in-between with these guys, is there?" he whispered, using up the last of his film.

Scribbling furiously in my notebook, I looked up at him. "What do you mean?"

"Well, it seems like they're either hiding and smirking up their wings, or throwing themselves in front of your camera. Look! The one on the left is closing his eyes! Unbelievable! I think he's actually going to sleep."

"Maybe it's a commentary on our stimulating company," I remarked with a mischievous smile.

Kelt grinned back in accord. "There's a humbling thought. I wonder if they've got a nest around here."

I scanned the trees. "Hard to say. I don't see any cavities from where I'm sitting. . . . Do you see any whitewash?"

"Nothing except what's underneath them." Kelt pointed to the right. "But what's that over there on that branch? A feather?"

Halfway up the leeward side of the canyon, we hit pay-dirt. An ancient Douglas fir, with a deep cavity high in its venerable trunk, stood watch over the landscape. A wide splash of whitewash stained the thick, corky bark, and the pile of pellets below confirmed tenancy. I pocketed a few for further study.

"How do you know that this is a spotted owl nest?" Kelt asked.

"I don't. Not for certain, anyway. But we haven't seen or heard any other owls around here. Spotted owls usually mate for life; they occupy the same territory and sometimes use the same nesting tree for several years. It's a good bet this is their tree, but we'll have to come back again to be absolutely sure."

"I thought that most owls would have laid all their eggs by now," Kelt said, a little disappointed that there was no sign of young.

"Don't worry about it," I consoled him. "It's quite

possible she's a late bloomer. In the long run, it doesn't really matter. We've found a potential breeding pair here, and that's more than anyone else can say." I threw out my arms in joyous enthusiasm. "Think about what that means, Kelt. The spotted owls in this forest are not just lone strays; they're actually breeding here!"

Buoyed by my exuberance, Kelt laughed. "So, we get our names in the bird books now?"

"You bet! Fame and fortune will be ours! Well, maybe fame, and Dave did promise a fancy dinner. But, if all goes well ... it's goodbye to Seidlin clear-cutting!"

"Amen to that!" he replied fervently.

"I think we deserve more than just our names in a bird book," I began.

Kelt broke in. "Right now I'd settle for a hot breakfast."

I grinned. "Hey, I'll even throw in dry socks. C'mon, let's head back. I don't want to disturb the owls any more than we have to."

"Oh yeah, they really look disturbed," Kelt snickered, pointing back to the pair, who were now snoozing heavily in the golden sunshine. "I can almost hear them snoring!"

I chuckled. "They're pretty relaxed, aren't they?"

"Relaxed?! They're practically comatose!" He shook his head in amused disbelief. "Let's go. I can hardly wait to tell Kaye and Ben!"

As it turned out, news of the spotted owl pair had to wait. Twenty feet from the car, Kelt slipped in the snow and fell heavily to the ground. He laughed and cursed good-naturedly, then rolled over to push himself up. Poking out from under the snow was a pale-colored sleeve.

Another body? I stood frozen in midstep, like one of

those ice sculptures you see at winter festivals. Kelt dug frantically into the packed, wet snow. With a yank made sharper by fear, he pulled. The entire coat came out in one tug. At least, what was left of the coat came out.

It was empty. No body this time. I almost fainted with relief. Then I took a closer look at what we had found. I gaped, staring in stunned disbelief at the snow-covered coat in Kelt's hands. It had been torn from shoulder to waist; smeared stains of an evil reddish brown soiled the cream-colored fabric. As Kelt held it up, pink-tinged snow plopped down in wet clumps at his feet.

CHAPTER 10

"I'm beginning to have second thoughts about this impact assessment," I told Kelt unhappily.

We had decided to leave the coat where it had been buried and bring the police directly to the site. The ride back to town had been silent, each of us lost in our own morbid thoughts. At least mine were morbid. Given our grisly discovery, I could only assume that Kelt's were as well. It was just before nine o'clock when we pulled into the parking lot of the RCMP station.

"Why?" Kelt demanded with forced cheerfulness. "We found spotted owls, didn't we?"

"Yeah, but it seems like every time I find an owl, there's some sort of unpleasant discovery right around the corner. If this keeps up, I won't be surprised if they put me on the RCMP payroll." I got out of the car. "Either that or toss me in jail," I added under my breath.

The RCMP detachment was busy that morning. Officers strode in and out, intent on various aspects of the investigation. Reporters trailed after them like hungry baby birds. Both interrogation rooms were occupied. Somewhere a deep voice boomed out in anger. A higher, lighter voice broke in, its tone calming, then both fell to a muffled murmur. Inspector Danson was nowhere to be seen, but Sergeant McIntrye sat at one of the desks compiling a list of names. Possible suspects, I surmised, then wondered if I was on the list.

His eyebrows shot up as we made our report. "Again!?" he exploded incredulously.

I colored under his gaze. "I know, I know!" I replied. "I never thought finding evidence for a murder would be an occupational hazard."

McIntyre shook his head slowly. "You know exactly where you found the coat?" he asked, gathering up a notebook, map and pen.

"Oh yes," Kelt assured him. "We built a little cairn at the side of the road to mark the spot."

"Good thinking." McIntyre pulled on his coat and stuffed the map in his breast pocket. "Let me round up a few more people and we'll head out."

An hour later, I finally understood what people were talking about when they spoke of *déjà vu*. Driving out to the site, watching as the Plastic Baggie Team combed the area, answering questions, and making a statement—it was all horribly familiar. The only difference was the reporters' fluttering presence. Fortunately, Sergeant McIntyre managed to keep most of them away from me.

I felt conspicuous among the police officers—like a gopher sitting on the snow—conspicuous and jumpy. I was especially wary of the falcon-like Inspector Danson. He'd poked his head out of one of the tiny offices just as we were leaving the station, and, when McIntyre told him about our discovery, he'd latched onto our group immediately. His questions were pretty general, unthreatening, but I could feel his eyes on me the entire time we were at the site, and it was everything I could do to keep from squirming. The Tape Team was tying their yellow ribbons around the trees by the time Kelt and I were given the go-ahead to leave.

"I don't think Inspector Danson likes me much," I confessed to Kelt as we drove off. "He keeps looking at me with a nasty, suspicious glare."

"You're imagining things," he tried to reassure me. "He was perfectly fine with me."

"Yeah, well, you didn't find a body in the woods."

"You've just got a natural case of paranoia. It's like when you're driving...."

"Is this going to be another cheese-slice theory?"

He grinned. "No, no. Just picture yourself happily driving along the freeway. Suddenly you notice a police car behind you. What's the first thing you do?"

"Uh, I don't know.... Make sure I'm not speeding, I guess."

"Exactly! The first thing you do is check your speedometer. Now, you're a law-abiding citizen, logically you know you haven't been speeding, but as soon as you see those blue-and-white cars, bam! Your paranoia kicks in and you start to feel guilty.

"It's the same principle here. You find a body—completely by accident—then you find something that might be crucial evidence in the case. Both times it was just random chance. You *know* that you didn't have anything to do with the crime, but as soon as you see the police, in this case our icy-of-countenance Inspector Danson, you start to feel guilty."

I regarded him doubtfully. "I guess so...."

"I *know* so. Besides, if you want to get technical, *I* found the coat. So you see, you have nothing to feel guilty about. It's all in your mind. By the way, you're speeding."

"What!?" My eyes flew to the speedometer. "I am not!"

Kelt smirked. "See?"

"Funny. Okay, Sigmund," I said, trying to relax, "is this when you tell me all my guilt stems from a deprived childhood?"

Kelt worked his eyebrows up and down furiously and assumed a truly vile Austrian accent. "Oh, no, not zee childhood, no. Zee paranoia ees deerectly related to zee repression of zee sexual impulses."

"Cute." I rolled my eyes. "I don't know about you, but I want to go back to the motel and change into some dry clothes."

"And breakfast? I distinctly remember being promised breakfast."

I quirked up one side of my mouth in a half-smile. He even sounded hungry. "Yes, and breakfast," I assured him.

The motel lobby was deserted, apart from a small battalion of half-empty Styrofoam cups. Either the news crews had finally succumbed to the motel's coffee or everybody was over at the RCMP station. I hoped it was the latter; I wasn't up to finding any more bodies.

"Any messages?" I asked the desk clerk, a young teenager clad in a Pearl Jam T-shirt. He tossed aside his magazine, stood up, and strolled unhurriedly over to the counter. His black jeans were so baggy I half-expected them to slide right off his narrow, adolescent hips, but he made it to the counter safely with dignity intact. Who says there's no magic left in the world?

"Nobody from th' outside," he mumbled. "But m'uncle Jaime phoned. Said you'd know what he was callin' for."

"Your uncle's Jaime Cardinal?"

"Yep. Need his number?"

"Please."

Back in my beige room, I dumped my backpack and binoculars on the hard, fabulous-fifties-style armchair. So, the mysterious Jaime Cardinal finally surfaces. As I peeled off cold, clammy jeans and wrapped myself in my Big Bird robe, I reviewed what I knew about the man.

Jaime Cardinal's family had lived in the town as long as there had been a town to live in. Jaime himself was part Native, part Scottish, a former logger turned environmentalist, and owner of the town's single gas station. He was also the guy who had first seen a spotted owl in the area. He had contacted the BCWA immediately with the news. I was curious about how the townspeople had taken that. Or if they knew.

Dave had described Jaime as an amiable man, talkative and helpful. Apparently he loved birds. That was how he'd gotten involved in the Wilderness Association in the first place. He was going to be pleased about the owls. I wondered what he'd have to say about the murder.

"Big Bert's Shoes and Cheese."

"What? Uh, I'm sorry, I must have the wrong number. ..."

"Oops! Thought you were someone else. This here's Jaime's Gasbar."

I smiled. "All right then. I guess I do have the right number. I'm trying to reach Jaime Cardinal."

"Try no more, sweet thang, you're speakin' to him. And who do I have the pleasure of addressin'?"

"My name's Robyn Devara . . . ," I began.

"Robyn Devara! Good to hear from you! Heh, heh.

Sorry about that shoes and cheese thing; I thought you were my cousin."

"Hey, no problem. I got my chuckle for the day. I heard about your accident. How are you feeling?"

"Already bored outta my skull, to tell you the truth. And the damn leg'll have me laid up for weeks yet!"

"I'm sorry. I heard it was bad."

"Yeah. I'll survive but it's gonna make it hard to stay on top of things. Hell, I never even knew you were in town till this mornin'."

"I've only been here since Thursday night, and my colleague, Kelt Roberson, came in on Saturday. We were giving you a few days to recuperate before we inflicted ourselves on you. We didn't want to bother you."

"Bother me? *Bother me?*! I *need* to be bothered! Can't do a damn thing right now. I'm goin' absolutely bug-f ... uh, crazy."

"Well, if you want, we could come out and compare notes today. We've just gotten back in from one of the survey blocks ..."

"And?" His voice brimmed over with impatient excitement.

I smiled. "And I think you'll like what we have to tell you."

I held the receiver away from my ear as Jaime let out a wild whoop of delight.

"All right! That's the best thing I've heard all through this sorry-assed week! Say, you guys eaten yet?"

"No, we were just about to head over to Irene's."

"Why don't you come on over here instead? I'm the best bean-burner in these parts. Besides, I've got a huge pot of coffee on, and all the fixins for my world-famous omelet."

He was irresistible. I knew that I was going to like Jaime Cardinal, but then I'd always been a sucker for men who wanted to feed me. "Sounds marvelous," I told him. "How do we get there?"

CHAPTER 11

Jaime's house was located at the south end of town, about a hundred yards from his gas station. Both buildings were small but solid-looking. The house was essentially a log cabin, well constructed with white mortar in between dark, unfinished logs. Bright green awnings decorated and protected the windows. It had a welcoming sort of air about it.

I was born and raised in a city, so the first time I had ever done any fieldwork I'd been a little taken aback by the overwhelming friendliness of small-town inhabitants. While city people may toss you a smile as you pass them on the street or pause to exchange a brief greeting over the fence, town and farm folk were just as likely to invite you in for a coffee, offer you vegetables from their gardens, and haul out their scrapbooks to show you photos of their daughters decked out in Harvest Queen finery. I found the unfailing hospitality of these people quite irresistible and I quickly learned to look forward to their warmth, soaking up their kindess like a new and improved Bounty paper towel. I was therefore delighted when Jaime Cardinal proved every bit as friendly in person as he'd seemed on the phone.

He was medium-sized—probably about as tall as I was

when he wasn't in a wheelchair—with skin the color of Kraft caramels and soft, dark, owl eyes. His hair was more silver than brown, and the skin around his eyes was crinkled with the lines of one long familiar with the outdoors.

He greeted us like old friends, pumping our hands amicably and settling us down with enormous mugs of richly fragrant coffee. We sat in a large, open kitchen where cool green counters were warmed by golden oak cabinets. In terra cotta pots along each of the two window ledges, tiny bushes of fresh herbs opened their leaves to the morning sun. It was the kind of room where you could easily chat away an afternoon or two. Jaime maneuvered around expertly in his wheelchair, refusing all offers of help, his right leg sticking out slightly, rigid in its fresh white cast.

"Okay, you got coffee. Anybody take cream or sugar? Yep? There you go. You know, it's great to finally meet you both."

"It's nice to meet you too," I told him. "I'm just sorry you won't be able to come out with us."

Jaime sighed. "Yeah. I was really lookin' forward to helpin' with the survey and all. I don't get out too much since I took a walk down the road—quit the loggin', you understand. I kinda miss it sometimes—the bein' outdoors part, I mean. I sure don't miss bein' a hairy-assed BC logger."

Hairy-assed? Kelt and I exchanged amused glances.

"When I slipped on that stupid ice, I think I was more mad than anything." Jaime paused to snort in disgust. "Figures I'd sprain the other leg too. Huh! Sourdough bread okay with breakfast?"

We nodded enthusiastically.

"It's nice of you to cook breakfast for us—" Kelt began.

Jaime waved it off. "Not a problem. I was kinda surprised when Dave told me you were already here. The way they were talkin' the other day, they were gonna can the whole survey till I was up and mobile again."

"I heard they're in a hurry for our results," I said.

Jaime shook his head in mock despair. "Ah, you know these environmental groups. Their heart's in the right place, but a lot of the time their administration skills are up their butts, not to put too fine a point on it. But I guess there's no real harm done; you're here safe and sound."

"And we've already hit the jackpot." Kelt smiled.

Jaime beamed back. "I'm all ears."

Obediently, Kelt and I related our early morning find, excluding any mention of the jacket. There would be time enough for that later. Jaime, busy chopping vegetables at the counter, uttered intermittent groans of delight as we described the owl pair.

"Ah, that's just goddamn wonderful. Wonderful," he sighed. "I wish I could have seen them. I never got a decent look at the one I found." He shook his head mournfully, then brought a couple of onions out from under the sink and began slicing them in a quick, rocking motion. Obviously a man who knew his way around a kitchen (more than I could say for myself). When he had a generous pile, he pulled an enormous, black, cast-iron frying pan out of the cupboard and put it on the stove.

As the onions began to sauté, the savory scent wafted out to tantalize my nose. Grumpily, my stomach reminded me that half a stale granola bar was a patently unacceptable breakfast. "So what about the owl you saw?" I asked Jaime, trying to cover up the sounds of my increasingly impatient stomach. "Whereabouts were you?"

Jaime launched into a brightly detailed description of the sighting. He'd been watching birds since he was a kid, he told us with a smile, but this had been his first spotted owl. His excitement was still evident. He'd gone out with one of his city cousins just to walk around. The owl had been a surprise for both of them. As he talked, he buttered thick slabs of sourdough bread, covered them generously with homemade strawberry preserves, and sprinkled grated yellow cheese over the now puffy, golden omelet. He topped up our coffees, and with an exaggerated flourish, he served us. "There now, that oughta warm your innards."

I looked at my laden plate with delight. "Wow!" I said. "And to think I was expecting shoes and cheese!"

Jaime guffawed and thumped my shoulder.

I forked up a piece of omelet and put a little bit of heaven into my watering mouth. "Mmmmph," I said, unable to speak coherently. My taste buds were in paroxysms of delight. I looked across the table. Kelt's eyes were half closed in ecstasy.

Jaime watched us indulgently for a moment before picking up his fork and burrowing into his own plate. "Eat up while it's hot. I like to see a body enjoyin' good food."

The bread tasted like it had been baked that morning. The preserves were tartly sweet with the sunny flavor of wild strawberries. The omelet itself was a feather-light concoction, bulging with a delectable mixture of onions, garlic, fresh basil, peppers, mushrooms, and sun-dried tomatoes, and blanketed with a rich layer of melted cheddar. I think I'd fallen in love.

As we stuffed ourselves, a hush descended on the room as effectively as if the Cone of Silence had been activated.

Finally Kelt mopped up his plate with the last of his bread. "That was absolutely incredible," he proclaimed with a surreptitious belch.

I added my enthusiastic praise to Kelt's, and Jaime beamed with delight. "Glad you liked it. More coffee?"

"Maybe in a bit," I said. "How about if Kelt and I take care of the dishes?"

"Oh no," Jaime protested. "I can do 'em up later."

"Forget it!" Kelt said. "You cooked, we clean. It's only fair."

"Well . . . guess I can't argue much with that." Jaime poured himself more coffee and leaned against the table, watching as we started to clear away the dishes. "So you saw the pair of owls this mornin'. Have you seen any other ones?"

I hesitated, then dropped the bomb. "Yes, I found another one. Right over Bill Reddecop's body."

"*You're* the one who found him?!" Jaime was shocked. "Alex never told me *that*."

"Alex?"

"Sergeant Alex McIntyre. We've been friends for years and years."

"Oh. Yeah, I was the one who found him. Kelt hadn't arrived yet and I was out by myself. It was pretty awful." I managed to suppress a shudder. "Did you know him?"

"Yeah." His voice was flat. "Yeah, most everybody in town knew Bill."

Tea towel in hand, I turned to face him. "You didn't like him," I said with some surprise.

Jaime snorted in disgust. "You could say that. Bill and

I were never real close, even when we were growin' up. The situation got a lot worse about a year ago."

"Oh?"

"You see, the Reddecops live right behind me. A number of months back, I got myself a dog. A real nice Lab pup, black as night. Sweet personality. Didn't chew stuff neither. Well, not much. Anyhow, she never liked Bill at all—kept barkin' whenever she laid eyes on him. She was kinda excitable, but you expect that from a real young dog. Huh! I guess Bill was never overly fond of dogs. Her barkin' pissed him right off. Once, I even caught him haulin' off to give her a boot."

Kelt looked up from the dishes. "I haven't much use for a person who kicks an animal," he said.

Jaime nodded his head. "You and me both, partner. Bill and I had words. Awful loud words at that. For a while there, I thought it was gonna come to blows. Then Alex came cruisin' by and broke things up. A week later, my pup disappeared."

"What?!" I stared at Jaime. "Did he do something to her?"

Jaime threw up his hands. "I dunno. I never found out. She hadn't run away before, and her rope wasn't chewed. She was just gone. I had my suspicions but no proof, y'know. I never trusted myself to speak to him ever since."

I dried the last dish thoughtfully and put it in the cupboard. "What about the other townspeople? Did they like him?"

Jaime finished his coffee as he considered the question. "Well, now that's kinda complicated. The Reddecop family's been around since Marten Valley was founded. You see, there were three partners that formed Seidlin

Lumber. Morris Young, he's dead now; Bert Chase; and Bill's old man—actually Bill Sr. was pretty much the drivin' force behind the whole thing. A lot of people owe their high-payin' jobs to him. He was a great guy, and the town respected him and his family.

"Havin' said that, I don't think too many folks cared much for Bill Jr. personally. He always had a real mean temper even as a kid. His brother Greg was a whole lot friendlier, y'know, more outgoin'. He's sure a hell of a lot more popular in town than Bill could ever've hoped to be."

Kelt's cheese-slice theory seemed to be holding up. "Mr. Reddecop Sr. is dead now?" I asked.

"Yeah, he passed on . . . lemme see, must be about ten years ago now."

"Is the brother still around?"

"Nah, not so's you'd notice. He's a hotshot architect down in Victoria now. Comes up every now and again for a visit. Not so much since Bill got hitched."

"Really? Too busy being a hotshot?"

"Could be. Myself, I figure he wasn't overly fond of Bill's wife."

Kelt gave the countertop a last wipe and draped the cloth over the faucet. "Ta da! Just call me Mr. Clean."

Jaime smiled. "Thanks, partners, that's great. Huh! Did a better job than I do. Come on." He spun his wheelchair around. "Let's retire to the livin' room."

Jaime led the way down a bright, narrow hall and into a large room on the right. I stepped into the room and stared, awestruck.

Jaime's living room was filled with birds. Warblers, chickadees, sparrows, owls, eagles, woodpeckers, ducks. They perched on every available surface, their forms lovingly shaped from wood. Some were extremely realistic, each feather separate and distinct, smoothed down or ruffled by the memory of a summer's breeze. Others merely suggested form: the shape of an owl dozing on a branch; a nuthatch making its inverted way down a trunk. They were exquisite.

"Jaime!" I exclaimed softly. "Are these your work?"

His face glowed with pleasure. "Yeah, I like to do a bit of carvin' in my spare time. This way I always got birds around, even in winter."

"Spare time?" Kelt sputtered. "You must have a lot of it on your hands. These are great! Where'd you learn to carve like this?"

Jaime shrugged a little self-consciously. "I dunno. I taught myself, I guess."

"You're kidding!"

"No, it's not that hard. You can always see the shape in the wood before you start. It's just a matter of carvin' off the excess."

"Uh huh," Kelt said. "Seems to me that Michelangelo said something like that."

I stroked a small warbler asleep on a bookshelf. It gleamed with the deep color of burnished bronze. "Birds all through the winter," I murmured. "What a lovely thought."

"Okay, okay." Jaime was starting to get a little self-conscious. "Quit your gawpin' and take a load off."

We settled ourselves into plump hunter-green chairs. Kelt sighed appreciatively. "You've got a wonderful place here, Jaime. I envy you."

Jaime looked around the room with a gentle smile. "It's home," he said simply. "Look, why don't you stay here while you're in town?"

"Really?" I was surprised and touched at the offer.

"Yeah! That motel is kinda depressin'. All those old beige rooms." He wiggled his fingers in disgust. "Nobody ever stays there if they can help it. I got plenty of room, and with this damn leg, it'll be kinda nice to have some help. Besides, I gotta go up to the hospital in Quesnel this comin' Sunday to get the leg looked at. If you don't mind, you can run me up there; y'know, as a kinda exchange for stayin' here."

Kelt and I looked at each other and smiled.

"You've got a deal," I said to Jaime. "Thanks. We'd be delighted to stay with you."

We relaxed for a while, but time wasn't waiting for man or woman, and Kelt and I had to heave our overstuffed selves out of Jaime's overstuffed chairs, go back to the motel, gather up our things, and check out. We returned only to discover that Jaime had taken relaxation one step further. A scrawled note taped to the kitchen door informed us that he'd gone for a nap, and urged us to make ourselves at home.

We took our coats off and hung them on wooden pegs by the door. Even the pegs were beautiful, carved in the shape of duck heads, their bills extended to catch the coats.

"A nap sounds pretty appealing right about now," Kelt remarked, shooting me a reproachful look. "It was an *awfully* early morning."

I grinned, unrepentant. "Yeah, but look what we found."

Kelt smiled back and leaned over to pick up his camera case. His shirt stretched taut across his back. Suddenly I could think of other things to do that afternoon. Things that weren't necessarily restful.

I gulped and cleared my throat. "You know, we should probably cook dinner tonight," I commented. "We" meaning him, of course.

Kelt nodded and took the bait. "Okay. I make a pretty good stir-fry, but that breakfast is going to be a hard act to follow."

"Just look on it as a challenge," I suggested helpfully. I was a helpful sort of person.

Quietly we dragged our luggage down the hall to our respective rooms. They were immaculate and tastefully decorated, mine done in forest green and copper, Kelt's in lovely shades of navy.

I dumped my duffel bag by the window and looked out onto a back yard that, though moderately sized, boasted a small forest of Sitka spruce. Decorating the trees were birdhouses and feeders both large and small, painted and plain. Quite an improvement on the Rest EZ. I looked around at the cozy room again. No dial phone, though. I snickered. Maybe I should complain to the management.

A nap did sound good, but I decided to work a little on my report first. By the time I'd finished typing up my field notes on my laptop, the house was quiet, the soft *tick tick* of a wall clock faintly audible in the hush. Both Kelt and Jaime were deep in slumber. One of them—I couldn't tell which—snored gently.

Surrounded now by peace and quiet, I wished perversely for their light-hearted presence. For the first time since that morning, I was alone with my thoughts. They weren't happy ones. I kept telling myself that Bill Reddecop's murder was none of my business, but the gods seemed to be doing their immortal best to make it my business. First I find the body, then it turns out I know the man's wife, and now a bloody coat pops up under my very feet (well, under Kelt's feet). All in all, I was beginning to think that somebody up there was trying to tell me something, and I found myself wishing I could just plug my ears.

Too jittery to take a nap and unable to concentrate on a book, I rooted through my coat pockets and came up with the owl pellets we'd found earlier. I rummaged through my duffel bag, found an exacto knife and a Petri dish, and sat down at the desk to dissect one of the pellets.

When owls eat, they swallow their prey whole. The nutrients are absorbed and digested, while the indigestible parts like fur and bone are regurgitated as pellets. Although most pellets are only about the size of my thumb, they often contain the prey animal's entire skeleton.

A spotted owl eats anything from flying squirrels, to woodrats, to deer mice, to small birds and insects. In the 1980s, three separate studies reported that larger prey, like squirrels and woodrats, played an important role in a spotted owl's reproductive success. Though I had a few problems with the reports (inadequate collection methods, small sample sizes, fluctuations in prey populations), the idea, in general, made sense. An abundance of large prey equals healthier owl parents and less competition among the young.

The pellets I'd picked up that morning all looked like they might contain the remains of larger prey. Woodrats, perhaps? I'd have to ask Kelt when he woke up. I picked a femur out of the dense mass. Definitely larger prey, though. I liked the idea that our owl pair had a good chance of breeding successfully. I smiled, imagining row after row of fuzzy, wide-eyed owlets shuffling along scaly branches as they waited for their parents to return with a fine squirrel lunch.

Soothed by the quiet work, I decided to try to settle down for a nap. I snuggled deep under the thick duvet, willing myself to relax. Despite my best efforts, my thoughts kept flitting about, whirling around spotted owls and Bill Reddecop's dead body, and settling on the torn, bloodied coat.

It didn't belong to the murdered man; that had still been on his body. A hunter? No, a hunter wouldn't have worn a white coat. And even if he had, it was unlikely he would have tossed it. Besides, the coat had been lying on snow, so it had been ditched during the winter. I didn't know of any open hunting season in the winter.

It had to be the murderer's coat. There had been a struggle; Inspector Danson had told me that much. Was that why the coat was so badly ripped? The murderer fought with Bill, killed him, and abandoned the coat once he realized it was covered in blood. Did Jurgen own a white parka?

CHAPTER 12

I woke a short while later. The house was still quiet. A brief nap had succeeded in banishing unpleasant thoughts of murderers and bloody coats, and I felt rested and alert. I got out of bed and stretched luxuriously. A little fresh air might be nice. I could stroll over to the grocery store and pick up some food for dinner. It was the least I could do. The gods knew I couldn't cook.

The outside air was revitalizing, though the sky hung low and heavy with the promise of more snow. A lot more snow from the looks of those clouds. Strolling back down Main Street, brown paper bags of vegetables in my arms, I noticed a sandwich-board sign outside Irene's Diner.

SPECIAL TODAY!

HOMEMADE BUMBLEBERRY PIE $1.95

Hmmm. A buck ninety-five for a piece of homemade pie? That sounded like a hell of a deal. My stomach gurbled encouragingly. I looked down at it in surprise. "After that huge breakfast?"

Gruffly, it informed me that breakfast had been hours ago and dinner was probably hours away. Powerless in the face of such logic—and reluctant to be seen arguing on the street with my stomach—I went in and ordered pie and coffee.

Monday afternoons were not a busy time for Irene's Diner. Except for another woman just finishing off the remains of a late lunch, I was the only patron. When the pie came, my jaw not only brushed the floor, it polished it and scrubbed it too.

The slice of bumbleberry pie was, in fact, almost a full quarter of a pie. A thick slice of berry heaven, it bulged with tangy raspberries, luscious strawberries, and plump blueberries whose dark juices flowed out to stain the white plate.

After the first bite, I resolved to buy a whole pie for dessert tonight. Kelt and Jaime would love it! After the second bite, I considered buying a whole pie and not telling them.

I was halfway through the slice when I became aware of someone standing over me. It was the other patron. She was a short, solid-looking woman with shoulder-length auburn hair and dark eyes. The eyes were friendly, echoing a wide, white smile.

"Hi!" Her voice was low and husky—quite beautiful, really—with a hint of Scottish brogue. "I'm Ella, one of Jaime's cousins," she said. "You must be Robyn Devara. I see you've discovered Irene's pies."

Her smile was infectious; I quickly licked pastry flakes from my lips and grinned up at her purply. "Hi, Ella. Care to join me?" I offered.

Her smile stretched wider and she slid into the seat across from me. "Thanks. I haven't had any dessert yet and . . . ooh, that pie looks good." She signaled the waitress for pie and coffee and turned her attention back to me.

"So, I hear you're looking for spotted owls," she began pleasantly. Obviously Ella was not one to beat around the bush.

"Uh, yeah," I replied cautiously. "That's right."

I must have looked ill at ease. I know I felt it. Suddenly Ella burst into peals of laughter. I smiled at her uncertainly.

Finally, she wiped her eyes and wagged her finger at me. "Ha, if you could see your face! I'll bet you feel like you've got the word 'environmentalist' stenciled across your forehead!"

I relaxed and returned her grin. "I've noticed they're not exactly popular around here."

Ella sobered. "No, especially after what's been happening. I'm sorry, Robyn, you've every right to be cautious. It was my brother Jess who was out with Jaime when he saw the owl," she explained. "That's how I knew who you were. Well, that was one of the reasons; the Marten Valley gossip hotline was fair burning up with the news."

"And to think I'd hoped to be here and gone before anyone knew what I was doing," I observed glumly.

"In a little wee town like Marten Valley?" Ella was genuinely surprised. "You don't come from a small town, do you?"

I shook my head.

"Well, even on a normal day, there're few secrets kept in such a small, isolated community. But with something like this? Environmentalists and spotted owls . . . everybody's worked up. Thing is, everybody knows what's happened in the States with this owl thing. And everybody's of a mind the same thing's going to happen here."

"But owls don't *have* to mean the end of logging in Marten Valley," I argued. "Maybe just the big clear-cuts, and they're on the verge of going out anyhow. There's still selective cutting or shelter cutting. Besides, what about infestations? From what I understand, you get one serious beetle epidemic and the whole section has to be fired, unless you can get to it in time to log it. A few spotted owl reserves aren't going to take up much more room than that."

Ella was shaking her head. "You don't have to convince me. I'm not overly fond of the clear-cutting either. But how much work is going to be left for the loggers if it stops? How many will get laid off? What will it mean for the town? There're still a lot of questions. And it's been so long since we had a beetle problem here that most don't even remember what it was like."

I looked at her sharply. "You haven't had any recent infestations?"

"Not since the early seventies. I remember my dad talking about it back then, but there's been none since. So you see, people aren't likely to be thinking of the owl reserves in those sorts of terms. The main trouble is, the world's changing and the old-growth loggers aren't quite sure how they'll fit in." She scooped up a piece of berry pie and paused, fork lifted halfway to her mouth. "Have you heard about the Alaska widows?"

I shook my head. "No, I don't think so."

"Well," Ella continued around her mouthful of pie, "they're living down in Oakridge, Oregon. Down where the logging stopped because of the owls. It's a town very similar to Marten Valley. Most everybody owns their own house, but the whole reason for the town being there was because of the logging. When the logging stopped, so did the work. Now all the loggers, the truckers, and the mill workers have to head up to Alaska to find work. They go up for ten months each year, while their wives, the Alaska widows, stay in Oakridge with the house and kids. A lot of the local businesses and stores have failed. Even if you wanted to sell your house, who would buy it?"

"And people here are afraid the same thing will happen to them," I concluded gloomily. My pie lay unfinished on the plate.

"Most believe that Seidlin's hardly going to stick around if there's no money in the logging."

"What did people do before Seidlin came in? The town's been here longer than 1956."

"Aye, but when you've grown used to having the kind of money you make from logging, it'd be very difficult to go back."

"How do you feel about all of this?" I asked her. "Your family's been here a long time, haven't they?"

"Me? Well, I'm not as pessimistic as some. The Marten Valley forest is awful big. I figure there's room enough for owls and loggers both."

"Are you a company worker?" I asked.

"Of course," she said. "Pretty much everyone around here works for the company in one way or another. I'm a crummy driver."

"Uh, I take it you're not commenting on your driving skills."

Ella laughed. "Oh no! No, I drive a bus that takes the crews out to the site. It's called a crummy. It *is* a bit unusual to have a woman crummy driver, but the big boss, Mr. Chase, he's very much an equal-opportunity employer. Actually his wife's very forceful about the whole thing—she can be a bit of a termagant—so I don't think he ever had much choice in the matter. I'm just as glad, really; it's a lot of fun being a crummy driver, though the return trip can get a little rowdy sometimes, especially when payday falls on a Friday."

I gestured towards her wedding band. "What about your husband? Is he a company man too?"

Ella chuckled. "No, Nat's the exception. He's not from around here, so he's never been bitten by the logging bug."

"Oh?" I prompted.

"We met at university," she explained. "I was getting a degree in sociology—useless as tits on a bull, my dad said, but I enjoyed myself. I couldn't find work in it once I'd graduated, but by then I'd met Nat. Marten Valley needed a teacher so we came back here and I started driving for Seidlin. It's good money, you know, but it's not my whole life. Not like most of the others. I guess that's why I can see both sides."

"I've heard the money's great."

She finished her coffee pensively. "You've heard right. And I expect I'd miss it a bit if it goes, but I don't believe that Seidlin will just pull out. With that new Forest Practices Code, they'll have to give up the clear-cutting in a few years anyhow. Besides, I've never been too comfortable with the idea that old-growth forests are useless just because they've no big-game animals in them."

"Far from it," I agreed. "In fact, North American old-growth forests are one of the most complex ecosystems in the world. There's a guy who actually climbed up into the canopies and discovered all kinds of strange stuff—unknown insects, weird aerial plants."

"Really?" Ella's eyes brightened with interest.

"Yeah, it's fascinating. They've got a huge research crane now that lifts the biologists up hundreds of feet to the canopy."

"Oooh, I'm not sure I'd like to ride a crane up that high."

I smiled and shook my head in heartfelt agreement. "No, I'm not crazy about heights myself. But it just goes to show you that old-growth forests aren't some kind of biological desert. One of the plants they've found doesn't even grow unless the forest is more than 150 years old. There could be anything up there . . . a cure for cancer, AIDS, even the common cold. Problem is, everybody knows we should save the tropical rainforests, but nobody seems to see—let alone want to save—what's in their own back yard."

Ella scraped up the last crumbs of her pie. "And I guess most loggers don't see beyond the owl."

"No, and that's been a problem with the whole campaign, both here and in the States. The spotted owl is really more of an indicator species, sort of like canaries, but in the forest instead of down a coal mine. They provide a good focus for the public, though. They're cute, cuddly-looking, and mysterious without being too weird."

"So, protect the owls and you help protect the other beasties who aren't so cute."

"That's about the size of it. It makes sense. It'd be kind of difficult to get people worked up about saving the red tree vole."

Ella laughed. "I must admit, I never really thought about it like that. You've an interesting way of putting things."

I smiled back. I liked Ella. She reminded me a lot of her cousin. She even talked almost as much as he did. A family trait? Oh well, it was a likeable one. She really seemed to have a feel for what was going on in Marten Valley.

"People seem pretty hostile towards spotted owls

here," I said. "I've seen the T-shirts and the bumper stickers. Do you think this murder has anything to do with it?"

"Bill Reddecop?" Her sunny expression darkened. "Now there's a terrible tragedy. I tell you, Robyn, around here, you expect to hear about an accident or a fatally in the forest. Most folks don't realize it, but logging's an awful dangerous line of work. A lot of good men get killed or hurt. That's why I always try my best to get the lads home on time—so their wives don't get to worrying, you see. No, you expect to hear about accidents and the like, but you sure don't expect to hear about a murder. It's not like we're Downtown, after all."

"Downtown?"

"It's what we call Vancouver around here. Was it Jaime that told you about Bill?"

"No, I was the one who found him." The words weren't getting much easier with repetition.

"You did?" She shuddered. "Ooh, poor you. Yes, I guess you'd be wondering about the connection then, wouldn't you?"

"Well, if I'm going to be hiking around looking for owls, I'd sort of like to know if I should be keeping an eye on my back too. I've heard that a lot of people think it was Jurgen Clark or, at least, one of the other environmentalists."

Ella nodded glumly. "Aye, you've heard right. Mr. Clark's not well liked in town. Not at all. To be frank, I don't really blame people. It's hard to find room in your heart for someone who accuses you of getting your jollies by killing trees and wee animals. But I don't know whether Bill's murder has anything to do with the owls, and that's the honest truth. I wouldn't rule it out, but my instincts tell me no. I think there're a lot of other reasons why it could have happened. If it's any comfort, I don't think anyone'll be taking a potshot at you. Especially now that Jaime's taken you under his wing."

"Oh? He's popular in town, is he?"

She chuckled. "Popular? He's related to just about everyone in some way, shape, or form. Besides, he's a good man and people trust his judgment."

"He is nice," I agreed. "But I've been wondering. What is his accent? I can hear the Scottish in yours, but I can't figure his out for the life of me."

Ella laughed. "I know, I know. We sometimes make a joke about it. Calling it the BC loggertalk. I don't know why, but all the lads seem to acquire it and then never lose it, even if they go to other jobs. I tease Jaime and tell him it's because they've all been hit on the head with branches and they're not quite right anymore."

I joined her laughter. "Well, I don't know, he seems pretty sharp to me—and he makes incredible omelets."

"Oh ho! He's made you one of his Italian specials, has he?"

I smacked my lips in remembrance. "Yeah, he invited my colleague and me over for breakfast. After he enslaved us with his omelet, he insisted that we stay with him while we're here. He said he could use some help while his leg was broken, but I suspect he just likes to have company."

Ella snorted. "That sounds like Jaime, all right. Not happy unless he's got folks around. He's always inviting the nieces and nephews to come and stay for a spell. Ah, well, the kids love him, and he's good for them. Doesn't let them get away with anything. Mind he doesn't talk your ear off while you're there, though." She glanced down at her watch. "Heavens! I've got to run. I didn't realize it was getting so late."

I stood and held out my hand. "It's been a pleasure talking with you, Ella. I hope we can get together again before I leave."

As she shook my hand warmly, her mouth curved up in a wicked grin. "Friday's strawberry-rhubarb pie day. It's really one of Irene's best. 'Twould be a pity to miss it."

"It would almost be inexcusable," I said gravely. She caught my eye and we burst out laughing, already fast friends.

"Friday at two all right with you?"

"Sounds perfect!" I assured her.

I watched as Ella paid for her meal and left with a cheery wave. She'd given me a lot to think about; not the least was the fact that Marten Valley hadn't had a bark beetle infestation in over twenty years. If that was the case, why had that clear-cut been so large?

The dead, or at least the exhausted, had arisen by the time I got back to Jaime's. Jaime looked rested and ready for action, but Kelt looked like death warmed over and left sitting under heat lamps.

"I guess these mammal biologists just don't have what it takes to keep up with us birders," I *tsked*, shaking my head. "Whatever happened to Mr. Alert? Looks like Mr. Lethargic now."

Jaime hid a smile behind his hand as Kelt made a rude face at me.

"Look!" I brandished the bags of vegetables. "Stir-fry ingredients! And . . ." I pulled out the pie box with a flourish. "Dessert!"

Jaime's reaction was instantaneous and gratifying. "Bumbleberry pie? Sweet thang, you found the key to my heart!"

"Hmmm," I drawled, eyeing his joyous antics suspiciously. "Seems like Irene's pies are well known in these parts. How did you know it was bumbleberry?"

"Monday's always bumbleberry day. And as a bachelor, you get to know these kinda things. Besides, bumbleberry's my favorite!"

"It's pretty wonderful," I agreed. "I also met your cousin Ella while I was at the diner."

Jaime was delighted. "Did you? When you were gettin' your stuff from the motel, I called her up and told her about you. I knew she'd want to meet you."

"She's great fun. We got along like a wildfire on the prairies. Sat and yakked for a good hour. She's an interesting woman."

"Ella knows more about what's goin' on in this town than anybody. Gotta watch her, though; she'll talk your ear off if she's got half a chance."

"Funny," I snickered. "She said the same thing about you."

"The rat!" Jaime exclaimed. Then he laughed sheepishly. "Huh! Probably true at that." He wheeled over to the refrigerator and pulled out a green bottle of Canada Dry. "Anyone for a splash of ginger ale? Sorry, no alcohol; I never drink the stuff."

"Ginger ale's great," I said, plunking three glasses down on the table. Jaime and I sat sipping our fizzy drinks and watched as Kelt prepared dinner.

"Ella doesn't seem to think that Bill Reddecop's murder has anything to do with the environmentalists," I commented.

Jaime took a long swig of his drink and nodded. "Yeah, I know. Not so sure of it myself."

"Oh? What do you think happened?"

He leaned back in his chair and looked at me. "I told you before Bill wasn't exactly what you'd call popular," he explained. "Thing is, it wasn't a real big problem so long as he was just one of the guys. He started out as a chokerman same as most everyone."

"A chokerman?"

"Yeah, that's the fella that rigs up the log with cables so's it can be yarded to the landing. Seemed like a fine idea for Bill to go into loggin', seein' how his old man had founded the company and all. Trouble was, in the grand peckin' order, the boss's son is low man on the totem pole. Most of the guys were kinda hard on Bill at first.

"Al and Norm were Bill's partners. You're always partnered up if you're a greenhorn. Till you prove yourself, you're just another name in the rain, as they say. Anyhow, Al and Norm were always playin' pranks on Bill—nothin' hurtful, of course; you don't do crap like that out there—just kinda embarrassin' stuff. Bill didn't take it real well, and that just made them laugh even harder. One day, as a joke, Norm filed an accident report with Workers' Compensation sayin' he'd busted a hernia and pissed himself crackin' up over the green kid."

Kelt and I burst out laughing.

"That's not the half of it!" Jaime chuckled. "Workers' Compensation actually sent some guy out to investigate!"

"No!"

"Yep, the guy had a pickle up his butt the size of one of them English cucumbers. Wantin' to know all the details about Norm's 'hernia' and what had happened to make it burst and how long he expected to be off work.

Norm played along for a while, till he couldn't hold it anymore. He started havin' a shit-fit laughin' and almost really did piss himself. Of course the rest of us were already rollin' on the floor."

"But Bill didn't laugh," I guessed.

"No, ma'am, he did not. Young Bill took himself real serious, and sure didn't like bein' the butt of so many jokes—'specially one like that. God, we laughed about that one for months! I still laugh! Many's the beer that's been bought in exchange for that story. Even guys on the island heard about it.

"Of course Bill never saw the humor in it, just like he never saw that other guys got razzed same as him. He didn't stay a chokerman for long; he up and took off Downtown to go to school. From what I hear, turned out he had a real head for numbers. But it didn't take too long before he figured out he just wasn't much of a city kinda guy. Huh! Guess we're the same in that respect. To make a long story short, he missed the loggin', so he learned how to be a surveyor, came back, and did that for a spell. Then, just before his old man died, Bill made foreman. That's when hell and all the little devils broke loose. He turned out to be a power-tripper—awful hard on the fellas below him."

"Paying them back for past insults?" I suggested.

Jaime nodded. "That's what I always figured. I tell you, it's one thing to take bullshit from some fancy-assed outsider. It's a whole different thing to take it from a guy you used to work beside."

"I can see why his crews didn't like him much, but killing a guy just for being an asshole? It doesn't seem like enough of a reason for murder," Kelt broke in.

"Well, no, not so's you'd think, but it sure adds to the

bad feelins, if you know what I mean. And then, of course, there were the fights."

"Fights?" I asked. Bill Reddecop was beginning to sound like a real honey. "I overheard somebody at Irene's say that Bill got into some sort of fight with Jurgen. Did he make a habit of doing things like that?"

Jaime laughed mirthlessly. "As I understand it, that particular fight was over some loggin' equipment. Seems somebody was sneakin' around to the Cats and pourin' sand into the gas tanks. Bill figured it was Jurgen and his gang."

"He was probably right," I sighed.

"Yeah, I thought so too. But in all fairness, Bill had a habit of gettin' into fights. Seemed to feel his week wasn't complete without some kinda nastiness." He shrugged. "You see, Bill was your basic jealous type. You seen his wife yet?"

Kelt pointed at me with the paring knife. "Seen her? She went to university with her! They met again in the police station after the murder."

Jaime regarded me with surprise. "That so? Well, isn't that the damndest thing?" He colored. "Here I been blatherin' away about her husband and you were *friends?*"

I shook my head. "Hardly that. We were classmates for a year but we didn't get along that well."

"I can't imagine anyone not gettin' along with you," Jaime said gallantly.

"Wow, I guess chivalry isn't dead after all," I grinned, before explaining. "Lori and I managed to be civil to each other until she slept with my boyfriend."

Kelt turned in surprise. "You never told me that."

Jaime was nodding in understanding. "That kinda thing's liable to put a crimp in a friendship."

I shrugged. "The guy was a creep; I was well rid of

him. But, in all fairness, I don't think she knew I was see-ing him."

Jaime's face darkened. "I'd be none too sure of that. She's got a reputation around this town that'd make any other woman blush purple. Seems she likes the men well enough, and not too picky about whether they're married or single. In fact, rumor has it she prefers 'em married. Less complications, y'know."

"I would've thought a married man would have more complications. A wife, to name one."

"So's you'd think, but look at it this way: if he was hitched, he'd be less likely to be on at her to leave Bill. Always seemed a bit conky to me, but she never seemed real interested in leavin' her marriage."

"Are you sure this isn't just small-town gossip?" I asked. "Ella told me about the Marten Valley hotline."

Jaime was already shaking his head. "Ella's right about the gossip. It buzzes around here worse than the mosquitoes do in the summer. Lori's been what you'd call a hot topic of conversation ever since she came. But I never heard nothin' about any affairs till after Bill was made foreman. Most of the guys that ended up goin' with her also worked under Bill. I dunno what *she* thought she was doin', but I always figured the guys were kinda gettin' back at Bill for bein' such an asshole."

"There were a lot of them?" I sighed. In many ways it wasn't so different from what had happened in university. Men still couldn't see past good looks, and the Loris of this world never changed. They always seemed to land on their feet, or their backs. Meow.

Jaime nodded solemnly. "Oh yeah, there were a bunch of 'em. Say what you will about her, Lori Reddecop's a fine-lookin' woman. Easy on the eyes, if you know what I mean."

I groaned. "Not you too?!"

"Nah, don't worry, sweet thang, your place in my heart is secure."

I batted my eyelashes at him, while Kelt rolled his eyes and made retching sounds.

"Did Bill know about Lori's infidelities?" I asked.

Jaime shook his head. "I don't think so. I always figured he was kinda suspicious—that's why he took to pickin' so many fights. It's funny, but if anyone in this town was to have showed up dead, I woulda laid money on it bein' her. And half the women out celebratin'."

"Maybe one of her single conquests wanted the husband out of the way," Kelt speculated as he tossed a colorful mound of vegetables into the wok.

Jaime nodded. "That's pretty much my thinkin' too. Although I gotta tell you, the idea of Jurgen Clark as a murderer is a whole lot more appealin' to me than the thought of someone I've known all my life."

I stood up and started setting the table. "Well, who was her latest? Someone single?"

"Well, now, that's what I can't quite figure," Jaime said. "Last I heard, she was seein' . . . well, I don't wanna name names here, but he was definitely hitched. Wouldn't dare get himself divorced either. The families are friendly, you see. Before him, it was another married guy. It just doesn't make a whole lotta sense. Ah well"— he poured more ginger ale all around—"Alex knows all this stuff. They'll find the guy who did it. Come on, Kelt, surely that wonderful-smellin' thing's ready now!"

After a superb dinner, Jaime and I made short work of the dishes while Kelt relaxed at the table, propping his head up on one hand. Once again, after the dishes had been scrubbed and put away, we retired to the living room's overstuffed chairs. Even Jaime hoisted himself out of his wheelchair and onto a deeply cushioned loveseat. When the phone rang, we all sat motionless for a moment, unwilling (or perhaps, unable) to bestir ourselves. I was the first to move.

"Big Bert's Shoes and Cheese," I answered, with a whimsical wink at Jaime.

"Is that you, Robyn? Aah, that silly man. Don't tell me he's got you doing that shoes and cheese thing now?"

"Ella?"

"Aye, it's me. And I can tell that you've been hanging around with my cousin a bit too much lately. Ah well," she said in mock regret, "I suppose it was bound to happen sooner or later, with you staying there and all."

I laughed. "He really is a bad influence, isn't he?"

"The worst! Why, I could tell you stories. . . ."

"Stories, eh?" I said with a sideways glance at Jaime. "Sounds interesting."

"You can just tell that Ella I got some real good stories of my own," Jaime broke in, obviously feeling that things had gone far enough.

"He says he's got stories of his own," I repeated obediently.

"Aah, but they're not as good as my stories. . . ." Ella laughed wickedly. "Still, I guess 'twould be rude to embarrass him in front of his guests. And actually, I phoned to talk to you, not to embarrass his great silly self, tempting though that idea may be. I think I told you this afternoon that my husband Nat is a schoolteacher here?"

"Yes, you did mention that."

"Well, Nat and I got to talking tonight about the little chat you and I had. You seem to know a great deal about the owls and suchlike. Most of the kids that Nat teaches have parents or siblings in the company, so they're only getting the one point of view in all of this.

"With everything that's happening, Nat was thinking it might be a good idea to present the other side to them. Sort of let them know how there's two sides to the issue. He's also wanting to encourage the girls in science and the like. I guess he thinks that having a professional woman biologist in town is too good an opportunity to pass up. Anyhow, he was wondering if you and your colleague would care to come in and talk to the kids about it."

"What a great idea!" I responded. "I'd love to. Hang on a sec; let me ask Kelt."

Kelt was more than amenable to the idea, and after a bit more discussion, we agreed to go in at eleven on Thursday morning to talk to the kids of Marten Valley. I had a few slides kicking around in my duffel bag, and I was sure I could scare up a few great horned owl pellets for Nat's students to dissect.

"And don't you be forgetting about Friday," Ella warned before she rang off. "Remember we've got a pie date!"

I laughed. Ella took her pies very seriously. "How could I forget?" I assured her.

CHAPTER 13

"Figures they'd pick today to feel bashful," Kelt said, tossing his pack into the car in disgust.

I couldn't really blame him. We'd risen at three a.m. to get all the way out here—quite a feat for me and, I was beginning to suspect, even more so for Kelt. So far, he was proving to be a decidedly non-morning type of person.

Last night, Jaime had dragged out an old map and shown us where he'd seen the spotted owl. It was a good twenty miles from where we'd been working so far, and about three miles from the only access road—three miles of dense, wet, mossy forest unspoiled by anything so unsightly as a path. Oh, there were a few wildlife trails, of course—faint, winding pathways trampled flat over the years by the odd mule deer—but neither Kelt nor I was terribly deer-like and we found the going difficult.

The only owl we could boast today was a tiny saw-whet, huddled deep within a dense tangle of bush. We'd found a few pellets, even some whitewash, and a couple of likely-looking tree cavities. But without the owls themselves, or even a feather, it was virtually impossible to identify any one species. Slogging through messy terrain was a standard part of field biology. Unfortunately, all too often, so was coming back empty-handed.

To make matters worse, Kelt was acting as if all the gods and their cats were pissing on him. At first I'd put it down to the earliness of the hour. But when an entire thermos of Jaime's ambrosial coffee failed to revive him, I resigned myself to a long morning. That was another downside to field biology. If one partner was in a foul mood, you could pretty much lay money on it infecting the other faster than Borg nanoprobes could assimilate other species. The ride back to town was very quiet.

As we coasted down Main Street, it was Kelt who finally broke the silence. "Hey, look, isn't that Jurgen and the ND gang?" He pointed to a small group of people standing on the corner by Irene's Diner. They were warmly dressed in wool shirts and fleecy pullovers. Faded backpacks and puffy rolls of sleeping bags were piled around their feet.

I glanced over just as Jurgen looked our way. He smiled in recognition and gestured us towards him.

"Pull over a minute, Kelt. It looks like Jurgen wants to talk."

Kelt eased the car to the side of the road and I rolled down my window as Jurgen trotted up, Bonnie trailing along behind him.

"Robyn! I was hoping to see you."

"Hey, Jurgen." I greeted him cautiously, remembering all too well his earlier anger. "What's up?"

"I, ah . . . I wanted to apologize for the other night."

Was hell experiencing a sudden cold snap? I stared at him in disbelief.

He stretched his mouth into a big smile. It looked like it was going to crack his face. "I just, uh, got a little rattled. Heh, heh, you know how I can get sometimes. I didn't mean to fly off the handle at you."

"He's really been under a lot of stress lately," Bonnie broke in quickly. A little too quickly? "And—"

"Anyway"—Jurgen seized the stage again—"I just wanted to make sure there were no hard feelings. You know, seeing as we're working for the same side and everything." He pulled up the corners of his mouth again into a sort of guarded smile that waited to see if the apology would be accepted.

I managed a half-grin back and shook my head slowly. "No hard feelings," I told him.

His smile widened, and he squeezed Bonnie's arm. "Good. Maybe we can get together sometime while you're here," he said, including both Kelt and me in the invitation.

"Yeah, maybe," I responded, trying to watch Bonnie from the corner of my eye. She had sagged against Jurgen as if in relief.

As we drove off, Kelt looked at me, one eyebrow raised. "Did that seem weird to you?"

I nodded. "I've never known Jurgen to apologize to anyone."

"I wonder what's going on."

He wasn't the only one.

Although it was technically my turn to cook, I was saved from poisoning everybody by the simple fact that Jaime had already mixed up a batch of Belgian waffle batter. He must have been watching out the window for us: the first golden waffles were just coming off the iron as we trooped in. A small keg of real maple syrup (no buttery-flavored table syrup here) sat waiting on the table, along with a deep dish of blueberry sauce and a pot of whipped butter. I could get used to this.

"I could get used to this," I told Jaime with a grateful smile.

Overcome by the mouth-watering sight, Kelt had fallen to one knee. "Marry me!" he begged Jaime. "I promise, I'll take care of you."

"No, me! Marry me!" I piped up, tipping Kelt over unceremoniously. I went down on bended knee. "He can cook too. I need you more!"

Jaime just looked at us and laughed.

Breakfast was an absolute wonder. Maybe it was a good thing Jaime had laughed off my marriage proposal. If I kept eating like this, I wouldn't win a beauty contest against the Michelin Man.

"Find anythin' today?" Jaime asked as he served up his sixth waffle.

Stuffed to the eyeballs, I had stopped at four. "Just a little saw-whet. And a lot of hard work it was too."

Jaime made sympathetic noises. "Those spotted ones aren't real easy to find, are they?"

I nodded in agreement. "We'll try again tomorrow," I said. "There were a lot of promising-looking spots up in that section."

Kelt paused mid-waffle. "Are we going to have to get up at three again?"

I laughed at his dismayed tone. "No, maybe not quite so early."

"Y'know," Jaime began conversationally, "when I was workin' for the company, I had to get up at four o'clock every mornin' just to catch that damn crummy."

"What made you leave the company?" I asked.

Jaime used his last piece of waffle to soak up the syrup

on his plate, then finished it off pensively. "Well, it was a couple of things. But I guess what settled my mind was this one particular day.

"I was out with a couple of other guys markin' the boundary lines for a new cutblock. Accordin' to the maps, we were supposed to take this one line right down to the river. I didn't know dick about watershed protection back then—hell, probably never even heard the term—but I did know my way around a forest. Anybody could have seen the line we were markin' was gonna cut right across a grizzly trail. It was an old trail too. Bears had been usin' it for years. Well, it just kinda struck me how these poor bears had been hikin' down this trail all this time, and here we were gonna come in and wreck it in a day.

"I took myself over to the foreman—a real asshole he was too—and pointed it out. Y'know, all we had to do was move the line over to the south a few hundred yards. It never woulda made much difference to the company, but it woulda meant a hell of a lot to the bears." He paused and sipped slowly at his coffee.

"They refused," I said softly.

Jamie nodded. "Damn right they refused. Gave me shit for causin' a fuss too. That's the day I yarded my last turn."

We sat silently for a minute, Jaime sunk in his memories, and Kelt and I not knowing what to say.

"Good thing I'd socked away some cash," Jaime continued with a dry laugh. "Even headed Downtown for a spell. Found out real fast that big cities aren't for me. My family's here, my home's here. When I came back, old Frank Pennick—that's the guy who used to own the gas station—let on that he was lookin' to retire. I bought the station, fixed it up a bit, and here I am."

He beamed at us. "And when I found that owl, I never wasted my time tryin' to tell the Seidlin boys about it."

I smiled back at him, feeling a close camaraderie with this retired logger. In many ways, Jaime was the older brother I'd always wished Neil could have been. "Got a little of your own back, eh?"

He grinned. "Well, y'know, they don't have to be clear-cuttin' around here. Still plenty of money harvestin' trees the other way. More labor-intensive too. Besides, who knows, maybe spotted owls'll start bringin' in the tourists."

Jaime paused and directed a sly wink at Kelt. "Y'know, some of them crazy bird-watchin' types'll go anywhere to add another bird to their list."

"Hey!" I exclaimed, intercepting the wink. "We're not *all* crazy." Then I thought about my savings account, specially earmarked for a trip to the bird mecca of Point Pelee in Ontario. "Well, maybe a little," I amended.

CHAPTER 14

It was later that day, after dishes had been washed and naps had been taken, that I first met Bill Reddecop's son. In the light-hearted company of Kelt and Jaime, it had been easy to forget about the murder. In fact, I had been actively trying to forget about the murder. The sight of the sandy-haired boy standing on the front porch brought it all crashing back down.

I had opened the front door expecting one of Jaime's cousins or perhaps the ever-smiling nephew who worked at the gas bar. I certainly wasn't prepared to come face to face with the living consequence of sudden, violent death.

Todd Reddecop was a slight boy, about eight or nine years old, with Lori's delicate features and blond hair tangled from the blustery afternoon. His soul stared at me from eyes as brown as dark-roasted coffee beans before he dropped his gaze to the floor.

"I . . . I'm looking for Jaime." His voice was soft, just a whisper really.

"You must be Todd," I said gently.

Still looking at the floor, he nodded shyly.

"Hey, Todd, I'm Robyn. Come on in. Jaime's in the kitchen."

Todd wiped his feet carefully on the mat and followed me down the hallway.

"Hey, partner!" Jaime's smile was warm and welcoming. "How's it hangin'?"

Todd's dark eyes shone. The corners of his mouth curved up into a shy smile. "Good."

"Glad to hear it! Haven't seen you around for a few days now. I was startin' to wonder where you'd got to!"

Todd looked at the floor, smiling.

"Now I'd hazard a guess that you're droppin' by today to work on that carvin' of yours."

When Todd nodded silently, Jaime continued. "I figured as much, but y'know, partner, carvin's hard work. A body needs a little strength before it can even *think* of doin' work that hard. Now, what kinda thing would be best. . . ? Carrots?" Jaime tapped his chin thoughtfully. "Nah, carrots are good—don't get me wrong—but I don't think they'd work real well in this case. I dunno . . . how about hot chocolate. . . ? Maybe I can scare up a couple of peanut butter cookies. . . . Yeah, that oughta do it. What do you think, partner?"

Todd's little face had lit up at the mention of cookies. "Okay."

I left the two of them to their cookies and cocoa. Todd was obviously a regular visitor here. I wasn't sure whether his reticence was due to my presence or to the boy's natural reserve, but I *was* sure that he needed Jaime—especially now. It seemed best to leave them alone.

I found Kelt in his room, rummaging through the dresser drawers. "Ah ha!" he exclaimed finally, pulling out a thick white sweater. "I knew it!"

"You're cold?" I asked incredulously. Jaime kept the house so warm, I'd exchanged my sweaters for T-shirts.

"I'm ... AACHPHEW!"

I leaned against the door frame and regarded Kelt in dismay. "Gods! Don't tell me *you're* getting sick now!"

He cleared his throat thickly and sneezed again. "If I am, it's all your fault," he accused me.

"*Mine?* I was better by the time you showed up."

He sniffed huffily but I could see a twinkle in his eyes. "Excuses! I never get sick; it must be your fault."

"Uh huh, just like you never sleep in, eh?" I asked archly.

"Humph."

"Humph yourself. Jaime's busy with a guest. Want to dissect some owl pellets?"

"Oh sure," he grumbled. "When other people get sick, their friends bring them flowers or candies, maybe a magazine or a video. What do I get? Owl barf."

I rolled my eyes. "It's not barf! It's the regurgitated—"

"Yeah, it's regurgitated. That means barf."

"Don't be silly!"

"I'm not," he protested. "When I drink too much beer, I don't hork out beer pellets."

"Oh, very nice," I replied sarcastically. "Look, how about if I give you a Mars Bar for helping me? I think I've got one in my duffel bag. ..."

Kelt agreed so quickly, I decided I'd been had. Oh well, if I gave him my Mars Bar, he would owe me. I rather liked the thought of Kelt owing me a favor. I wouldn't necessarily insist on repayment in chocolate, either.

I went to my room and returned with pellets, exacto knives, Petri dishes, and chocolate. We spent the afternoon sitting quietly beside each other in his room, picking through dried, tubular masses of owl barf. My love life, I reflected, was at a definite low ebb.

I'd just started pulling apart a second pellet when I heard a light knock at the front door. It was Lori.

"Oh!" Her red lips pursed in surprise when she saw me. She wore a wine-colored sweater dress that matched her lipstick and clung close to the curves of her body. Her feet were encased in the most delicate burgundy pumps; her tiny waist was accentuated with a heavy gold chain. I would've looked like a tarted-up grape in the same outfit. She just looked gorgeous.

"Robyn! What are *you* doing here?"

I felt like one of those strange new life forms one occasionally finds forgotten in the refrigerator. She hadn't lost her touch.

"Hey, Lori," I greeted her mildly. "My partner and I are staying with Jaime for a while. Are you looking for your son?"

She hesitated for a moment. "Uh, yes. Yes, is he here?"

"Yep, he's with Jaime."

Lori stepped daintily into the entranceway and slipped her shoes off. Even her toenails matched her outfit.

"I didn't get a chance to ask you the other day," she began, "but what are you doing in Marten Valley, Robyn? I just about fell over when I saw you."

"You've heard about this whole spotted owl thing?"

She nodded.

"I'm the one doing a survey to find out if the spotted owls are really here."

"Oh." Her tone was uninterested. Then her brow furrowed faintly in puzzlement. "But weren't you studying something else . . . fish or crabs or something like that?"

I smiled. "That was a long time ago. Things change; now I study birds."

"Things change . . . ," she echoed, and fell silent.

Inwardly, I cursed myself for reminding her. "Come on back. I think Jaime and Todd are in the kitchen."

Lori entered the kitchen, bringing with her a spicy cloud of Dior's Poison. Todd looked up briefly from his carving and smiled, his brown eyes shining.

"Hi, Mom."

"Hi, guy, I thought I'd find you here." She went over, laid her hand on his head, and turned slightly so she was facing Jaime. "Jaime, how are you?" Her voice throbbed.

Jaime looked at her without expression. "Afternoon, Lori. I'm doin' okay. Me and Todd here have been hangin' out for a couple of hours. We've been carvin'."

"So I see. How's your leg?"

"Gettin' better every day, thanks."

"You'll let me know if you need anything, won't you?"

When the women of Marten Valley had found out about Jaime's accident, they'd promptly marched to his house bearing an army of frozen casseroles. I wasn't sure what Lori was offering, but somehow—maybe by the way she breathed the word "anything"—I didn't think she meant a frozen lasagna.

Jaime flicked a long-suffering look my way. "Thanks anyhow, Lori, but I got a bunch of help stayin' here with me now."

Lori glanced towards me. "I see." She pouted slightly. "Come on, Todd, it's time to go home for . . ."

I looked up to see what was wrong. Kelt was standing in the doorway. The white cable-knit sweater set off his dark good looks; his emerald green eyes regarded us calmly. He looked as scrumptious as a triple chocolate fudge sundae with sprinkles. And Lori looked like a dieter just itching to fall off the wagon. I wondered whether it would be polite to offer her a towel in case she started drooling.

"Hello." She turned the full power of her gaze on him.

I was amazed at how much could be insinuated by a single word. Kelt bobbed his head, uncomfortably I thought (hoped?).

"Lori, this is my partner in owls, Kelt Roberson. Kelt, Lori Reddecop."

"Kelt." Her voice was a silky caress.

I gritted my teeth.

"It's so wonderful to finally meet you," she oozed.

Finally?

"I hear that you're looking for owls in the forest. How fascinating!"

Kelt shrugged. "It's really Robyn's survey. I'm just the slave."

"Really. And what do you do when you're not slaving?" Her tone implied that whatever it was, she'd be delighted to help out. I could feel my teeth clenching together again.

"I study small mammals."

"Small mammals? Like squirrels and things?"

"Yeah, and bats."

She shuddered delicately as her flawlessly manicured hands rose to touch her gleaming curls. "Bats? Oooh, I don't think I'd like to study bats."

Kelt grinned. "Oh, come on. You'd be surprised at how interesting they are."

I didn't think Kelt had said anything particularly amusing, but Lori laughed a low, silvery laugh.

"Mom, I'm kind of hungry," Todd piped up softly, having ignored the conversation till this point.

Lori turned around to look at her child. She bent down to kiss his brow, a move that also, incidentally, showed off the round firmness of her buttocks. I rolled my eyes and gritted my teeth again. If this kept up, I might have to search out the local orthodontist.

"Okay, hon," she said, her voice returning to a semblance of normality. "I've got some spaghetti sauce simmering, made especially for you with no mushrooms. Let's go home and have dinner."

As Todd got up and started to tidy away the carving tools, Lori turned her attention back to Kelt and Jaime.

"Thank you so much for taking care of Todd."

Jaime waved away her thanks. "No problem. He's a great kid, and I sure enjoy havin' the company." He clapped Todd lightly on the back. "Come back and see me real soon, partner!"

Todd looked at the floor and smiled.

As they turned to go, Lori raised her sapphire eyes up to Kelt. "Bye for now," she murmured.

For a brief second it seemed that she would brush against him on her way out, but Kelt stepped back and the moment was lost.

"That happen often?" Kelt was asking Jaime as I returned to the kitchen.

Jaime grimaced. "What? Todd or Lori?"

Kelt grinned. "Both."

Jaime busied himself putting empty cocoa mugs into the sink. "Well, Lori's stopped droppin' by so much, thank god, but Todd's here a fair bit. Probably three or four times a week."

"That seems like a lot," Kelt said. "Doesn't he have any friends closer to his age?"

Jaime shook his head. "Nah, not really. I know you're not supposed to speak badly of the dead and all that, but Todd's old man sure went a long way to ruinin' that boy's self-confidence. Always callin' him an idiot, and tellin' him he was stupid. I figure Todd started comin' here to get away from his old man—and y'know, I never found it in my heart to blame him. The upshot of the whole thing is that Todd's real quiet, even with guys his own age. Only seems to loosen himself up when he's with me."

"Maybe it's because you do all the talking," I suggested.

Jaime flicked a dishtowel at me. "Ha, ha. You're obviously hangin' around with Ella too much. Don't worry, I make sure Todd gets in a word here and there." He frowned a little before continuing thoughtfully. "I think there's somethin' buggin' him, though. Probably not so's anybody else can tell, but he was a whole lot quieter than usual. Barely let out a peep."

"His father's death?"

"Could be." I could tell Jaime wasn't convinced. "But he came wanderin' over on Sunday morning, after they'd found his old man, and he never folded up his face that tight then."

"Maybe it hadn't sunk in yet," Kelt said. "It can take a while for kids to fully realize something like that."

"Yeah. . . ." Jaime still looked a little doubtful. Then his expression cleared. "Y'know, he's a great kid. Take a look at his carvin'." He wheeled over to a cupboard and pulled out a small knob of wood. Half-finished, the shape of a great horned owl was instantly recognizable.

"That little kid did this?" Kelt was impressed.

So was I. The carving was crude, but already Todd's skill was apparent. Given a few more years of experience, Todd Reddecop would be a carver to be reckoned with.

Jaime smiled proudly. "Yeah, and quite a few others. The boy's got himself some real talent."

"It's great that you spend so much time with him," I told Jaime with a smile.

"Aah, I sure don't mind gabbin', eatin' cookies, and carvin'."

"Speaking of eating . . ." Kelt's voice rose hopefully.

As one, Kelt and Jaime turned and regarded me.

"Oh no!" I said, fending off their expectant looks. "If you guys want me to do dinner, we're going to Irene's."

"You can't be *that* bad." Kelt's tone was disbelieving.

I figured it was time to burst a few bubbles. "Hey, I once ruined hot dogs," I told them.

"*Hot dogs!?* How do you ruin hot dogs?"

"Forgot to put water in the pot. They burned black to the bottom. I wrecked the pot too."

Kelt and Jaime dissolved into gales of laughter. I thought they were being a little excessive.

Finally, Jaime wiped the mirth from his eyes. "I never heard of anybody wreckin' hot dogs before," he told Kelt. "You think maybe we should save her from herself?"

"Yeah," Kelt agreed. "Do you want to marry her, or should I?"

I looked at Kelt's rakish grin and dancing green eyes. In my dreams.

CHAPTER 15

After a succulent dinner of grilled peppers and fettucine à la Kelt, the chef decided to retire for the night with a couple of Aspirin and a mug of Neo Citran for company. I had a feeling we wouldn't be getting up to go owling the next morning.

Jaime had to go through some accounts, so I plunked myself in front of my laptop and my notebook, ostensibly to type out some field notes. I should have known myself better than that. Instead of coordinates and descriptions of owls, I found myself instead jotting down names and tying them together with arrows and lines.

Ever since I'd seen Todd's haunted eyes that afternoon, Bill Reddecop's murder had been weighing heavily on my mind. Up till now I'd had my head in the sand like the proverbial ostrich, but the truth of the matter is, in real life, ostriches don't put their heads in the sand. I finally had to admit to myself that finding somebody's corpse sort of makes you feel like you've got an obligation to them. Like it was up to you to figure out who made them a corpse.

After a while, I sighed and looked down at the doodles on my notebook. Bill Reddecop's name dominated the page. Who would want to kill him? The environmentalists?

Specifically Jurgen, of course. His name appeared to the right of Bill's. He was a tough one. My gut told me he wasn't a murderer, but gods, that temper! Danson said Bill had fought with his killer, and Jurgen was certainly capable of *that*. And he'd been acting pretty strangely lately. When it came right down to it, I really didn't know him at all. I wondered if I could get Bonnie talking.

Bill's workers were next on the list. An unknown quantity. From what Jaime had said, Bill could be a vindictive s.o.b. Had he gone too far and someone decided not to take it anymore? Maybe Jaime would know more about that.

Okay then, who else? Lori? I'd scrawled her name to the left. She sure hadn't seemed like a bereaved widow that afternoon. I grimaced. On one hand, I didn't like her much, and it was difficult not to let that color my perceptions. On the other hand, she was pretty slight. I thought it unlikely she could have overpowered her husband in a fight.

Lori's paramours were next on the list. I'd need legal-size paper if I wanted to fit all their names on one page. Catty maybe, but probably true. Who were they? Had one of them wanted more than just a brief fling? I should be able to get their names from Ella, but I couldn't see any of them answering my questions. What did I mean, "answering my questions"? Just how far was I prepared to go for this "obligation"? Had I watched too many *Columbo* episodes as a kid? Who the hell was I to investigate a murder?

No, not investigate a *murder*, I thought slowly. But perhaps a life. All I'd seen of Bill Reddecop was a dead body. What had he really been like? Both Ella and Jaime seemed to think he was a jerk, but weren't there always two sides to any story? *Somebody* must have liked the guy. Who? The clues to his death were in his life. Maybe . . .

"Hey, Robyn, I'm all finished out here. You want a cup of joe?" Jaime tapped at my door.

"Decaf?"

"Of course!"

I looked down at my doodling. There were way too many question marks. Fun to draw, maybe, but not particularly helpful. Well, I wasn't accomplishing a whole lot sitting here. If I wanted to understand Bill's life, I'd have to talk to the people who'd been a part of it.

"Sounds great," I told Jaime. "I'll be there in a sec."

We'd just sat down in the kitchen with our steaming mugs of decaf (brewed with a cinnamon stick for flavor) when we heard a soft rap at the kitchen door. I opened the door to a towering figure dressed in a long, blue-gray parka.

In the manner of very tall people, he was stooped slightly, as if constantly on guard against banging his head on low-slung door frames. His hair was of medium length, dirty blond with broad streaks of white along the temples. He was slim to the point of skinniness, and had a grizzled face that, though long and drooping, was kind, with bright, warm eyes.

"Halmar!" Jaime's tone was pleased. "About time you dropped by! Come on in; we got a pot of coffee goin'."

Halmar ducked into the room and shed his coat.

"Yoost came to see how da leg was doon," he said with a crooked grin. "Da fellas wants to know eff you got effrything you neet."

"I'm doin' just fine," Jaime answered. "Halmar, this here's Robyn Devara. Y'know, the one doin' the owl survey. Robyn, this's my buddy, Halmar."

"Hey, Halmar." I smiled up at him, then looked at Jaime. "What? No relation? I thought everybody here was related to you."

Halmar chuckled, a deep, hearty sound. "Nice to meet you, Robyn. I heart a lot about you. None of da guys told me you were cute like dis, dough, or I come sooner to visit. Him . . ." Halmar jerked his thumb toward Jaime. "He's not much for looking at."

I laughed as Jaime faked a punch to Halmar's slight frame. Despite his flattering comments to me, Halmar was obviously here to see Jaime. Once he was settled at the table, a mug of coffee comfortably in hand, he got down to business.

"Da guys dey want you to know dere's gonna be a beeg demonstration tomorrow," he told Jaime. "You know, show dem green cuckoos how effryone feels."

Jaime looked skeptical. "It's not gonna be another one like last week, is it?"

Halmar was already shaking his head. "No, nobody wants anodder fight, not like dat anyhow. Always we are wanting to be peaceful. Besides, dat beeg cop says we gotta be calm, focks up his day eff we get into trouble."

"No kiddin'," Jaime grunted.

Halmar agreed. "Wid dat Bill getting himself kilt, all dose noos guys are gonna be all offer da place. Eet's goot for us, I guess. For da demonstration."

"What if Jurgen and his gang show up again?" I asked. "I saw a crowd last Friday that looked pretty ugly, and he was smack in the middle of it."

Halmar nodded. "Yah, I was dere too. Things yoost got outta hant. I don't think eet will happen like dat again." He smiled humorlessly. "Not while da noos guys are around."

Jaime agreed with Halmar. "Bill's murder pulled everyone up real short," he explained to me. "With all the media hangin' around, folks are gonna be a whole lot more careful about what they say and do. Nobody wants Marten Valley to come out lookin' like some hick hillbilly town. I figure everyone'll keep a lid on their temper, even if Jurgen does show his face."

"Oh, I think you can bet good money on him being there," I told them. "He wouldn't miss an opportunity like this. Not with the kind of media attention you'll be getting. I think you can probably count on him showing off his black eye too."

Halmar got up and poured more coffee all around. He sighed as he sat back down. "Yah, I think yoor right. He's telling some noospaper guy all about dat fight in da bar."

"What happened there, anyhow?" I asked. "Jurgen told me that Bill punched him without provocation."

Halmar's eyes were wary as he looked at me. "You know dis Yoorgen Clark?"

"Superficially," I told him with a reassuring smile. "In my line of work, you meet all kinds. Don't worry, I'm not a Nature Defence spy."

"Of course not!" Jaime snorted at the idea.

Jaime's reaction seemed to have more effect on Halmar than my own assurances. Halmar's expression eased. "Sorry, Robyn, eet's yoost dis whole thing about da owls. Eet gets you all twist't around." He smiled apologetically.

"That's okay, Halmar," I said. "It's not an easy situation. So what exactly happened in the bar that night? Was Jurgen mouthing off?"

"Does he ever shut his mouth?" Jaime asked sarcastically.

Halmar smiled. "Well, he neffer said much at first—

not to us—but den he was talking wid a loud voice to all his buddies. He was saying dat we were rapists. Of da forest, you know."

I was unsurprised. Diplomacy had never been one of Jurgen's strong points. Still, it took a lot of balls—or perhaps stupidity—to go into a loggers' bar and make comments like that.

"Anyway," Halmar continued, "we yoost kept drinking and not paying attention to him, until Bill show't up. Bill was already mat. Jaime, you know what eet was like; he came in yoost looking for a fight. Went right up to dat Yoorgen and start't screaming about dose tree spikes."

"Tree spikes?" I gulped in horror, remembering all too well the spike sticking out from Bill Reddecop's chest.

Halmar seemed oblivious to my reaction. "Yah," he said, puzzled. "I haff no idea why he was so mat. Nobody effer put dose things around here—yoost a few of dose environmentalists climbing trees dat we haff to cut, or sometimes dey chain demselves to da Cat. Maybe Bill figur't da spikes were next, I guess." He shrugged. "Bill shout't and he shook his fist a lot, but dat Yoorgen yoost stoot dere wid a nasty look on his face. Finally, he got mat, I guess. He said something to Bill—I haff no idea what—but den he start't calling Bill a chickenshat asshole."

Jaime shook his head and whistled. "I bet that got Bill goin'."

"Going! Ha! He haul't off and socked dat Yoorgen smack in da eye. Surprise' da hell outta him too."

"Bill never could stand to be called a chickenshit," Jaime observed. "Even when we were kids."

Halmar nodded his agreement. "Yah, remember da time dat new kit call't him dat? I dought his nose was neffer gonna stop bleeding. Well, as soon as dat Yoorgen pick't himself up, he's screaming bloody murter—" Belatedly, Halmar realized what he'd just said. "Not *dat* kinda murter," he hastened to assure us. "Yoost dat he was gonna sue da pants right off Bill. Den he stomp't outta da bar to get da police."

"And did they come?" I asked.

"Yah, dat beeg cop came and hadda look around, but already Bill had left. Went home, I think." Halmar sighed. "I neffer thought about it till yesterday, but dat was da last time I effer saw Bill."

"You were friends?" I asked quietly.

Halmar's eyebrows rose in surprise. "Wid Bill? No, we were neffer really friends. I knew much better his brodder Greg, even dough I was neffer friends wid him much."

"You weren't friends with Greg Reddecop?" I asked. "From what Jaime told me, I thought everybody liked *him*."

Halmar shrugged. "We neffer hit it off too good. I dunno why. Not effryone likes him. Joe Neibuner, he neffer liked him. 'Specially when Greg triet to borrow money from him a couple years ago when Joe went down to da island. Greg was hard up for cash, I guess. Got all mat when Joe said no." He shrugged again.

"But you didn't like Bill either."

"No. He was always so mat. But I did know him many years. No madder what kinda guy he was, he didn't deserf to die like dat."

"Didn't Bill have *any* friends?" I asked.

"Dere were a few guys he hung around wid, but . . ." Halmar shrugged.

"He never really made himself too likeable," Jaime explained.

145

As epitaphs went, it was pretty pathetic. No real friends, and an undeserved death. What a waste of a life. We finished our coffee in silence; then Jaime cleared his throat. "So what time's this demonstration tomorrow?"

"Four-thirty. Effrybody's early off work for it. After dere's gonna be a beeg barbecue for da whole town. Dey gotta tent set up outside of Rusty's. Dey're gonna haff drinks and food and stuff." Halmar looked at me. "Eef you like, you come along too, Robyn."

I smiled and shook my head. "Thanks, Halmar, but under the circumstances I don't think it would be wise."

Halmar seemed relieved, and I was glad that I'd refused. Although he might not hold my environmental leanings against me, the other townspeople were another matter.

The conversation then turned to talk of general things: the ineptitude of the local hockey team, the length of the winter, and the short-sighted stupidity of politicians. Even in a different province, some things stayed the same.

"What do you do at Seidlin?" I asked Halmar during a lull in the conversation.

"I'm da scaler," he replied. "First I measure da logs to see how much is there of da wood. I figure out what kinda trees dey are and how good is da quality. Den I grade dem."

"The logs are graded based on quality and species?"

"Yah, dat's how dey figure out how much dey're worth. We hafta pay stumpage to da province, you know, for da right to cut da wood. Some of da really good stuff, like da Sitka spruce, can be worth a lotta money. Odders, not so much."

"What sort of price difference are we looking at here?"

"Well, for da really good stuff, da stumpage ees about a hunnert bucks for effry cubic meter. For da lowest stuff, eet's about twenny-five cents effry cubic meter. Da lumber dat dey get from da timber ees worth much more after eet is process't. Like maybe ten times more. Depends on da market."

I whistled. "That would make quite a price difference between the high- and low-grade stuff. What makes wood a lower grade?"

"Lotsa stuff," Halmar answered. "Eef da trees are dead when dey're cut, den dey're only good for pulping. If dey're sick wid a fungus or a disease, den dat will bring da grade down."

"What about a bark beetle infestation?"

"Yah, dose liddle bugs can really fock up da trees. Dey bring a kinda fungus wid dem, makes da sapwood all blue. Den you haff to grade da logs lower 'cause of da blue stain." Halmar shook his head slowly. "Dey're liddle bastarts. I hadda bunch of dem when I was working on da island. Had to cut da trees and move 'em and grade 'em before da bugs flew."

"You never had to deal with that here?" I asked carefully.

"Here? No, I been working for da company for offer fourteen years; dere hasn't been a trouble since I been here. Da guy before me said he hadda problem with dem, but dat was before my time. Good thing too. Dose bastarts are hard to get rit of."

Interesting. "When I drove out here from Vancouver, I saw signs up all over the place warning about them. I'd wondered if they were a problem in Marten Valley."

"None of dem blue trees here," Halmar assured me. "Not for years and years."

Before he left, Halmar had a few last words for me. "Robyn, eet was nice to meet you," he said, shaking my hand warmly. "I hope effrything goes good wid your work here. Yoost make sure yoor careful out dere."

I raised one eyebrow quizzically. "Are you warning me?" I asked.

"No, no . . . well . . . I dunno, wid da murter and effrything. . . ." He shrugged uncomfortably. "Hell, I know dere're guys who are mat about dose owls. Dey scare't," he said, "and scare't guys go funny sometimes. Yoost be careful."

Jaime's expression had darkened during this exchange. "If any of those assholes even *thinks* of layin' a hand—even so much as a finger—on Robyn, they're gonna answer to me," he exclaimed.

Halmar looked down at Jaime's cast pointedly. "Yah, but dere's not much you can do right now, I guess. And a few of da guys blame you for dis whole thing."

"*What?!*" Jaime sputtered in outrage. "*Who* blames me?"

Halmar laid a placating hand on his shoulder. "Eet's probably yoost a lotta bullshat. You know how some of dose guys can get."

Halmar sighed. "Me, I don't think eet's serious, and I neffer woulda said anything if I knew you would get all mat. I yoost thought I'd tell you guys dat people are a liddle pissed off right now." He stabbed a finger at Jaime. "You found dat owl in da first place." He jerked his thumb at me. "And she tries to find more of dem. Of course some of da guys are mat! Eet's nothing serious; yoost be careful, dat's all." He zipped up his parka decisively.

"Thanks for the warning, Halmar. We appreciate it." I opened the door for him.

Halmar looked back at the still-sputtering Jaime. "I neffer meant to make him mat," he said.

"Don't worry," I assured him. "He'll understand as soon as he's calmed down."

I gathered up coffee mugs and rinsed them out while Jaime continued to mutter to himself. I was a little surprised at his indignation. What had he expected? Finally I turned around.

"What did you expect?" I demanded.

"Not this!" he snapped back. "Aah, I'm sorry, Robyn. But jeez, these folks are my family. Never thought they'd go and turn against me."

"That's not what Halmar said."

"Maybe not so's it was out in the open, but it sure came through loud and clear." Jaime sighed dejectedly.

I sat down across from him and squeezed his hand. "You know, when I was in Washington state, I saw the same kind of thing going on down there. The loggers versus owls movement split towns in two."

Jaime seemed surprised. "I thought the towns were pretty much united against the environmentalists."

I nodded. "Yes, in most cases that was true. But some of those towns had environmentalists living in them, same as here. When that happened, the townspeople started fighting each other as well as the outsiders. I know of at least one family that broke up over it. But Jaime, Washington was a different situation. The logging had stopped completely. That's not going to happen in Marten Valley. There might be a little less work for everyone, but the town is *not* going to die."

"Try tellin' that to the town."

"Well, maybe you should," I declared. "You know as much about this as I do. The BCWA doesn't want to stop all the logging, just the clear-cutting. Now, correct me if I'm wrong, but didn't you say selective cutting is actually more manpower-intensive?"

Jaime nodded.

"There you go," I continued. "Then the loggers and everybody else will still have work. So they'll have to leave a few undisturbed owl sites; it's no big deal."

"So long as Seidlin decides it's still worth their while."

"True. But the company's been here a long time. They've got offices, a sawmill, and a willing workforce. I think it would take a lot more than this for them to pull out of Marten Valley. Besides, they'll have to stop clear-cutting when the new code comes into full effect. The owls are just hurrying things along a bit."

"I know," Jaime said miserably. "I just hate the thought that this damn thing'll be hangin' around my neck for the rest of my life."

I thought back to the angry confrontation I had witnessed on Friday. The townspeople had been furious, but they'd been up against outside environmentalists. Surely they wouldn't be like that with one of their own. After all, the logging wasn't in any immediate danger of ending. Still, what exactly had happened in the forest last Thursday night? And, maybe more importantly, why?

CHAPTER 16

As predicted, Kelt was in no shape to go owling. I'd tapped lightly at his door about five-thirty. No response. A louder knock still yielded nothing. Gently, I pushed the door open. Even from the doorway, his rasping breath was audible. Best to just let him sleep.

Briefly I considered going out alone. I'd been out owling before by myself; I knew what I was doing. But if Kaye found out, I'd never hear the end of it, and to be honest, Halmar's warning the night before had left me . . . maybe shaken was too strong a word, but cautious. Definitely more cautious.

If Bill Reddecop had been murdered because of the spotted owls, I wasn't about to tromp around a deserted forest by myself. I'd been having rotten luck lately, yes, but I wasn't ready to start checking out cemetery plots just yet. Never one to pass up an opportunity, I crept back into bed and burrowed under the blankets.

I should have known better than to go back to sleep. At five-thirty I had been awake and alert. When I woke again at eight, I felt groggy and out of sorts.

The sun shone brightly in an azure sky. In the sleeping trees outside my window I could see house sparrows perched like chubby buds along the branches. A strong wind was blowing—from the north, I guessed. All the sparrows had lined up facing that direction so their feathers wouldn't be ruffled by the chill. It would have been a great day for fieldwork.

I was grouchy and getting a little stressed about the survey. Yes, we'd found a few spotted owls, but the work was far from over. Kelt's illness was only the latest in a sequence of events that seemed to be conspiring against me. I'd hoped this would be a relatively quick job, but here I was almost a week into it with well over half of my work still ahead of me.

And I hadn't forgotten about that big clear-cut. I could maybe see a crummy driver not knowing about a beetle infestation, but Halmar hadn't known about it either, and he was a scaler. Had the forest been cleared for another reason, or had Seidlin lied about an infestation? Was such a thing even possible? My spidey senses were off the tingle-o-meter. It was time to find out.

Feeling better now that I had a plan, I threw my robe on, tiptoed down the hall, and hit the shower. Neither Kelt nor Jaime was up by the time I left the house.

It was after nine o'clock now. Seidlin's offices should be open and ready for business. Mine was probably not what they had in mind.

I walked over to Main Street, planning out my strategy. As an independent surveyor, I had every right (and, in all honesty, an obligation) to go in and ask someone about logging activities in the area. After all, I didn't want to stumble inadvertently on a work site during the course of my survey. I had a 1:100,000 map delineating the entire survey area as well as more detailed 1:25,000 maps that showed each section of five square miles. I'd brought them along to compare with Seidlin's maps of their current activities. While I was comparing the two, hopefully I'd be able to slip in a few questions about bark beetle infestations.

Being an environmentalist or at least the closest thing to one, I was expecting a cool reception at best. I certainly wasn't prepared for the vice-president of public relations, Mr. Gus Nickerson (just call me Gus) to come out and pump my hand.

"It's great! Great that ya came to see us here. Really appreciate it, y'know. Lots don't. As if we bite or something. Ha, ha, ha."

Gus Nickerson was a huge man, with a booming voice to match. A stereotypical logger, he possessed a broad expanse of shoulder and no discernible neck. His face was florid, and boasted a thick, gingery mustache waxed and curled at the tips.

"Really appreciate ya coming," he repeated, giving my hand a last bone-grinding squeeze before releasing it. "Can get dangerous out there if ya don't know what yer doing. Lots don't. Lots more don't realize it. Can I get ya a cup a' joe to start?"

"Thanks. That'd be great," I answered, trying inconspicuously to rub some feeling back into my hand.

We walked down a long hallway past numerous tiny cubicles where secretaries and clerks paused in their work to have a peek at the visitor. A few smiled uncertainly at me.

"We got sugar and that powdered cream stuff. What would ya like?"

"Black's fine," I answered.

"Don't blame ya." Gus boomed. "Can't stand that creamer stuff either." He patted his ample middle. The guy was built like a tank. "But the real stuff's too fattening, y'know. Not that a little thing like you has anything to worry about along those lines. Ha, ha, ha."

A hearty fellow, Gus. A real pal.

After we'd poured our coffee, he took me back down the hall to a small room off the main lobby. The walls of the room were almost completely covered with framed sepia photos of logging operations long past.

"Our museum," Gus announced proudly. "Got photographs here from Seidlin's very first days. See here? My dad. Best faller this company's ever had. This one over here's Mr. Chase back when he helped found the company. Only founder left now. Eighty-three years old and still comes into the office every day!"

Remembering what Ella had said about his wife's shrewish tendencies, I wasn't surprised that Mr. Chase still dragged his carcass into the office. In fact, I almost expected to see Mrs. Chase's picture in the "museum," but there were just two photos of her husband—the one that Gus had pointed out, and another, more recent picture showing a much older man with a thick crop of snow-white hair. His gray eyes seemed a bit shifty, but maybe I was just projecting that onto him.

We spent a little more time in the room, Gus pointing out this person or that person who had made some sort of significant contribution to the company. It was interesting, but the loquacious Gus threatened to go on all day. I waited for him to pause. The man had to draw breath at some point.

"Can we compare maps now?" I asked sweetly when Gus had finally run down. "I'd really like to make sure I don't get in anybody's way out there."

"Sure, sure. Let's go on up to Planning and Development. Got a big map up there. Shows all the sites."

The map had been posted in the planning department's luxuriously appointed boardroom. I sank into a padded leather chair and spread my maps across the oak tabletop. I'd been hoping that Gus would appoint some low-level (preferably talkative) clerk to help me do my comparison. I'd even been secretly hoping for someone who had known and was willing to talk about Bill Reddecop. But apparently two birds had no intention of being killed with one stone. Instead, Gus leaned back in another chair and continued his monologue as I worked.

It was difficult to concentrate. Gus was swiftly becoming an irritant. The map, however, was quite helpful. I could see immediately that I'd have to skirt around a few blocks, but it wouldn't be a big deal.

"I don't think we'll have any sort of conflict," I told Gus. "For the most part, my survey blocks aren't in the areas that you guys are working in."

"Great. Great."

"Gus," I began on a friendly note, "I took a drive up to the Wolf Creek area the other day—it's on my survey plan—and, well, I couldn't help but notice that big clearcut. Can you tell me why it was so large?"

It would have been easy to miss Gus's reaction. His open, friendly expression didn't change a bit. But I was watching him closely. As soon as I mentioned Wolf Creek, he blinked rapidly a few times before covering up with a loud guffaw.

"Ha, ha! Bet you noticed that! Couldn't help it. Don't blame ya. It's one mother of a clear-cut." He smiled broadly and patted my hand. "Truth is we had a problem out that way last year. Bark beetles. Know anything about them?"

I shook my head. "Not much."

"Nasty things. Hard to get rid of. It was cut or burn. Had the access roads, so we cut."

"That's odd," I said. "A friend of mine's a crummy driver. She said there hadn't been a beetle infestation in over twenty years."

Gus waved it off, though his cheerful smile was beginning to look a little weary. "Crummy drivers! They don't know what goes on at a site. Got thirty-three crews working for us. Lotta crews. Can't expect them all to know what's going on everywhere."

True. But Halmar had also told me there hadn't been a beetle infestation in years—and he was a scaler. There couldn't be *that* many scalers, and they all worked in the same place. If there had been an infestation, Halmar would have known about it.

I decided to make my escape while the going was good. I thanked Gus for all his help and managed to keep my smile as he gripped my hand in another crushing handshake. No, I certainly didn't want to antagonize Gus any more. At least not right now, not until I knew a little bit more about what had happened at Wolf Creek. And that meant talking to the crews. But first, I needed to go to the town library and see what I could find out about bark beetles.

Marten Valley's librarian turned out to be a young man sporting dyed black hair and alternative-punk clothing. At first I thought he was a patron until I realized he was the only other person in the library. He even had a gold stud embedded in the tip of his tongue. I tried not to think about hot soup and ice-cold Slurpees.

Pierced tongue notwithstanding, he was extremely

helpful and quite knowledgeable about his collection. Ten minutes after I'd asked tentatively about bark beetles, I found myself seated at a table with a small stack of books and assorted provincial and federal government documents. I settled down to read.

Bark beetles, it appeared, were pernicious little beggars (or "bastarts," as Halmar had labeled them). There were a couple of different species, the mountain pine beetle being the most destructive in western North America. Most of the trees around the Wolf Creek cutblock had been pines.

Mountain pine beetles prefer live, otherwise healthy trees. According to one book on tree pests and diseases, there were a number of ways to tell if you've got a beetle problem, including pitch tubes (eighth-inch holes) in the tree trunks and red boring dust on the ground and in bark crevices. Later on, the foliage turns from green to greenish yellow to an unhealthy reddish brown. Another reliable sign is a marked increase in the population of beetle-munching woodpeckers. As the birds move in for the all-you-can-eat buffet, they strip much of the bark away from infested trees. Easy enough to identify, I thought with a shrug.

The trees are killed within a year of infestation. The blue fungus Halmar had mentioned was called *Ceratocystis montia* and is carried by the beetles as they skip happily from tree to tree. When the beetles build their egg galleries in the bark, the sapwood is infected with the blue fungus. The beetles hang out at the beetle singles bars, do their thing, and lay their eggs. By mid-July the new adults chew their way out through the bark and fly off to start the whole process again.

As Megan had discovered and Gus had confirmed,

there were essentially two ways of dealing with a severe epidemic—burning or sanitation cutting. The massive clear-cut in the Cariboo Region a few years earlier had, in fact, been undertaken to control a bark beetle epidemic. Some environmentalists had labeled it "the clear-cut you can see from space," but it could have just as easily been "the forest fire you can see from space."

Perhaps most interesting (at least to me) was the fact that despite sanitation harvesting, it was virtually impossible to eliminate an entire infestation. Clear-cutting was undertaken to control the worst areas, but adjacent stands were likely to be infested as well, albeit more lightly.

I stretched and tilted the chair back thoughtfully. On one hand, I hadn't seen any signs of beetle infestation in the area adjacent to the clear-cut. On the other hand, neither Kelt nor I had known to look for pitch tubes and boring dust. Perhaps I should take another run out there. On yet another hand, it was sort of hard to miss discolored foliage and signs of a strong woodpecker presence. There hadn't been any of either, I was sure of that.

I brought the chair back down with a muffled thud. I had long since run out of hands. I needed to talk to someone from the crew that had worked out there, and for that, I needed to talk to Jaime.

I started closing books and gathering up my things. As I closed the volume on tree pests and diseases, I caught a flash of bright blue on the inside cover. Curious, I opened the book again. The blue turned out to be a donation sticker. *A Guide to Tree Pests and Diseases* had been donated to Marten Valley Public Library by none other than Bill Reddecop, Sr.

"Did the senior Bill Reddecop donate many books to

the library?" I asked the librarian when I returned the books to the front desk.

"Oh yes," he assured me. "Old Mr. Reddecop was a great believer in libraries. Probably close to a third of our collection was purchased with money that he donated. He figured you could never have too much knowledge."

"He sounds like a smart man."

"He was a good man," he agreed. "It's terrible what happened to his son."

"Yes."

"I tell you, I'm kind of glad he wasn't around to see it. He always cared so much about his family and his employees."

"Did you ever work for him?" I asked.

The librarian shook his head. "No, not me. I've never been bitten by the logging bug. But my dad was a company man for over thirty years. He always said Mr. Reddecop had safety and learning on the brain long before it was fashionable."

"Really?"

"Oh yes, he was implementing safety procedures years before they became mandatory. He was also replanting before anybody else ever thought of it. He was a good man," he repeated.

A good man. I wondered what he would have said to my growing suspicions about his company.

CHAPTER 17

I walked thoughtfully back to Jaime's along Marten Valley's quiet residential streets. Perhaps a little too thoughtfully, I realized, looking up and not recognizing anything. I'd begun to retrace my steps when I spied the slight figure of Todd Reddecop entering a large, cream-colored bungalow.

"Mom?" he called out as the door slammed behind him.

On impulse, I turned up the driveway. I hadn't liked Lori when we were schoolmates, and so far I hadn't seen anything that might make me feel differently. But ever since I'd decided to pull a Columbo, she'd been lurking around in the back of my mind. If I was trying to find out about Bill Reddecop's life, what better place to start than with his wife?

"Robyn!" Lori seemed nonplussed to see me standing on her porch. She was dressed relatively normally in faded jeans and an old UBC sweatshirt. Her bright hair had been pulled back into a ponytail; her face was devoid of makeup. Her features were still very attractive, despite the lack of artifice. Her eyes were still brilliantly blue, but for the first time I noticed the fine lines around her mouth and the faint crow's-feet around her eyes. She seemed smaller somehow, more insecure. I found myself uncomfortable with the change.

"Hi, Lori, I, uh . . . was just taking a walk and I saw Todd, so I thought I'd stop by and see how you were doing."

"Oh. Well, that's nice of you. Do you want to come in? I was just going to make some coffee."

"That would be great," I told her. "It's a little brisk today."

She showed me to the living room and disappeared down the hall to put the coffee maker on. I looked around the room and let out a low whistle.

Lori's expensive taste in clothing and jewelry had seeped over into her taste in furniture. The room was a mixture of antique and modern. Gorgeously carved tables surrounded ivory leather couches. A huge oriental carpet of ivory, hunter green, and dusty rose covered a hardwood floor that had been burnished to a deep, coppery red. I was admiring a shelf of beautiful Inuit carvings when Lori came back carrying a tray of coffee and muffins.

"You've got a lovely place, Lori," I remarked. "This room is marvelous!"

"Thanks. I just had it redone." Lori's tone was strained. "Bill didn't see the point. He . . . well, he didn't think we should do it."

I looked at her more closely, noting the dark circles under her eyes.

"I'm sorry about what happened," I said gently. "Are you okay?"

She shot me a tremulous look, then dropped her gaze to the coffee pot. "Is anybody ever okay after something like this?"

I waited for her to continue.

"I guess I didn't really realize until this morning." She perched on the edge of one of her ivory couches, as if afraid to let herself sink into its comfort.

"I keep expecting him to walk in the door. I feel like I'm on automatic pilot. People keep coming over and looking at me, just waiting for me to fall apart. But you don't, you know, at least not right away. How can you?" Her voice was thick with unshed tears.

In university it had been easy to dismiss Lori as a self-centered flirt. I had disliked her as much for her apparent lack of complexity as for her lack of morals. Ever since I'd recognized her in the RCMP station, I had been judging her through the eyes of my younger self. But as I sat in her living room, I came face to face with my prejudice. I found I didn't know how to respond to this new, vulnerable Lori.

"I don't know," I answered finally. "I've never been married myself."

She looked at me a little defiantly. "It wasn't perfect. I'm sure you've heard all the stories."

I squirmed.

"But whatever it was, that was between Bill and me."

"Do you have any idea who might have done this?" I asked.

She shook her head helplessly. "I don't know. Everybody says it's the environmentalists."

I nodded. "I've heard that too. But what about the townspeople? Did Bill have any enemies?"

"There were a few," she admitted. "Nobody really serious. I think the worst fight Bill had was with Jaime Cardinal, but he was already in a cast by the time Bill was . . . by Thursday night."

"There was no one else?" I pressed, wondering if she knew about Bill's history of fighting for her somewhat dubious honor. It was hard to imagine that she could be ignorant of those conflicts.

"Nobody," she said firmly. "To tell you the truth, Robyn, I think it *was* the environmentalists. That one man especially. Jurgen Clark." She shivered. "He seems so angry all the time, and he and Bill had a big fight in the bar."

"Yeah, I heard about that. Jurgen wouldn't win any personality contests, that's for sure," I told her. "But it doesn't necessarily mean he's capable of murder."

At the word "murder," Lori seemed to collapse in on herself. I cursed myself for being so blunt.

"I don't know, Robyn," she whispered. "I don't know what to think anymore."

"Mom?" Todd stood in the doorway.

Because I was looking right at her, I could see the heroic effort Lori made to pull herself together.

"Hi, hon," she managed, her voice quivering just a bit. "What's up?"

"Can you help me glue this?" Todd held up an intricate-looking model of the *Starship Enterprise.*

In the next few minutes, Lori rose higher in my esteem as I watched her help her son. Another person might have just glued the model herself to be done more quickly. Lori helped Todd patiently, holding the pieces and passing him the glue, guiding him along without doing the work for him. She knew all the *Star Trek* characters (a fact that sent her up another notch in my books), and her praise of the finished model was warm without being cloying. Under Lori's loving attention, Todd opened up like a spring tulip.

Unwilling to intrude any longer, I finished my coffee, licked away the last few crumbs of my muffin, and said my goodbyes. Clearly I needed to re-evaluate my feelings about Lori.

I arrived back at the house by twelve-thirty. At 12:35, the front doorbell rang. Jaime and I were in the kitchen, waiting for the coffee to percolate. Kelt had yet to make an appearance.

I waved Jaime to stay where he was, padded down the hallway to the front door, and peered out the window. It was the same turkey vulture of an RCMP constable who had rapped on my motel room door the other morning.

I opened the door. "Yes?" I asked cautiously.

"Ms Devara." His gravelly voice was reproving. "They told me at the motel that you'd come here to stay."

"Yes, I didn't know that I should have notified you," I said half-jokingly.

He didn't even crack a smile. "That's okay. Will you be stayin' here now while you're in Marten Valley?"

"I . . . yes."

He nodded. "We'd like you to come down to the station to answer a few more questions."

"Hi, Pete." Jaime had poked his head out of the kitchen. "What's up?"

The constable (Pete?) looked past me and smiled. "Jaime! How's the leg?"

Jaime wheeled down the hallway. "Ah, this damn leg! Can't do anythin' with it." He shook his head mournfully. "I see you met one of my house guests. This is Robyn Devara. Robyn, this here's Pete Lenarden. He and I grew up together. He's usually part of the Quesnell RCMP detachment, but he managed to get himself posted here on some kinda temporary assignment."

"We've sort of met already," I told Jaime. "Pete brought me to the RCMP office the other morning to answer some questions, and now it looks like they want me to answer a few more."

"*More* questions?" Jaime's voice registered surprise and disbelief. I could have kissed him. "Ah, c'mon Pete. Robyn's good folks."

Pete shrugged. "Orders from the Vancouver inspector," he explained. "It's not up to me."

I went to my room to get a sweater and returned to the sunny kitchen to find Jaime and Pete in deep conversation. Their expressions were serious and they broke off their talk as soon as I entered the room.

"I'll come by later for a longer visit," Pete promised, getting to his feet.

Jaime smiled at me and clouted me on the shoulder. "See you, Robyn. If Kelt drags his butt outta bed anytime soon, I'll tell him where you are."

I smiled back gratefully. "Thanks, Jaime. Need me to pick up anything on my way back?"

"Well, now that you mention it . . . see if Irene's done bakin' the pies for today."

"A whole pie or just a slice?"

"A whole one, of course. I hafta share with you and Kelt now, don't I?"

Pete chuckled. "You always did like those peach-raspberry ones."

"Ever since we were kids." Jaime grinned.

I began to revise my first impressions of Constable Pete Lenarden. He'd seemed suspicious of me earlier, but maybe Kelt's paranoia theory could explain that away. Pete and Jaime were obviously the best of friends. And Pete knew that today was peach-raspberry pie day at Irene's. He couldn't be all bad.

I wasn't sure I could say the same about Inspector Danson. I got into the RCMP van with a distinct feeling of trepidation.

"How would you describe your relationship with Lori Reddecop?" The raptor-like eyes of Inspector Danson raked me over.

I was sitting in the same hospital-green interrogation room that I'd been in before. Today, somebody had opened the venetian blinds to the bright sunshine. The golden rays only made the room seem more dreary. Inspector Danson and Sergeant McIntyre sat across from me again, their faces serious and businesslike. No glimmer of friendliness from McIntyre today. I guess they were playing bad cop, bad cop.

I considered the question carefully. "I'm not sure that 'relationship' is the right word," I answered. "It seems a little strong for Lori and me. We're really more like acquaintances, and not very good ones at that."

"Could you elaborate on that, please?"

"We knew each other in university ten or eleven years ago, but even then we weren't what you would call friends. We were lab partners, that's about it."

"How well did you get along with her?"

"Not very," I replied. "But we weren't enemies or any-thing. I just avoided her when we weren't in class."

"And after she slept with your boyfriend?"

I gaped at the inspector, shocked into silence.

"Come, Ms Devara," Danson said sarcastically.

"Surely you can't expect us to believe that it had no effect on your relationship ... ah, pardon me, your *acquaintance* with Mrs. Reddecop?"

I swallowed, my throat suddenly parched. "I . . . no . . . how did you know?"

McIntyre leaned forward. "Lori told us about the affair yesterday."

"*Lori* did?!" It seemed I would have to do a little more re-evaluating.

Inspector Danson folded his hands together on the table and stared at me. "Perhaps you would like to explain to us why you didn't see fit to tell us yourself?" he asked icily.

I took a deep breath. This wasn't just a matter of Kelt's paranoia theory. I was definitely under suspicion here. I squirmed under the inspector's piercing gaze. How could I have been so stupid?

"I'm sorry," I began lamely. "I never thought it would be relevant—"

"You had a grudge against a woman whose husband has been murdered, and you don't think that's *relevant?!*" Danson's tone oozed with derision. Even McIntyre looked doubtful.

"No—"

"No? You've just said that you didn't think it was relevant."

"No, it wasn't like that—"

"Well, maybe you could explain to us just what it was like," he snapped.

I took another breath, attempting to calm my rising temper. "I'm trying to explain, if you would just let me speak."

Danson leaned back in the chair and waved me to continue. "By all means," he said. "Speak."

"The incident in question happened over ten years ago," I told them. "*Ten* years! I don't know about you, but I don't *hold* grudges that long, and even if I did, it wouldn't have mattered in this case. Yes, I knew that Lori had a fling with Guido. But it was a one-night thing. She had a steady boyfriend—some law student or something. And, up until now, I'd always thought that she hadn't known who Guido was. That I'd been seeing him, I mean."

"And this is why you didn't think it was relevant to our investigation?" McIntyre asked mildly.

I nodded. "Well, that and the fact that I stopped dating Guido ten years ago, shortly after his fling with Lori. That affair was just one of many. The guy was a total loser, with a capital L. I blamed him more than I blamed her." I paused. "Actually, I never really blamed her at all. Like I said before, I didn't think she knew."

Danson still looked skeptical and very serious. "But obviously she did know," he observed clinically.

"Yes . . . obviously," I echoed. I was still trying to get my mind around that one. It seemed that Lori could still be a galaxy-class bitch when she wanted to. But, no matter what she had said or done, I was still well rid of Guido, though I did wonder why she'd chosen to tell Inspector Danson about the affair. Did Lori honestly think that I'd had something to do with her husband's murder?

I brought my attention back to the two RCMP officers. "Look," I told them. "That particular incident happened so long ago, it feels like another life. I'm not harboring any secret grudges against Lori Reddecop, even after what you've told me just now. I didn't even know she was married—let alone to Bill Reddecop—until after he'd been murdered! And I certainly didn't have anything to do with *that*, except find the body, of course."

"And a jacket covered in his blood," McIntyre added.

"I . . . what?" I asked weakly.

"The jacket that you and your colleague found was covered in blood. It was Bill Reddecop's blood."

I must have turned green, but the surprises weren't over yet.

"We also found Bill's pickup truck in the general area where you found the coat. You wouldn't happen to know anythin' about that, would you?"

McIntyre rummaged around in an olive green file folder and pulled out a photograph. The picture was out of focus but clear enough to reveal a battered blue pick-up truck partially hidden by bushes. There were large rust stains along the edges of its wheel wells, deep dents on the fender, and a smashed left brake light. With a sick feeling in the pit of my stomach, I realized I'd seen this truck before. More importantly, I knew when.

I raised horrified eyes and looked at McIntyre. "I've seen this truck! I saw it on the night of the murder."

"Why didn't you tell us sooner?" McIntyre asked, exasperation creeping into his tone.

"I'm sorry," I apologized quickly. "I didn't remember until now. I was pretty sick that night. I had a terrible cold, and I wasn't thinking straight or paying much attention to anything except getting back to the motel and going to bed. I'm really sorry."

"Where did you see the truck?" Danson asked.

I thought for a minute, trying to dredge up the faint memory. I'd been so intent on getting back to the motel. . . .

"Close to that Seidlin Lumber Mill sign," I said finally.

"You know the big yellow one? I saw it as I was leaving the site. I didn't go any further down the road; I just turned around and headed back to town. I figured the truck had just been abandoned."

"What time was this?"

I shrugged apologetically. "I didn't look, so I'm not really certain ... maybe somewhere around nine-thirty or ten."

Danson returned to the subject of Lori again. How well had I known her? When had I seen her last? Why hadn't I liked her? Had I met her husband? I was sure getting a lot of exposure lately to *déjà vu*; it seemed to me that I had already answered most of these questions before. Maybe they were checking my statement. It was a chilling thought.

At last, even Inspector Danson seemed to run out of questions. As I rose to leave, I paused, struck by something McIntyre had said earlier. "You mentioned that the truck was found near that coat?"

McIntyre nodded.

"But that wasn't anywhere near where I saw it!"

McIntyre let out his breath in a long sigh. "Yeah, I know," he said. "Now we've got to find out when it was moved. And who moved it."

"Well, aren't there fingerprints or something?" I asked. I felt like I had a vested interest in this investigation.

McIntyre regarded me steadily. "Oh yes, we've got prints from the dead man, his wife, his son, his brother, his best friend, even his boss. In fact, just about everybody in town seems to have been in Bill's truck at one time or another. We even know that he had a dog in the truck. Any one of them could've moved the truck, except maybe the dog."

Danson leaned forward and tapped the photograph. "That's assuming the murderer was in the truck," he said, looking at me pointedly. "The time of death isn't very exact. It's quite possible that Bill Reddecop was killed after the truck was moved and the murderer drove a different vehicle. As far as we've been able to determine, your rental car and this old truck were the only vehicles out there that night."

I gulped. There didn't seem to be any question anymore; I was definitely a murder suspect. "I didn't see any other cars," I said, trying to be helpful.

Danson's expression was unreadable. "Please make sure to tell us if you happen to *remember* another one."

CHAPTER 18

Somebody thought I was a killer. The idea alone was enough to send my blood plummeting below room temperature. Somebody believed I had the remorseless conscience and cold cruelty of a murderer.

It was difficult to get my mind around it. I'd always thought of myself as an ordinary person. I liked to read and watch movies and sit gossiping with friends in coffee houses. Sometimes I worked too hard. I owned a cat. What the hell was I doing involved—no, *suspected*—in a murder investigation? The gods were certainly having their little joke. I wasn't laughing.

Dark thoughts matched steps with me all the way through town. At the entrance to Irene's Diner, I took a deep breath and squared my shoulders. The RCMP could believe what they wanted. I was innocent, and if I had to prove that to the falcon-like Inspector Danson, then so be it. I opened the door to the diner and was engulfed in a cloud of sweet-smelling heaven. The peach-raspberry pies had just come out of the oven.

I inhaled deeply with lungs and diaphragm, willing away the tensions of the last hour. There was a long line of flaky golden suns behind the counter. What did one call a group of pies, I wondered. A succulence? The pies were still too hot to go into a box, so I decided to have some tea and a sandwich while I waited. Lunchtime had come and gone while I'd been in the RCMP station.

The diner was busy, filled with people enjoying afternoon coffee and cinnamon buns of gargantuan proportions (another Irene special?). A man sat at a central table, a large crowd gathered around him. Although balding, he wasn't one of those types who grow their hair long on the side and then not-so-cunningly comb it over their bald spots. Instead, what was left of his light brown hair had been neatly close-cropped. I could only see the back of his head, but he looked like a younger man, stylishly dressed and obviously popular in Marten Valley. Something I couldn't say about myself.

It wasn't that the Marten Valley folk disliked me, Robyn Devara. But Robyn Devara, environmental consultant and spotted owl biologist, was another matter. I understood their reasons, but understanding didn't make it any easier to deal with unwelcoming stares and turned backs. I was never going to get dates or win any popularity contests around here. Hell, at this point, I'd have even settled for a friendly smile.

But eyes remained wary, and mouths thin-lipped and disapproving. I found a table by the window and slouched into the chair.

My thoughts naturally turned to the murder. Had Bill Reddecop really been killed because of the spotted owls? Why had Jurgen changed the subject so quickly when we'd been talking about the murder? What about that uncharacteristic apology? And what was the matter with Bonnie? Did she know something about the murder? Why had Lori told the RCMP about her affair with Guido? Who else had been in the forest that night? And what did that massive clear-cut have to do with anything? Questions buzzed around like black flies, whining and stinging, with answers just out of reach.

"Excuse me, Ms Devara?"

I glanced up and found myself drowning in a pair of eyes the exact color of rich, dark chocolate. Expensive European chocolates. The kind that are so luscious, you want to smear them all over your body. I gulped.

His body was muscular, trim with the look of a physically active man. His charcoal pants were well-fitting; his snowy dress shirt accentuated his athletic physique. I estimated his age to be late thirties. He sported glasses rimmed with thin gold wire, and his bald head, far from appearing strange for a man his age, merely served as a more effective setting for those stunning eyes. Ever since Captain Jean-Luc Picard had taken command of the *Starship Enterprise,* I'd discovered in myself a devastating attraction to bald men—some of them anyway. Apparently this was one.

I cleared my throat self-consciously, suddenly aware that I had been staring. Hopefully I hadn't been drooling too. I suppressed the urge to wipe my mouth. "Uh, yes," I managed to say at last. "I don't believe we've met." I was moderately proud of the steadiness of my voice.

He smiled warmly, the skin around his eyes crinkling a bit at the corners. "No, we've not met before. I'm Greg Reddecop." He held out his hand.

"Greg Reddecop," I echoed, reaching out to shake it. "Bill Reddecop's brother?"

His eyes clouded. "Yes, that's right. May I sit down for a moment?"

"Please do," I said, indicating the chair opposite me. I

eyed his expensive clothes as he settled into the seat. Remembering what Halmar had said about him, I didn't think that Greg Reddecop looked like a guy who was particularly hard up for cash.

"I'm sorry about your brother," I told him.

He inclined his head, acknowledging my sympathy. "Thank you. I apologize for intruding on you like this. . . ."

"That's okay," I assured him quickly. "I was just waiting for the pies to cool."

He smiled again, a heart-stopping little grin. "I'd heard that you were staying with Jaime Cardinal. Now I'm sure of it!"

"He likes his pies," I agreed.

Greg's chocolate-colored eyes twinkled. "When he got back from Vancouver, we all thought he was going to set up camp in Irene's kitchen."

I laughed. "Withdrawal symptoms?"

Greg chuckled and shook his head slowly. "Like none I've ever seen." He took a deep breath and his expression sobered. "I just wanted to talk to you briefly, Ms Devara. About my brother."

"Please, call me Robyn."

He smiled gratefully. "Thanks, Robyn. I understand from the RCMP that it was you who found him."

I nodded. "Yes, I . . . yes, I did."

Greg's eyes grew bright with unshed tears. "It was pretty bad?" he asked, his voice trembling.

I nodded again. "I'm sorry."

"You didn't find anything else? Nothing that might indicate who did it?"

I shook my head miserably. His pain was almost palpable, and I wished I could tell him something—

anything—that might help. I had never fully realized before how inadequate "sorry" could be.

"My colleague and I found a jacket that the police think is connected, but it was quite far away from ... where I found your brother. I'm afraid that when I found him, I really didn't think to look around."

Greg bowed his head and blinked rapidly. When he raised his face to me again, his eyes were swimming. "Thank you for finding him," he said simply. "At least we know what happened and we aren't sitting around waiting for him to come home. At least the police have a good chance of finding out who did it." He struggled visibly to get his emotions under control.

"Have you just come in from Victoria?" I asked, trying to steer the conversation to subjects less painful.

He swallowed hard and blotted his eyes with a paper napkin. His hands were attractive for a man's, well shaped and strong-looking. In order to become a field biologist, I'd trained myself in the skills of observation. I couldn't help but observe the third finger of his left hand was devoid of rings.

"No, I arrived on Monday," he said. "I couldn't get a flight to the mainland until Sunday night. How did you ...? Oh, of course, Jaime."

I nodded. "He told me you were a hotshot architect in Victoria."

Somewhat recovered, Greg snorted in amusement. "Hotshot architect, eh?"

I smiled. "Those were his very words."

"How is he, anyhow? I heard he busted up his legs."

"Sure did," I replied. "Broke one of them in three places and sprained the other one. He's getting around in a wheelchair right now."

Greg winced at the description of Jaime's injuries. "I'll have to come and see him as soon as I get a chance."

"I'm sure he'd like that," I said.

"How did you come to be staying with him?" Greg asked.

Briefly I explained about the spotted owls and my meeting with Jaime. Now that we'd stopped talking about his brother's death, Greg had managed to get himself under control. He seemed genuinely interested in the spotted owl situation in Marten Valley. Surprisingly, he showed little regard for the loggers' concerns. Maybe he'd been living in big cities for too long.

"And so you walk around the site to see if you can spot an owl."

"Well, there's a little more to it than that," I told him. "I've got to do quite a few walk-arounds to make sure I'm sampling enough of the area. I describe the habitat and any significant micro-habitats, and try to determine if there are any particular areas the owls are more partial to. Plus, of course, I've got to get as accurate a count as possible."

"That makes sense."

I nodded in agreement. "Yes, but most importantly, I've got to look for breeding evidence. Courtship behavior, nests, copulation, that kind of thing." Someone had once said to me that field biology involved watching everything else have sex except yourself. As I looked at Greg, I sighed a little for the accuracy of such an observation.

"And if the owls are breeding?" Greg asked intently. "What does that mean for Marten Valley?"

Maybe Greg wasn't as disinterested as I thought.

"I'm not really certain," I admitted cautiously. "I'd

imagine the area would be designated as an active owl site, at which point Seidlin would have to submit a new development plan, possibly even reclaim some of the forest."

"But the logging won't stop, will it?" Greg asked, then smiled at me reassuringly. "Don't worry, I haven't really got a personal interest in this. A good number of my friends work for the company; I'm wondering how they'll make out."

"In my opinion, the logging will be affected," I told him. "But not in a big way. You see, one of the problems with an impact assessment is that the impact is often determined to be either minor, major, or negligible."

"Open to interpretation, in other words."

I nodded. "Right. And if a project is very profitable, its effect is too often judged as negligible."

"You sound a little cynical."

I shrugged. "I've just seen it happen a few too many times. I'm all for sustainable development, but so often it seems like there's a hidden agenda at work. And it all has to do with profits both for private industry and government." I stopped and smiled at Greg. "I'm sorry," I apologized. "I'm up on a soapbox again."

"Not at all," he assured me with another disarming smile. "It's fascinating." He paused for a moment, gazing thoughtfully at me. "I think I'd like to see a spotted owl," he said finally. "I don't believe I've ever seen one before."

"They're awfully hard to find," I advised him. "You probably wouldn't have any luck."

"What about if I had an expert along to help me?" His tone was suggestive.

Flustered, I lowered my eyes and fiddled with the lid of my teapot. "Uh, I don't know . . . ," I began uncertainly.

Greg turned the full force of his warm gaze on me with devastating effect. "I'd really appreciate it if you'd take me on one of your walk-arounds," he said. "I'd like to see what has the whole town so worked up." His face darkened. "I'd like to see this owl that my brother was killed for."

I hesitated, considering his request. Under the circumstances, I wasn't sure how I felt about going into the woods with a strange man—even one as attractive as Greg Reddecop. But Kelt would be there, and Greg was an old friend of Jaime's.

I was also very much aware that an important part of conservation was education. If you couldn't get people to care about something, you had very little chance of saving it. If I could get the people of Marten Valley to look at the owls as something other than an impediment to logging, I would go a long way to helping the BCWA in their fight to establish a forest reserve. That was, after all, one of the reasons I had agreed to speak at the school.

On another level, I also had to acknowledge Greg's request in terms of his brother's death. If our positions were reversed, I'd want to see the owls too.

"Well," I began cautiously, "it's not really certain that your brother was killed because of the owls."

"Why else?" His tone had sharpened.

I shrugged uncomfortably, unwilling to go into it with him. "I don't know," I said. "But I guess if you want to see owls, I'll take you out sometime. I can't guarantee that we'll see any, though. They're pretty elusive, even for experienced field biologists."

"Thanks." He smiled at me.

Just then a young waitress came up to the table, a square, white, cardboard box in hand. "Here's your pie now. You tell Uncle Jaime to hurry up an' get better."

Another relative? I could see now what Jaime meant when he'd said that Marten Valley was home. I didn't even *have* this many relatives. "Thanks," I told her with a grin. "I'm sure this pie will help along the healing process."

"I'm sure it will," she giggled before winking saucily at Greg and flouncing away.

"I should get going," I told Greg, pulling out some bills and tucking them under the napkin dispenser. "Jaime's going to be wondering where I am."

Greg rose with alacrity. "It's been a pleasure talking with you, Robyn," he said, shaking my hand. "Thank you again for what you did."

I smiled up at him. "It was very nice meeting you too," I told him. "Jaime has spoken of you fondly."

"Tell him I'll be by as soon as I get the chance. You won't forget your promise to show me an owl?" His dark eyes were bright with anticipation.

I shook my head. "Not a chance," I assured him.

As I turned up the street to Jaime's Gasbar, I recognized Bonnie's pale figure standing at the pumps. Slumped against the side of a beat-up, green vw van, she was filling the tank and staring down at her feet. Jurgen was nowhere in sight. Recognizing a golden opportunity when I saw one, I stepped up my pace and reached the van just as she was finishing.

"Hey, Bonnie, how's it going?"

She jumped and stared at me for a moment, her eyes wide and frightened. "Robyn! God you scared me!"

I concentrated on projecting friendly warmth, the kind that inspires confidences and the sharing of secrets.

"Sorry about that. I was just sort of surprised to see you here. Actually I'm glad I ran into you."

"I'm in a bit of a hurry," she said nervously, her gray eyes darting around. To see if Jurgen was nearby?

"I just wanted to chat for a second," I assured her. "Are you guys going to make an appearance at this demonstration today?"

"Oh yes," she replied with an air of relief, obviously believing that the question was my reason for stopping her. Foolish girl.

"Wait till you see what Jurgen's got planned," she said, lowering her voice confidentially.

"Uh huh, I can just imagine," I said. "Look, Bonnie, it's Jurgen I want to talk to you about."

Bonnie grew still. Her eyes flew to my face. "Jurgen?"

"Yeah, you know—that little guy you hang around with," I said in a feeble attempt at comic relief. A dismal failure.

"What . . . what about him?" she whispered, huge eyes threatening to take over her face.

"I'm a little worried about him, that's all," I said, slipping into the role of concerned friend. "With the murder and everything, it seems like things are getting a little dangerous around here."

Although I wouldn't have believed it possible, Bonnie's pale complexion whitened even further. Ye gods, was she going to pass out on me? I could see Jaime's smiling nephew watching us from his booth.

"I've got to get back," Bonnie said finally, her tongue tripping over the words in her haste. "Jurgen's expecting me and we've still got some stuff to do before the demonstration." Clutching her purse tightly to her chest, she turned towards the gas bar's booth, forestalling any further conversation.

"Bonnie."

She stopped and turned slowly, her expression closed and tight.

"I know you're in a hurry," I said. "But if you need anything, I'm here. You know, in case you run into some trouble you can't handle."

She ducked her head in acknowledgment and scurried over to pay for the gas. I shrugged mental shoulders and turned back towards Jaime's house.

I had wanted information from Bonnie—a lot more information—but Bonnie was obviously not in a talkative mood. I got the feeling that I'd handled the situation badly. But what was I supposed to say? Hi, Bonnie, what's bugging you? Did Jurgen really kill that logger? Right. All I could do now was wait and hope she would take me up on my offer.

Pie box in hand, I arrived back at Jaime's to find that Kelt had emerged from his room, downed two glasses of juice and three Aspirins, and returned to his bed.

"He looked kinda rough," Jaime told me. "That's one hell of a cold you gave him."

"Me? I was better by the time he got here!"

Jaime grinned. "He's sure ornery when he's sick."

I smiled back and shook my head. "So much for Mr. Tough Guy, eh?"

Jaime chuckled, then gazed at the white pie box. "I want to hear about that Vancouver inspector, but first . . . do you think that pie's still warm?"

I laughed and cut us a couple of generous wedges while Jaime put the kettle on for tea.

Jaime delved into his pie with obvious relish. Easy enough for him; he wasn't a murder suspect. I looked down at my own slice and found my appetite had deserted me. I wondered if Bill Reddecop had liked Irene's pies. Morosely, I picked at the flaky crust.

"You gonna eat that pie, or just play with it?"

I smiled crookedly and shrugged one shoulder. "I guess I'm not that hungry."

"How'd it go with the Mounties?" he asked.

My stomach lurched but I managed a light tone. "Oh, they just wanted clarification on my statement," I said easily. "It was no big deal."

Jaime gave me a long look. "Why didn't they just phone you?"

I shrugged again with studied indifference. "I guess they wanted it in person. I think they were a little put out at having to track me down here."

"Ah, don't you be worryin' yourself about that," he told me, taking another sip from his mug. "It's just Pete playin' the cop."

"I met another friend of yours today," I said, forcing my tone toward cheerfulness. "While I was waiting for the pie, Greg Reddecop came up and introduced himself."

Jaime's face brightened. "Greg! I heard he was comin' back." Jaime's expression sobered as he remembered the reason for Greg's return. "How's he doin'?"

"About what you'd expect. He's pretty cut up about his brother's death. He thanked me for finding Bill. Said he was glad that at least they knew what had happened."

Idly I played with the rim on my mug. "I never really thought about that aspect of it," I said. "If I hadn't found his body, his family would have been left wondering."

"Nice of Greg to think of thankin' you."

"Yeah." I smiled absently, recalling Greg's warm regard. "He didn't look at all like I expected, though."

Jaime took one look at my dreamy gaze and hooted with laughter. "Not again!"

I snapped my attention back to the present. "What?" I asked defensively.

"Just about every damn woman in this town seems to have a thing for Greg. He's *bald*, for cryin' out loud!"

"The better to entrap you with testosterone, my dear."

Jaime snorted.

I shook my finger at him. "Ah, but you're not a woman. I can see why the Marten Valley women are smitten. It's not just all that testosterone." I clasped my heart and struck a dramatic pose. "Those eyes . . . that charming personality. . . ."

Jaime rolled his eyes. "All right. All right. It's not fair! I tell you, even *Irene* starts bakin' special pies for him whenever he comes back to town."

I laughed. "Aha! At last we get to the root of your— jealousy!"

Jaime chuckled. "Ah, I'm just funnin' you. I've never really been jealous of Greg. He's a great guy, always jokin' and kiddin' but never pushes the limit, if you know what I mean. Most of the women who go around fantasizin' about Greg are my cousins and sisters anyhow. Besides," Jaime added smugly, "when I hurt my leg, Irene baked me *two* special pies."

"There's riches for you!"

Jaime poured another cup of tea. "So how come you're so smitten with Greg? I thought you and Kelt . . ."

"I'm not smitten with Greg," I broke in. "And Kelt and I are just work colleagues. And speaking of work . . ."

Jaime cocked one eyebrow at me quizzically at my abrupt change in subject, but his face grew serious as I launched into a description of the Wolf Creek clear-cut and my oh-so-friendly visit with Gus Nickerson.

"So lemme get this straight. You're thinkin' Seidlin lied about a beetle infestation and got permission to cut a bigger block?"

"It's the only answer I can come up with," I said. "What do you think? Is it possible?"

Jaime ran his fingers through his hair. "Well, I guess it might be at that. Most of the guys don't know squat about the new laws. But a scam like that would have to involve a couple of different guys. Not the crews so much, but the other guys. There'd be survey reports and probes and all kinds of paperwork that'd have to be faked. I dunno, Robyn, it's kinda unlikely, don't you think?"

"Have you got another explanation?"

Jaime shook his head. "Not offhand."

"What about this fabled Marten Valley hotline?" I asked. "If there was a beetle infestation, wouldn't people talk about it?"

"Maybe not," Jaime replied. "You see, with everyone workin' in the same industry and for the same company, folks don't really wanna talk about work outside of work. It's too much, if you know what I mean. The hotline's more for what you'd call the personal kinda gossip."

"So in other words, it's possible that somebody or several somebodies faked reports and got permission to cut a huge area, and nobody else would've wanted or known or cared enough to question it."

"But why?" Jaime asked.

"I think Halmar gave us the answer to that the other night," I replied. "What's the timber volume on a typical forest site?"

Jaime thought for a moment. "I'm really dredgin' up my memory here, but I think it's anywhere from seven hundred to one thousand cubic yards per acre."

"And Halmar said the stumpage rate for high-quality wood is about a hundred dollars per cubic yard. That's just the stumpage rate. Depending on the market, Seidlin could sell that timber for ten times that amount. twenty-four hundred cubic yards multiplied by a thousand dollars multiplied by almost one hundred fifty acres. That's a hell of a lot of money, Jaime!"

"What do you want to do?"

"That's where I need your help," I told him. "I want to talk to someone on the crew that cut that area. To see if there really was an infestation. I need you to get me some names."

Jaime rubbed his chin. "Seems to me there was more than one crew up there. . . ." His face brightened. "I can give Sheila a call. She's been workin' in payroll at the company ever since it started up. When you're on a crew, you have to write down on your timesheets where you been workin'. She'll probably be able to give me the names like that." He snapped his fingers.

"Great! Is it too late to phone her today?"

"I'm on it, partner," Jaime said as he wheeled down to the living room to make the call. I poured another cup of tea and waited at the kitchen table. He was back in less than twenty minutes.

"That was fast," I said, examining his face.

He looked troubled. "Yeah, that Sheila sure knows her stuff. All I had to do was ask her about the crews that worked up by Wolf Creek and she had their names for me in five minutes."

"And . . ."

He sighed. "And I figure you might have yourself a bit of a problem. All the guys on her list are dead set against environmentalists and spotted owls. I dunno if they'll even talk to you."

"What about you? Would they talk to you?"

Jaime shook his head. "Y'know what Halmar was sayin', about guys bein' pissed off at me? Well, these'd be the ones he was talkin' about."

"Okay, I guess I'll have to give it a try, then," I said. "I might get lucky."

Jaime handed me a scrap of paper. "I wrote down the names of guys that might consider talkin' to you. There were other guys on the crew, but I know they'd rather cut their own legs off than talk to a tree-hugger—'specially one that's lookin' for owls."

I was about to ask Jaime about the other problem I was supposed to be solving. About if any of Bill Reddecop's workers might have held a grudge against him. But further discussion was postponed by the chimes of the front doorbell.

Jaime glanced up at the kitchen clock. "That'll be Todd. Y'know, Robyn, you might wanna try givin' those guys a call now. Everybody got off early for the demonstration. They'll probably be at home."

As Jaime opened the door for the small boy, I cleared away our plates and mugs. Knowing that Todd and Jaime would want to carve, I greeted Todd with a warm smile and took myself down the hall to my room. I paused for a moment by Kelt's door, wondering if he was awake. A loud snore answered my question, and I continued regretfully to my own room, snagging the hall phone on my way.

The first call was not promising.

"Hi. May I speak to Al Garvey, please?"

"Yer speakin' to him."

"Oh, hello, Mr. Garvey. My name is Robyn Devara and—"

"You the one that's stayin' with Jaime Cardinal?"

"Yes, I—" I broke off as the phone went dead in my ear.

The second call was even worse. Lem Berman sounded like the hounds of hell were snapping at his heels.

"Where do you get off on phonin' me? I don't know anythin'! Just leave me alone!"

The next few calls were no better, though most of the other men were more polite than Al Garvey or Lem Berman had been.

"I'm sorry, I'd like ta help ya out," one said with a slow drawl. "I really would. But I'm sure ya understand why I can't."

I did, and although it was frustrating, I didn't blame him. It took me barely twenty minutes to scratch out all the names on my list. For the moment, I was stymied.

Jaime and Todd were still carving, and Kelt still snoozed away in his room. I dug out a stack of periodicals from my duffel bag and curled up on one of Jaime's overstuffed armchairs.

I had a lot of professional reading to catch up on, but I found it difficult to concentrate on the intricacies of the proposed Federal Endangered Species legislation. How was I going to find out if the beetle infestation was real or a fraud if nobody would talk to me about it? I sincerely doubted that Gus would give me access to their files. Had Bill's crew worked on that site? I hadn't thought to ask Jaime. And if his crew had been there, what, if anything, did that mean?

Fortunately Jaime had accepted my offhand explanation about this morning's invitation to the RCMP offices. That made me feel only marginally better. I was still a suspect in a murder investigation. In novels and movies, the heroine always manages to solve the crime herself. Working around incompetent police officers, she brings the murderer to justice by using her staggering powers of logic and intuition. Unfortunately, I hadn't really the faintest idea of how to accomplish such a feat. I had a hunch the townspeople weren't exactly ready to confide in me. Bonnie obviously knew something, but my attempt at questioning her had been pathetic. And what about the chatty Gus Nickerson and his non-existent beetle infestation? What did that have to do with any of this? Hell, I couldn't even decide whether Bill had been murdered because of the spotted owls, a logging scam, or something entirely different. And the only time I ever appeared to be endowed with any sort of staggering powers was when I first got out of bed in the morning. All in all, it didn't bode well. The gods, I decided grimly, would have a lot to answer for when I got my hands on them.

My own lack of concentration finally drove me from my reading. Halmar had told us the demonstration was at four-thirty. Though he had politely invited me along, I would, obviously, not be a welcome addition to the rally. But if I was going to solve this crime myself, I should take every opportunity to observe the suspects. The police were suspicious of me, but I knew that I hadn't done it. It had to be someone else, and whether the whole mess was connected to owls or not, chances were that "someone" would be at the demonstration. Welcome or not, I was going to the rally.

CHAPTER 19

Save for an ominous steely smudge on the horizon, the sky was colorless, bleached white by those icy winter clouds peculiar to the Northern Hemisphere. The air was chilly, blowing with a damp, penetrating wind, and I burrowed a little deeper into the warmth of my parka. I passed by Rusty's Bar. A huge red-and-white-striped tent had been set up in the parking lot for the barbecue that was to follow the rally.

The entire town had turned out for the demonstration. Main Street was lined with the colorfully scarfed figures of Marten Valley's mothers and wives; toddlers bundled to their bright, curious eyeballs had been tucked carefully into strollers. A few elderly people had come out, their lined cheeks pink with the cold, their eyes sparkling with the promise of new fuel for the Marten Valley hotline.

Teenagers, obviously forced to attend the rally, loitered on the edges of the crowd, clad in their uniforms of oversized jeans, smirks of carefully contrived boredom on their faces. Every so often, one or another of them turned from the group to spit noisily and derisively on the pavement. As I made my way through the crowd, I took care to stay well back from the line of fire. What did one call a group of teenagers? A spittoon?

The men of the town—and a few of the women—had gathered in front of Seidlin's offices. I watched them mill about. How many of them had worked with Bill? Had they liked him?

A podium complete with a silvery hedgehog of microphones had been erected in front of the carved oak doors. Stacks of placards and signs leaned against the building, waiting to be swept up in a surge of emotion. RCMP officers stood impassively along the sidelines. As predicted, the media were out in force. Camera crews fiddled with their equipment, and I could see reporters darting from one person to another, their microphones poking eagerly into the crowd like robins looking for a juicy worm.

I looked around but saw nary a sign of Jurgen and his gang. Puzzling. Not to mention disturbing. I wondered what they were up to. With so much media in attendance, I couldn't imagine Jurgen passing up the opportunity to get on his soapbox. Had a more sinister opportunity proved irresistible to him last Thursday night? He and Bill Reddecop certainly disliked each other. Hated each other? Was Jurgen a killer?

Briefly I spotted Ella, but the crowd swirled and eddied and I lost sight of her short figure. I recognized a few other faces: the gossipy cashier from the grocery store, the solid-looking Pete Lenarden, and there was Halmar towering benignly over his co-workers. His face lit up as he spotted me; he smiled and waved and gestured me over. I smiled back and shook my head. I was fine just where I was. I wanted to observe today, not participate.

Gus Nickerson appeared to my right, and I ducked behind the crowd before he could see me. My hand still hadn't recovered from his handshake. He was a strong man. Strong enough to drive a tree spike through some-one's heart? But why Bill?

A fur-wrapped Lori was there too, hemmed in by a comfort committee of Marten Valley's women. Bill's murder must have caused the women to put aside their dislike of her, at least for a while. I wondered if any of them were capable of murder. With Bill dead, it was unlikely that Lori would stay in Marten Valley. Without Lori, there would be fewer straying husbands. Still, in that scenario, it would have made more sense for Lori to turn up dead. I scanned the women's faces but saw noth-ing more than kind concern and excitement for the com-ing demonstrations.

The crush of the crowd grew stronger. Almost unconsciously, I found myself searching for another face. For eyes the color of rich chocolate. I finally spot-ted him standing on the other side of Main Street, on the sidewalk just outside Irene's. He was dressed casually in jeans and a royal blue parka, chatting easily with a small group of women both young and old, who appeared far more interested in his august person than in the demonstration.

Just then, a cry went up, and the crowd around Seidlin's offices surged towards the pile of signs. I craned my neck trying to get a better view.

I'd managed to find myself a fairly central spot a little way back from the crowd. Conscious of my status as both outsider and environmentalist, I had inserted myself between two groups of sullen teens, hoping to be over-looked in the general avoidance of those ill-tempered individuals. I hoped they wouldn't spit on me. I tweaked up the collar of my parka just in case.

The demonstration began with speeches. People who

had worked all their lives in the forest industry got up and told their stories. They spoke of the forest, about their lives in Marten Valley, and mostly about the people who supported their families by logging. As each speaker told his or her story, the other loggers waved signs and placards and the crowd cheered their support.

Finally the mayor of Marten Valley stepped up to the podium. He was a short, pudgy, little man, his waddling gait reminiscent of an overfed goose. But once he was at the podium, there was nothing awkward about him. He held up his hands and the crowd quietened immediately.

"My friends," he began softly. "You've heard a lot of stories today about the people in this town. About how they came here and found work and started families. About what the forest industry means to them. Hell, you've probably heard most of these stories before. God knows, I have." The man rolled his eyes and grinned as the crowd tittered at his long-suffering tone. He paused for a second and his voice became serious. "But these are stories that should be repeated! They are the stories of our lives. They are our roots. We've built a community here in Marten Valley, a place for families to grow and prosper. And we were able to do this because there are jobs here, because there is logging here.

"There are some who feel that we should stop this logging. They say that cutting down trees is evil. That the spotted owls need the trees. Well, let's take a look at that for a moment. They say that these owls are here, living in the forest. I've been living in Marten Valley all my life. I camp in this forest all the time. I've never seen *anything* that looks like a spotted owl."

A few in the crowd cheered their agreement. The mayor smiled and continued. "I don't want to sound cold and hard. Maybe there are a few spotted owls around here. Great! There's room enough for everybody. There's lots of forest and there always will be. We don't destroy forests! Oh, of course we cut some trees down—it's our job. But for every tree that's cut, another one is planted. I call it continuation.

"There's *plenty* of room here for owls and loggers. And what about these owls anyhow? Some people think the owls are endangered, but others aren't so sure. I just read about a guy who found four owls as he took a walk through a young forest—a *young* forest, not old-growth! And environmentalists want us to stop logging because the owls *might* be here and they *might* be endangered?! Well, what about us?" His voice rang with conviction. "If they stop the logging, I *know* our town will be endangered. If they stop the logging, I *know* that our people will have to leave to find other jobs. If they stop the logging, I *know* of many who will have to walk away from their homes. If they stop the logging, I *know* that Marten Valley will become a ghost town, and all those stories that you just heard will be forgotten. I *know* this. The logging must not stop."

I had to hand it to the mayor, he sure knew how to work a crowd. Whistles of approval shrieked out as people stamped their feet, shouted, and clapped. Even the spittoon of teenagers had temporarily put aside their sullen manner to cheer raucously at his words. That I felt uncomfortable was the understatement of the year. I'd glanced around, intending to make good my escape, when I caught sight of what was coming down Main Street.

At the far end of the street, a double row of men marched slowly towards the podium. Their expressions were sober, their pace measured and dignified. Between them and supported by them were the unmistakable shapes of coffins.

I counted fourteen crude, unfinished caskets. On each, a name had been scrawled in black paint. The crowd's cheering cacophony was silenced by the grim spectacle. By the time the first group of men approached the podium, a light drizzle had begun to fall, as if the sky itself wept in despair. The media people were beside themselves with delight.

The mayor stepped up to the microphone hedgehog again. "All of us here today know how dangerous it can be to work in the forest. We all know people who have been injured or killed. But these coffins," he said soberly, "represent the towns that died when the logging stopped. You've all read about them. You've read about the people who used to live in them. These coffins stand for those people who lost their way of life. There are only fourteen coffins here, but there were many more towns that died. Too many to make coffins for. Today, we will burn these coffins in memory of all the towns and of all the people that lived in them." His voice rose to a thunder. "And we will make sure that Marten Valley is *never* laid to rest."

As the mayor spoke, each coffin was piled on the street in front of Seidlin's office building. With his last words, he lit a torch, and, stepping down from the podium, he touched the flickering torch to the pile of coffins. The coffins must have been doused with gasoline. There was a great *whoosh*, and then the pyre was engulfed in devouring flames.

But the show wasn't over yet. As I turned to leave, I noticed a disturbance at the far end of the crowd. I caught sight of Jurgen and his group. The reason for their absence up till now was immediately apparent.

Somehow Jurgen had gotten wind of what was to happen at the demonstration. Sporting black arm bands, he and his followers now walked down Main Street with their own coffin. The names of endangered and extinct species had been painted in green on the weather-stained wood. Bonnie and a few other demonstrators walked alongside, carrying signs proclaiming "Nature Defence!" Jurgen's black eye was purpling beautifully now, adding more color to the bizarre tableau.

Jurgen's voice rang out. "And what about the animals that have died? Who mourns for them?"

His question met with angry shouts and jeers. The RCMP hastened towards the group of environmentalists, while the news people spoke rapidly into their microphones and scurried over, their cameras rolling.

Brazenly, Jurgen strode up to the funeral pyre. "This coffin is for the animals. For the species that died so you can have nice homes and fancy cars. What makes you think you're better than they are? What makes you think you deserve to live when they die? We're all in this together! It's not just the spotted owls; the whole ecosystem is endangered!"

At this point, many in the crowd of loggers found their voices. As environmentalists and loggers began shouting insults at each other, their cries and jeers soon merged to become an incoherent roar. The RCMP had formed a ragged but effective line between the two groups. It was impossible to see or hear anything more, and I wasn't at all sure I wanted to.

In one way I regretted my decision to come. I don't know what I'd expected. I hadn't spoken to anyone, hadn't learned anything about Bill Reddecop's murder. All I had seen was a crowd of worried people whose way of life was endangered as much as any spotted owl.

The only bright spot was an idea that had come to me as I watched the mayor give his speech in front of Seidlin's office building—an idea that was technically illegal. As the spittoon peeled off from the rest of the crowd, I followed them through the crush of people. If my idea had any chance of succeeding, I had to get back to Jaime's and start preparing.

CHAPTER 20

"You want to break into Seidlin's offices!?" Kelt gaped at me in shock.

"Not exactly break," I protested. "I'm not about to heave bricks through any windows. I was thinking more along the lines of sneaking in, having a quick look around, and getting the hell out. It's the perfect time. Everyone in town is heading to Rusty's for that barbecue."

"It is gettin' kinda dark out now, easy to sneak around," Jaime mused.

"And most if not all of the cops will be at the barbecue making sure Nature Defence doesn't crash the party," I said.

Jaime was nodding. "You're right, it'd be the perfect time, and I can tell you approximately where you'd find those files. . . ."

Kelt's eyes goggled out as he looked at us. "*You too?!*" he exclaimed to Jaime. "What the hell's going on here? I zone out for a day, and everybody turns into felons!"

It took a while to explain, but Jaime and I finally got the whole story out. The clear-cut, the beetles, and Gus Nickerson. Kelt still seemed a bit shaken by my proposition.

"But it's against the law, Robyn," he urged when we'd finished. "What do you think Kaye and Ben would say if they heard?"

"Well," I hedged, "it *would* be after work hours."

"*After work hours!?* Oh, I'm sure *that'll* make them feel a lot better! What happens if you get caught? Think about how that'll look for Woodrow Consultants."

I was trying not to. "Then I'll just have to make sure I don't get caught, won't I?" I said stubbornly.

Kelt threw up his hands in despair and tried another tack. "What do you think you're going to do with any proof you find? It sure won't be admissible in court!"

"I don't know yet, Kelt. If I could think of another way to get evidence I'd do it. But I can't, and we need some sort of evidence before we can take it any further. Hasn't it occurred to you that Bill Reddecop's murder may have something to do with this?"

Now both Kelt and Jaime looked at me in surprise.

"How'd you figure that?" Jaime asked.

"It's just a wild guess," I replied. "But, I've been thinking about a few things I've heard. The librarian told me Bill Sr. was a pretty straight and narrow sort of man. A good guy, he said. Bill Sr. donated books to the library, implemented replanting projects, and made sure his workers kept up safety standards even before they were compulsory. It sounds as if the company was more like a family than a business venture to him."

Jaime nodded slowly. "Yeah, you wouldn't be too far off to say somethin' like that."

"Well, then," I continued, "how do you think his son would've taken it if he'd found out his dad's precious company was veering off the straight and narrow?"

"And ruinin' his old man's good name and all that."

Jaime nodded again in comprehension. "You're right, he sure wouldn't have taken it well. Bill kinda worshiped his old man."

"So maybe he found out somehow. It wouldn't have been difficult. He was a foreman; he would've been in and out of the planning and development department. Maybe he was going to tell somebody and he was killed before he got the chance."

"That's a lot of 'maybes.' Why not just go to the RCMP with all of this?" Kelt asked. He was turning out to be quite the Mr. Straight and Narrow himself. Easy for him. Nobody suspected him of killing anybody.

"All what?" I argued. "I *know* it's a lot of 'maybes'; that's the problem. All we've got are suspicions, and if we try to go through legal channels, Gus and his cronies are going to have plenty of time to destroy or alter any evidence. We've got to get proof first and then decide what to do with it."

"So, what's your plan, sweet thang?"

I looked at Jaime and smiled gratefully. His light tone eased the growing tension in the room. "I thought I could try to jimmy the lock on one of those basement windows around the side of the building. Once I'm in, I'll have a quick snoop through the planning department's files."

"You might just try the door, y'know."

"The door?"

"Yeah, one of those big rectangular things with knobs."

"Funny. What do you mean?"

Jaime grinned, unrepentant. "I know things're kinda different in the big cities, but around here, we're not real persnickety about lockin' doors. Scotty Henson's the security guard in the buildin' and I guarantee you he'll be rushin' over to the barbecue. Probably lock the front doors before he heads over, but I betcha anythin' the little side one on the left'll still be open. He wouldn't worry so much about lockin' that one up till after he's et. You'd never see it unless you knew it was there."

Jaime snorted with laughter. "And to tell you the truth, Scotty'd be more worried about all the steaks bein' gone before he gets to the barbecue. He likes his grub." He patted his stomach significantly.

"Great!" I exclaimed. "Let's hope he stays away and chows down on the salad bar too. That'll make it a hell of a lot easier for me."

"For us," Kelt said, his jaw sticking out stubbornly.

Surprised, I turned to him. "Us? Are you sure?"

Kelt heaved a great sigh. "I can't let you do this yourself, Robyn, and Jaime here won't be much help with that cast. I don't like it much, but I like the thought of illegal clear-cuts even less. I'm in."

"Thanks, Kelt." I smiled warmly. "All right, now that we've got that settled, where can we find those files?"

Forty minutes later, Kelt and I slunk out the door on sneakered feet and headed over to Seidlin's office building. The night air was still, the stars bright diamonds on a navy velvet sky. Our breath puffed out in icy clouds. We had dressed in dark clothes and packed small flashlights that Jaime had dug out of a closet. I felt like something out of a *Pink Panther* movie, but we weren't after any diamonds, and Inspector Danson was no bumbling Clouseau.

Jaime had gone to the barbecue, both to socialize and

to keep Scotty the security guard engaged for as long as possible. By now, the party at Rusty's was in full swing. On the still air I could hear the distant sounds of laughter, singing, and the thumpa-thump of music. We ghosted down the alley towards our target. My hands were shaking a little.

Jaime's guess proved correct. The narrow metal door facing onto the alley opened easily, without so much as a squeak. Soundlessly, we slipped into the building.

The first part would be the most dangerous. Although the metal door entered directly into a concrete stairwell, the doors on each floor except the ground were locked (part of the reason why Scotty was not overly concerned with locking the side door). The planning and development department was on the fourth floor. We'd have to go up via the main staircase in the front lobby. The stairs were directly opposite the main doors, and the lobby was always kept brightly lit.

"This is it!" I murmured to Kelt as we paused by the door leading to the front. "If anyone sees us, we're toast."

Kelt just smiled grimly and nodded. I wondered if his heart was pounding as furiously as my own.

For the next thirty seconds, I thanked the gods that I was a field biologist. Practiced at moving silently through forests, I zipped through the front lobby and up the steps without a sound except the wild thumping of my pulse. Kelt followed closely and just as silently on my heels. We stopped to catch our breath on the first floor and to listen for any sign of alarm. Save for the low hum of the ventilation system, the building remained silent. We continued up the stairs.

At Jaime's suggestion, we split up on the third floor. Kelt continued up another flight to the planning department. I was going to see what I could find on the third floor, the floor where the scaling yard's files were kept.

Cut logs on a forest site, Jaime had informed us, are stamped with a timber mark. That way, you could identify which area they came from. Using the mark, logs could be tracked from the site to the scaling yard to the mill. I needed to find the scaling records for the Wolf Creek timber. Gus had already told me the area had been clear-cut because of bark beetles. But, if the records made no mention of blue-stained wood, I'd have solid proof of a scam.

I found the filing room at the far end of the floor. Although the tiny room was windowless, I didn't want to risk turning on the light. Instead, in true cat-burglar fashion, I flicked on my flashlight and started going through the cabinets. It took me less than five minutes to find the scaling records I was looking for. They were stored in a cabinet marked "Scaling Records, 1995-6." This burglar stuff was a cinch, I thought jauntily.

Unfortunately, that was the only easy part. It took a while for me to identify the Wolf Creek timber mark, longer to find the appropriate scaling records, and even more time to figure out the meaning behind the codes of numbers and letters.

Before we'd left, Jaime, a veritable mine of information, had explained a bit about scaling and grading. According to him, the highest-grade pine was Grade Code D. Blue-stained wood would be Grade Code H or I, possibly even J, depending on the condition of the entire log. Codes X, Y, and Z were for poor-quality logs good enough only to pulp.

As you might expect from an old-growth forest, the Wolf Creek logs varied from Code D all the way down to

z. But as I flipped through the thick file and scanned rows and rows of scribbled codes, it was obvious the majority of the timber had been Grade Code D—the highest grade for pine. "None of dem blue trees here," Halmar had said. It appeared he'd been right.

Some thoughtful clerk had stamped each completed form with "Data Entered" followed by a date and (even better) a file name. The Wolf Creek scaling records had been compiled in a single computer file. Yes! I punched the air with a victorious fist. I'd been intending to simply photocopy a sample of the records, but a computer printout would be much, much better. I checked my watch. We'd been here for forty-five minutes. I sent a small prayer to Jaime to keep the guard busy for a little while longer; then, almost gleefully, I skipped out to the reception area and flicked on the computer and the laser printer.

Seidlin used Macintosh computers, which meant finding the file would be cake. I moved the cursor to the *File* menu, highlighted *Find*, and typed in the sequence of numbers and letters. The computers were networked; the file was located on an external drive. A storage drive? Whatever, it took only a second to find it and a few more to launch the software. Within two minutes, columns of numbers and letters covered the screen. Perhaps I'd missed my calling, I thought whimsically. I sent the file to print and nervously tapped my finger against the desk. Perhaps not. We'd been here for almost an hour now. Time to get out.

I snagged the first pages off the printer and scanned them briefly. What the . . . ? According to this printout, most of the Wolf Creek logs had been graded much lower than the written records had indicated. I flew back to the filing cabinet and yanked out the file again. There! I wasn't mistaken! The two records were different.

"Robyn! What the hell are you doing?" Kelt's urgent hiss crackled across the floor.

I jumped, almost dropping the file. "I'm just about done," I whispered back shakily, poking my head through the file-room door. "Turn on that photocopier, will you?"

As the computer spat out its evidence of wrongdoing, I copied a selection of scaling records from the file. Kelt waited silently; I could tell from his face that he'd found something. I couldn't wait to get back to Jaime's and compare notes.

I was just about to copy another page when I heard the sound of water rushing through the pipes. A toilet flushing?

"Quick! The guard's back!" I squeaked as I grabbed up my copies and stuffed the originals back into the file. "Grab those printouts. Turn off the computer!"

I pelted to the file room and crammed the file back into the cabinet. Kelt was already at the stairwell door. I ran towards him before skidding to a stop. The photocopier! It was still on! I waved Kelt to go on ahead and turned, intending to sprint back across the room. I never made it.

As I spun around, I stumbled and smashed my hip against a desk. The metal in-basket hit the carpet with a muffled crash; papers and unopened mail whooshed out across the floor. Frantically I grabbed up handfuls of envelopes and memos, dumping them in an untidy pile on the desk. Maybe the secretary would think the janitorial staff had been careless. As I reached for the last envelope, my straining ears caught the sound of a merry whistle. The guard! Frozen in fear, I glanced down at the unopened letter in my hands and did a double-take. The letter was addressed to Bill Reddecop. It had been stamped "Personal and Confidential"; the return address was the Regional Manager's Office of the BC Ministry of Forestry. I barely had time to think about what it might mean. The whistle was getting louder.

I jammed the envelope into my pocket and urged my feet to move. For once, they listened to me. I flew across the floor and through the stairwell door. As I slithered down the stairs, I heard the guard open the main door.

"Hellooo?" His voice was deep; he even sounded big and burly. Just the sort of guy you'd want as a security guard. As long as you weren't a burglar.

The stairwell door closed with an audible snick. I reached the second-floor landing and pressed my back against the wall. I heard the door open above me.

"Hellooo?"

I held my breath. This was one Scotty I didn't want beaming me up.

"Hellooo? Anyone there?" He waited for a moment, then grunted. "Keerist, now I'm imaginin' things!" He belched long and loud and sighed heavily.

As my heart threatened to jump out of my throat, the door snicked shut again. I was alone in the stairwell. I let out my breath slowly. Maybe he wasn't the sort of guy you'd want as a security guard after all. But he was sure great if you were a burglar. I waited for another minute to make sure he wouldn't come back, then crept down the remaining flight of stairs.

As I slipped back into the night, I was suddenly swept up in a huge bear hug.

"*Goddamnit*, Robyn!" Kelt's angry hiss threatened to

become a shriek in my ear. "Where the hell were you! I thought you'd been caught!"

Much as I was loath to leave his arms, it wasn't the time and it certainly was not the place. I gently disengaged myself from his hold. "The guard came back, Kelt. I had to wait till the coast was clear again. Come on, let's get out of here."

CHAPTER 21

Kelt berated himself under his breath the whole way back to Jaime's house. I waited until the door was safely closed behind us before I spoke.

"I'm sorry," I apologized with a sincere smile. "I really didn't mean to scare you like that. But I had to hide in the stairwell till the guard left."

He harrumphed, plainly trying to find fault with my explanation. "I don't know how I would've explained *that* to Kaye and Ben," he said finally. "What possessed you to go back?"

"I'd left the photocopier on. But I bumped into a desk by accident and all the papers went flying. I was trying to pick everything up when I heard the guard coming. I never did get the copier turned off," I said glumly.

My face brightened. "But, Kelt, they fudged the scaling records, and look!" I dug the letter out of my pocket and showed it to him. "Why do you suppose Bill Reddecop would be getting confidential mail from the Regional Manager?"

Kelt looked at the envelope, then at me. "You found this on the desk?"

I nodded. "Yeah, I knocked it onto the floor with the rest of the stuff."

"Are you going to open it?"

I hesitated for a moment, a sudden chill tickling up my spine. After all, the letter was addressed to a dead man. I took a deep breath and tore open the envelope.

"Dear Mr. Reddecop," I read out loud. "In response to the concerns put forth in your letter dated February 28th, please be advised that investigations are to be undertaken with regard to the Wolf Creek forest site. . . ."

Kelt let out a whoop of jubilation as I scanned the rest of the letter.

"This looks like a preliminary notification," I remarked after I'd read it all. "They very carefully don't say what they're going to be investigating. But one thing's for sure: Bill Reddecop blew the proverbial whistle."

"And wait till you hear about all the stuff I found," Kelt exclaimed, his eyes sparkling. So much for Mr. Law-Abiding Citizen. I hoped I hadn't created a monster.

"It was pretty easy to find the Forest Development Plans for Wolf Creek," he said. "Say what you will about Seidlin, they've got great secretaries! So anyway, I'd found the Wolf Creek plans and all the background stuff, and you still hadn't come up yet so I thought I'd do a little more snooping around.

"I remembered that both Ella and Halmar had told you the last infestation was in the 1970s. It took a bit more digging to find it, but, get this . . . they're *the same!*"

"What do you mean, '*the same*'?"

"The data is all the same for both areas!"

"You're kidding!"

"I kid you not!" Kelt said solemnly, shaking his head in disbelief. "We're talking number of acres affected, the hazard risk, survey data, everything! They were too stupid to even think up some different numbers."

He grinned boyishly. "I really ran up the counter on the photocopier, but I've got copies of everything from the initial notification to the results of ground surveys and beetle probes. They're identical for both areas! Robyn, we've got those bastards by the short and curlies!"

Unbelievable! This was so much more than I had hoped for, and the revelations weren't over yet.

"That's not all. . . ." Kelt paused dramatically. "You'll never guess who was one of the junior surveyors from 1972."

"Who?"

"None other than your good pal Gus! Guess it wasn't much of a stretch for him to fake the reports."

I let out my breath in a whistle of disbelief. "How much of a stretch would murder be?" I wondered aloud.

"I think we can safely leave *that* with Inspector Danson." Kelt aimed a reproving look my way.

We were still exulting when Jaime wheeled through the kitchen door. Poor guy didn't even have time to hang up his coat before we descended on him, words tumbling out.

"The computer files were fixed—"

"And Bill knew about the clear-cut—"

"They copied data from 1972—"

Jaime's eyes widened under the barrage. "Slow yourselves down," he hollered finally. "You're gonna burst somethin'. Lemme get inside the house first."

Sheepishly, Kelt and I stepped back to let Jaime hang up his coat. We even let him settle at the kitchen table before we began telling him the whole story.

We sat around the table well into the small hours of the morning, discussing what we'd found, and what we should do about it. Was Bill's murder connected to the illegal clear-cut? It seemed so. Had it been the company's orders, or the decision of a few unscrupulous individuals? I didn't know, and in a way, it didn't matter. Regardless of specifically who was to blame for the murder (the powerful Gus Nickerson came to mind here), there was a definite connection. Once investigations had begun into Seidlin's industry violations, the truth about Bill Reddecop's murder would come out, and whoever was responsible for his death would be punished.

How best then to disclose the violations? Jaime suggested we wait to see what the Regional Manager would do. If little or nothing came from their investigations, then we could bring out our evidence. Kelt and I were skeptical.

"Maybe we should tell one of those reporters at the Rest EZ," I suggested.

Jaime looked doubtful.

"Look what happened a couple of years ago with Godfrey-Hall," Kelt said to Jaime. "The government became the company's single largest stockholder. Now tell me, how is the Ministry of Forests supposed to police the timber industry when they essentially own a big chunk of the company? Did you know that Godfrey-Hall has been cited over ninety times for violations? Everything from illegal dumping to logging on protected lands. And they've paid minimal fines—less than half a million dollars for everything! I'm sorry, Jaime, my faith in the Regional Manager is shaky at best. I checked into Seidlin before I came here. The government isn't the largest stockholder, but they're not the smallest either."

I continued the argument. "And what about the International Timber Company? They've been caught repeatedly logging in unauthorized areas—including spotted owl reserves. Again they only paid small fines, and they got to keep all their illegally cut logs."

The argument went back and forth. I sided with Kelt, but then, it was easier for us. We were just visitors to Marten Valley. In a few weeks, we'd go back to our homes in Calgary, and any changes or troubles in the valley would seem far, far away.

"I think we're gettin' away from what's really important here," Jaime said finally.

I raised one eyebrow. "Oh?"

Jaime rubbed his eyes, looking tired and dejected. "We're sittin' here blatherin' on about Seidlin and the clear-cuttin', but industry violations like this are happenin' all the time. I don't like it much, but I know they happen. Thing is, murder sure doesn't happen all the time. There's a *murderer* walkin' around this town."

Kelt nodded slowly. "So instead of blowing the whistle on the violations and waiting for the murder connection to be discovered . . ."

"We tell the cops about the murder and how we think it's connected to the scam," Jaime finished.

I was shaking my head. "How? We'd have to tell them how we got the information. We can't do *that!* They'd lock me up and toss away the key. I'd be the Birdwoman of Alcatraz!"

Jaime patted my hand. "Alcatraz is a tourist attraction now, and I'm not suggestin' we tell that Downtown inspector. I think we should be talkin' to Pete."

"Pete Lenarden?"

"Yeah, you see, ever since Pete up and joined the force, he started comin' across like this big, honest cop. But, I tell you, he used to be a bad-ass kid, always gettin' himself into trouble with the law. Heh heh, he carved his name in just about every piece of furniture in the station. Guess ol' Pete finally figured he was in that RCMP station so much, he might as well join 'em. Anyhow, the bottom line is, he's what you might call understandin' about things outside of the law."

I regarded Jaime skeptically. "So you'll just go up to him and say, 'Hey Pete, some friends of mine have evidence connecting Bill's murder to an illegal clear-cut. What should they do? Oh, by the way, they broke into Seidlin's offices to get it.'"

"Don't tell him it was us," Kelt interjected. "Well . . . maybe you can say it was her." He pointed towards me.

I shot him a withering look. "Thanks a lot."

"It *was* your idea."

"Funny. Seriously, Jaime, what do you think your friend is going to say?"

"I figure he'll give us all royal shit and then he'll go off and investigate."

"Royal shit, eh?" I looked down at my hands. "You're sure it won't be anything more than that?"

"We go back a long way, me and Pete. I'm positive."

I sat and stared at the oak tabletop, absently tracing the patterns of the wood grain. Jaime was right. The murder was more important than any industry violation, regardless of how blatant. Someone had killed a man, purposefully, savagely, leaving his wife a widow and his son without a father. And we had a good idea who it was. That was what was important. We couldn't just leave it until it came out in a general investigation of the company. We had to tell somebody now. And the best somebody to tell was Pete Lenarden.

"You're absolutely right," I told Jaime finally. "We'll tell your friend Pete tomorrow, right after the school visit."

I glanced over at Kelt to gauge his reaction. He curved his mouth up in a relieved smile and nodded. I wished I had his confidence.

Chapter 22

A late night of crime and an anticipated punishment notwithstanding, I got up early for another day of field-work. The survey was now well behind schedule. At the very least, we needed to cover a few more blocks, and I wanted to check on the owl pair again. Today's work would already be cut short; I had to be back at eleven to speak to Nat's students. I tried not to think too much about what would happen *after* the school visit.

I dressed in layers that could be easily peeled off as the day warmed up. I'd set the coffee maker on automatic last night, and the rich smell of fresh coffee was just starting to waft through the house as I emerged from my room.

Despite a nasty-sounding cough (no doubt brought on by the shock of committing a break-in), Kelt had insisted he was well enough to come along, though he'd bowed out of the school visit, not wanting to pass any germs to the kids.

I was glad he was well enough to join me on the sur-vey. Given what we'd discovered the previous night, I could kick myself for asking Gus about the Wolf Creek cut. Not to mention questioning members of the crews. I only hoped Gus's suspicions hadn't been aroused too much. Like maybe he thought it was just passing curiosity. Right. Not with my luck. Still, it was too late now to do anything about it—except, of course, avoid going into the forest alone. I certainly didn't fancy meeting Gus and his bone-crushing hands in an isolated ravine.

I tapped lightly at Kelt's door and poked my head in.

"Kelt?"

"Djrlunmhth?"

Déjà vu again. "Time to get up."

"Friumgl kwe gilb?"

"Yes, I've made coffee. I'm going to fill a thermos now. Get dressed and I'll meet you in the car."

"Kakhe."

In the kitchen, I rummaged through the cupboards until I found a box of granola bars. They looked as if they'd been around since *Archaeopteryx* flew the skies, but I stuffed a couple in my pocket for later. Hopefully they would be enough to fire up Kelt's synapses.

I filled the thermos with coffee and extra sugar for good measure, then padded down the hall to listen at Kelt's door. I could hear the faint sounds of movement and then a muffled curse. Grinning, I ducked into my room, gathered up binoculars, maps, camera, and notebook, and pulled on my coat. I'd wait for Kelt outside.

I swung the door open, stepped out onto the porch, and froze.

The mutilated body was spread across the hood of my rental car. Intestines had been smeared across the windshield. The dark eyes were half closed, their life extinguished. Blood soaked the feathers. It was a barred owl.

Superficially, the little woodland owls were similar to spotted owls; it was easy enough to mistake the two if you didn't know what to look for. Obviously someone hadn't.

It looked like the owl had been beaten. Its mangled body was torn and misshapen, most of its feathers broken or missing. I hoped the unfortunate bird had simply been hit by a car. I hated to think of somebody purposely inflicting this kind of damage on a living creature. I hated to think of it, but I had to. Beside the pathetic little body, the words "Go Home BITCH" had been scrawled in blood.

I was still standing on the porch when Kelt came out of the house and saw the broken body.

"Shit," he said.

I couldn't have put it better myself.

Kelt strode over to the car and bent to look more closely at the mess. "Blood's pretty much dry," he noted. "They must've left this here a while ago."

I forced my legs to move towards the car, trying to concentrate on the owl instead of the bloody message. "Was it hit by a car?"

"I don't know; it's kind of hard to tell."

"No, look!" I pointed to the owl's lower body. "Those are buckshot wounds."

Sickened, Kelt and I looked at each other.

"I guess it's a matter for the police, then," I said. Was this Gus's idea of a subtle hint?

Kelt nodded. "That message alone is enough to warrant their involvement."

I raised my eyes to look at the message that had been left for me. The blood-streaked letters were written large and clear so I would be sure to get the point. I did.

In my line of work, I'd been unpopular before. As an environmental consultant, I tried not to antagonize anybody unnecessarily. It was a job that required as much diplomacy as it did biology. Most of the time, people were fairly open-minded about conservation issues (and environmental consultants). Other times I'd had to deal with people who thought the world would be a better place if we just paved over the forests (and the environmental consultants). Still, this message was more serious than anything I'd encountered before. Using capital letters for the word "bitch" indicated not only anger, but hatred. I shivered and pulled my coat closer around my body.

Kelt took one look at my face and propelled me back indoors. "Come on. I'll get Jaime up and we'll have a cup of coffee."

Jaime was horrified by our discovery. When he wheeled himself to the porch and looked out at the dead owl, I could see his face whiten. I thought it was in shock until he turned and I could see the fury twisting his face into a parody of itself.

"Those sons-of-bitches!" he swore tightly. "I never would have believed they'd do this!"

"You know who did it?" Kelt asked.

Jaime shook his head. "No, but I can sure hazard a good guess. Son-of-a-bitch! I'm callin' Alex."

Kelt and I sat silently as Jaime put a call through to a sleepy Sergeant McIntyre. In a tone that was angry and clipped, Jaime described the dead owl and its threatening message. After he had hung up, he wheeled over to me and put a comforting arm around my shoulders. "Don't you worry yourself about anythin'," he said. "Alex is pissed right off and he's on his way over right now."

Alex must have been really mad. Though Jaime had obviously woken him with the news, both Alex (Sergeant

McIntyre to us murder suspects) and the young, blond constable I'd seen the other day arrived on the doorstep, fully uniformed, within twenty minutes. Trailing behind them like a skein of geese was a small contingent of media people.

"You'd think there would be other, more exciting news to cover," I said sourly, watching their progress from the living-room window.

Kelt stood and joined me. "What? More exciting than murder, demonstrations with coffins, and slaughtered owls?"

He had a point. I sighed and watched as lights were lit and cameras rolled to record the bloody mess. How had they heard about this so fast? Somebody probably had Alex's house staked out.

After they'd had a good long look at my car, the two RCMP officers came into the living room to ask a few questions. I was waiting for them. Now that I'd recovered from the initial shock, I was starting to get mad. I had a few questions of my own.

Unfortunately they were to go unanswered. Though McIntyre and Jaime seemed to have a good idea who was responsible, neither of them was voicing it. Or, at least, nobody wanted to tell *me*. I had my own suspicions, but, for obvious reasons, I was reluctant to voice them in front of Sergeant McIntyre. Instead, I had to make do with assurances that they would find out who had done it, that it wouldn't happen again, and that whoever was responsible was unlikely to try more persuasive methods to get me to leave. I can't say I was reassured.

A couple of the news people wanted me to make a statement. I didn't feel much like talking, so Jaime went out to fob them off. To make things worse, Kaye phoned just as Jaime reappeared at the door, and Kelt blurted out the whole story while I signaled wildly for him to stop. Great. Now I was in Dutch with the boss.

To my utter disgust, Kelt told Kaye everything. His explanation was a mastery of storytelling, complete with long pauses, allowing her suitable time in which to express her horror. The only thing he left out was our brief foray into the world of crime. Nevertheless, he told her about the bloody coat, the dead owl, the threatening message, even that I was a suspect in the murder. I shot a questioning glance at Jaime and he had the decency to look sheepish. Great. I was surrounded by conspirators.

"Robyn, Kaye wants to speak to you." Kelt extended the telephone receiver towards me, holding it as a snake-handler might hold a pit viper.

I winced. "Thanks a lot," I mouthed. I was on the phone for a long time.

CHAPTER 23

A few hours later, I drove Kelt's car across town to where the red brick schoolhouse stood surrounded by a stand of feathery cedars. I had forced the dead owl out of my mind for the time being. Nat's kids were looking forward to my talk, and I didn't want to disappoint them because of some criminal idiot. I was also trying not to think about the previous night—more specifically, about how I would explain the previous night to Constable Pete.

Everybody referred to the schoolhouse as The School, but as I pulled into the tiny parking lot, I saw the sign "Colonel Sanders Public School" peering over a mound of fresh snow. Colonel Sanders? I hoped it wasn't the same one that immediately sprang to mind. I had a brief mental image of classrooms of children with overdeveloped thighs.

Nat was a tall, thin man with sky-blue eyes and a thick thatch of strawberry-blond curls. He was every bit as friendly as his wife, and I warmed to him immediately. The kids in his Grade 3 class turned out to be a delight, with bright, curious minds and penetrating questions. Normal thighs, too.

Nat and I had decided on a loosely structured discussion rather than a formal talk. I'd come prepared to discuss the spotted owl controversy, but the kids were so interested in field biology that instead I ended up telling them about my job, my reasons for studying biology, and how many frogs I'd had to dissect in school.

After twenty-five minutes of this, Nat tactfully steered the conversation towards the spotted owls. Surprisingly, most of the kids believed the owls should be saved. I don't know why this astonished me so much—maybe because they were all from logging families—but their attitude towards the owls reminded me just how strong a connection exists between young children and wildlife.

The kids were squarely on the owls' side, but most were pretty worried about what their parents would do if the logging stopped.

"Why do we have to stop logging?" a little brown-haired girl asked. "Can't the owls just move to another place until the trees grow back?"

"It takes a long time for the trees to grow back that much," I told her. "How many of you know what old-growth forest is?"

A few tentative hands went up.

"An old-growth forest is exactly what it sounds like— a forest that's been growing for a long, long time. It has all sorts of neat stuff in it. There are old trees, younger, smaller trees, bushes and shrubs, and dead trees that have fallen over. Owls—and many other creatures—use all of these things at different times. Now, a young forest may have nice trees and even a few shrubs and bushes, but it won't have the deadfall—the trees that have fallen over. The ecosystem isn't the same and the spotted owls don't like it."

"My dad says there are lots of spotted owls in other places. He said these ones aren't important."

"Oh, they're important," I assured the child. "It's important to have a lot of any kind of animal."

"Even mosquitoes?"

I grinned. "Yes, I'm afraid so. A good example of this is the whooping cranes. There's only one flock of whooping cranes left in the whole world. Now, this flock flies around doing its own thing, but they all stay in the same general area. What happens if there's a big hurricane or a bad oil spill in this area?"

"All the whooping cranes die," somebody piped up.

"Right, but if there were a second flock of cranes, then the species would still survive."

"Is there another flock of whooping cranes?" a little girl asked, her eyes dark with concern.

"They're working on it," I assured her. "I used the whooping cranes as an example because they're sort of an extreme case, but the same goes for every species, including spotted owls. The more you have of a species, the less likely they are to become extinct. You all know what extinct means, don't you?"

"Gone forever," they chorused.

"That's right. But there is another side to this whole spotted owl problem," I continued. "If we set aside some forest to save the spotted owls, we're also saving the other plants and animals and insects that live in that forest."

"Why would anybody want to save insects?"

I laughed. "Oh, come on! Insects aren't all that bad. Well, maybe mosquitoes aren't the greatest, but a lot of birds eat them. If the bugs are gone, then the birds lose that food source. If there isn't enough food, then the birds will start to die. Besides, you never know what will turn out to be helpful. There are plants in the rainforest that people can use for medicine. Nobody knew about them twenty years ago. What if something like that is living in this forest?" I shrugged. "Nobody knows. There's still a lot we don't know about our forests here in Canada. So you see, it's important to save the spotted owls because it also means we're saving all of these other things too."

"How do you *know* if there are spotted owls in the forest?"

I described in detail how to spot owls and owl signs in the forest. When I pulled out my baggie of great horned owl pellets, most of the kids were delighted.

"Is it barf?" one dark-haired girl asked suspiciously. A child after Kelt's heart.

Patiently I explained the difference to her as Nat divided the children into groups and handed out dissecting tools and pellets.

I stayed on for a bit, chatting to Nat and supervising the dissection process. From the bones that emerged from the furry pellets, it looked like the horned owls were making good use of Marten Valley's population of woodrats.

Though the lunch bell rang at 12:20, the children were reluctant to leave. I was touched and gratified by their groans of disappointment when Nat told them I had to go back to work. But the groans quickly turned to cheers when he assured them the owl pellets would be waiting for them after lunch. The story of my life: second banana to an owl pellet.

In unison, the kids thanked me for coming and bringing the pellets. One little girl, prompted by a loud whisper from her friend, came up and shyly handed me a drawing. It had been rendered in crayon, the bright markings depicting a forest of improbably colored trees, complete with large-eyed brown splotches perched on the branches. "Save the spotid alow" was written across the top in neon orange. When I thanked her, her eyes sparkled and she blushed pink to the roots of her hair.

As I turned to leave, I glanced back and caught sight of the girl who had been suspicious of the pellet. Oblivious to both the lunch bell and my departure, she sat in the corner so engrossed in dissecting the pellet that her nose almost touched the furry mass. I smiled and went out the door.

CHAPTER 24

Constable Pete Lenarden's truck was already at Jaime's house by the time I got back. Kelt and Jaime sat in the living room, hands clasped tightly in their laps, eyes lowered. Constable Pete towered over them, his arms folded across his chest. The royal shit had, apparently, begun.

"So, the mastermind deigns to join us," Pete said sarcastically as I hung my coat and pulled off my boots.

Silently I came into the room and sat down. Neither Kelt nor Jaime met my eyes. No problem on that score from Constable Pete. He glared down at me like an ancient Greek Fury.

"Jaime and Kelt here have given me the bare bones," he said mildly, his tone belying his wrathful expression. "But why don't you fill me in on all the details?"

I gulped and started talking.

Constable Pete was not happy—far from it. But as I drained my conscience, I could see I'd managed to intrigue him. Corporate crime, conspiracies, murder—it would've intrigued me if I hadn't been in it up to my corneas.

By the time I'd finished my explanation and produced the Regional Manager's letter to Bill Reddecop, Pete was sitting quietly (he'd sunk down in a chair when I'd gotten to the part about Scotty the security guard). He held the pilfered letter lightly in his hand. The silence dragged on.

I drew in a breath to say something—anything to break the icy hush. Jaime caught my eye and shook his head.

Finally Pete inhaled deeply and sighed. "Well, I can't say as I approve of what you did," he began. "I don't know what it's like in Calgary, but Jaime, you, of all people, should have known better! Jesus! This is exactly why the force doesn't believe in posting officers to their home towns."

Jaime looked abashed.

"But in a way—and only in a way, mind you—I kinda understand why you did it." He scrubbed his face tiredly. "I must say, what you found is . . . interestin'. Very interestin'."

"So what can we do about it?" I asked.

Pete looked at me, his eyes like two frozen ponds.

"We?!" he exclaimed, his eyebrows shooting up incredulously. "We? You are going to do nothin'. That means all of you! I am going to investigate a little further— by myself! What I want all of you to do is . . . nothin'. Stay away from Seidlin, and stay away from Gus Nickerson. You"—he pointed to me—"don't go into that forest alone. And you"—he turned his finger towards Kelt—"don't be followin' her on any more nighttime excursions."

Pete stood then and turned to Jaime. "And as for you . . . "

"Pete—"

"I don't want to hear it," he cut in. "As for you, I want you to keep your face shut about this. You understand? Not a peep! Leave it with me for a day or so while I check things out. I'll let you know what I find. You've put me in a helluva situation, Jaime. Just make sure you keep your mouth in park for a change. I *don't* want any more murders around here!"

With that he bowed his head in a curt nod, put on his hat, and let himself out the front door, leaving behind three very chastened people.

When the ring of the phone split the silence, we all jumped guiltily.

"Uh, hello?" Jaime answered. "Yeah, hang on a sec."

He covered the receiver with his palm. "It's Gus Nickerson," he hissed. "He wants to speak to you."

"Tell him she's not here," Kelt urged.

"No, it's okay," I said. "I'd better find out what he wants."

"Hello?" I squeaked. I cleared my throat and tried again. "Hello?"

"Robyn Devara," Gus boomed. "Heard ya were stayin' with Jaime Cardinal."

"Uh, hi Gus," I replied cautiously. I could feel Kelt and Jaime's intent looks. "Yeah, I'm staying with Jaime while I'm in town. What can I do for you?"

"Gotta problem. Hope ya can help me with it. Kinda delicate."

"What's up?"

"Heard ya were asking some guys a bunch a' questions."

"Well, yes, I was," I admitted.

"Can't have that, I'm afraid. Mr. Chase doesn't like it. Too much going on right now. Gets the workers upset, y'know."

"I didn't mean to upset anyone," I protested.

"'Course not. Ha, ha. Knew you didn't. Just thought I'd call and tell ya to cut it out. Mr. Chase's orders, y'know. No hard feelins."

"Uh, no, of course not. I'm sorry I caused a problem."

"No problem anymore. All fixed. Anything you wanna know, you just ask me. It's what I'm here for."

Ask him? Not likely. Despite his jovial tone, Gus's laughter had an edge that hadn't been present the other day. I had never received a clearer warning in my life.

"Thanks, Gus," I told him. "But I don't have any questions right now."

CHAPTER 25

Todd came over again just before four o'clock, so Kelt and I took ourselves out of the kitchen and down the hall. We decided to go and pick up a few groceries. Jaime was a generous host, but feeding three people could get pricey, and we did have an expense account. The grocery store was nowhere near as large as the Superstores in Calgary, but it was well stocked with a pretty decent selection. We filled our cart with fresh fruits and vegetables as well as a few choice items from the gourmet section. By the time we got back, Todd had gone.

In the scant handful of days that I had known Jaime, I had come to rely on his unfailing good humor. Which made it all the more upsetting when I stepped in and caught sight of his face. His caramel-colored skin was pale, his dark eyes grave with concern.

"What's wrong?" I demanded.

He looked at me for a long moment. "I found out what's been botherin' Todd," he replied softly.

I arched my eyebrow. "Not anything good by the looks of you."

Jaime rubbed his eyes and let out his breath in a heavy sigh. "You got that right," he muttered. He wheeled over to the kitchen table and rested his head in his hands for a moment.

Kelt and I exchanged a long look and dumped our groceries on the counter. I shrugged off my coat and draped it over a chair. "Want some tea?" I asked.

Jaime nodded.

I put the kettle on while Kelt set mugs and milk on the table. As one, we slid into chairs across from Jaime.

"Tell us," Kelt said gently.

Jaime nodded. "Todd finally got around to tellin' me what's been buggin' him," he began, then sighed to a stop.

"And . . . ," I prompted.

He seemed to give himself a mental shake. "And it appears he saw Lem staggerin' down the street on Thursday night, the night Bill got himself murdered. Lem was right pissed to the gills."

"Lem?" Kelt asked.

"Yeah, Lem Berman. He's a faller, cuts down trees."

"He was one of the guys I spoke to on the phone, wasn't he?" I asked after a moment's thought.

Jaime nodded. "Yeah, he works—worked—under Bill."

"He was pretty hostile," I remembered aloud.

Jaime nodded again. "He can be sometimes. More so since Anna up and left him last year. He's got a real problem with the booze—always searchin' for the bottom of a bottle."

I lifted my shoulders in confusion. "So why is this suspicious?"

Jaime took a deep breath. "It wasn't just that he was drunk, Robyn. Todd saw Lem staggerin' around, crashin' into fences and the like. It's happened before; Lem goes on a bender and wanders around town singin' and hollerin'. Except this time he was covered in blood."

"*What!?*" Kelt exploded.

Jaime nodded morosely. "That's what Todd told me. Lem's jacket was all splashed and covered in blood. Said he could see it clear as day under the streetlight."

"What time was this?" I asked.

"Around nine or ten, maybe later. You see, ever since Todd got an astronomy book for Christmas, he's always sneakin' out of bed to look at the stars. Drives Lori crazy, from all I hear. Anyhow, that night he couldn't sleep. Lori had taken off somewhere, and he heard his old man leave sometime around seven or seven-thirty.

"Huh!" Jaime snorted angrily. "I know we don't have much in the way of crime around Marten Valley—at least not till recently—but jeez, leavin' a kid that young alone at night? What if there'd been a fire or somethin'?" He shook his head in disgust.

"Todd got kinda scared being alone and everythin', so he got out of bed and started lookin' at the stars. After a spell, he saw Lem stumblin' around. And when Lem came into the light, Todd saw the blood."

"And he waited this long to tell someone?" I was incredulous.

Jaime frowned slightly. "I know it sounds bad, but you have to remember he's just a little kid. And an awful quiet one at that. I don't think he even connected it with his old man's death till he overheard his mom tellin' someone how Bill had been killed—stabbed with the spike, you understand. It took forever just to get it out of him today."

"Do *we* even know that this is connected with Bill's murder?" I said. "What about Gus Nickerson and his bunch? What about that clear-cut?"

"I don't know," Jaime said. "But it's a hell of a coincidence, don't you think?"

Well, yes, I had to admit that. But I wasn't ready to let my pal Gus off the hook just yet. Not after what we'd learned the other night, not after that dead owl on my car, and certainly not after his oh-so-friendly warning earlier.

"You've got to tell the police," Kelt was urging him. Constable Pete's lecture was apparently still making its effects felt.

"I know," Jaime said miserably. "I just never thought of Lem as a murderer. I mean, *Lem?* The guy's squishier than a month-old banana!"

"Well, it sounds like Lem was pretty drunk at the time. You just said he was hostile when he drinks."

"No, no, not when he *drinks*," Jaime said. "You misunderstood me. Lem's what you'd call a happy drunk. He can get kinda mean when he's *on* the wagon, but I don't know that I've ever seen him mad when he's fallen off. Whinin' and cryin' maybe if he's real bad, but never angry. He usually just sings a bunch of old songs and passes out."

"Which just goes to show you he may not be a murderer at all," I insisted.

"I still think it's a police matter," Kelt said, shooting me a stubborn look of his own.

Jaime nodded. "I know. But I'd sure like to give him the chance to turn himself in."

Kelt looked doubtful. "How are you going to do that?"

"I figure I'll tell him what I know," Jaime replied. "I won't let on who saw him, of course. Just that he was seen all covered in blood on the night Bill was killed."

"Why not tell the RCMP yourself?" I asked. "Especially after the way your friend Pete read us the riot act."

Jaime waved off the lecture. "Ah, that was just Pete shootin' his mouth off." I had to admire his courage. Even I couldn't dismiss Constable Pete so easily.

"You see, I grew up with Lem," Jaime explained slowly. "His old man was a mean sucker, used to slap Lem and his mom around whenever things weren't goin' his way—which was just about all the time, it seemed. We all knew about it; nobody ever tried stoppin' it. We—the whole gang of us—were all too young, I guess, and Lem's mom never lodged a complaint. Found out later, she took to drinkin' a lot too. While Lem was at school, you understand. Anyhow, Lem was one of those geeky kids, y'know the ones everybody makes fun of? His clothes were always dirty, he didn't smell too good, and he was kinda slow in school."

"A social outcast," Kelt observed.

"Yeah, that's it exactly. You know how mean kids can get. Guess I've always felt bad about how I treated him when we were kids. Most everybody picked on him, but that's no excuse. It's not somethin' I'm proud of." He paused and sipped at his tea pensively.

"So what happened to Lem when he grew up?" I asked.

"He went to work at the company, just like his old man. Things were okay for a spell. Turned out he had a real feel for cuttin' trees. But come payday, just like his old man, he started lookin' for the bottom of a lotta bottles. Not seriously, not at first, but it got worse and worse over the years."

"You said Anna left him. Was that his wife?"

"Yeah, he met her Downtown on some vacation. She was cute but kinda flighty. You could tell she wasn't much of a small-town gal. Had itchy feet. When she up and left, I didn't figure Lem would ever pull himself together."

"Any kids?" Kelt asked.

Jaime shook his head. "Nah, just the two of them. When Anna left, Lem's drinkin' got a whole lot worse. I don't know." Jaime ran his fingers through his hair. "I feel like poor old Lem never had a break his whole life. Guess that's why I want to give him one now."

"Poor old Lem might have killed Bill Reddecop," Kelt observed grimly.

"I'm not convinced of that," I said.

"Me neither," Jaime added. "Actually, I don't know what to think, but whatever the truth is, it'd look a whole lot better if he told Alex about it himself."

I didn't feel great about Jaime's decision, and I could tell Kelt felt the same. I had never met this Lem, but I didn't buy the idea of him as a murderer. Why would a sad, drunken man suddenly become a vicious killer? No, Lem didn't seem to fit the profile, but I still thought the police should be informed. On the other hand, Lem was Jaime's friend; it was his decision. Besides, who was I to promote the straight and narrow path?

"What will you do?" I asked finally.

Jaime looked relieved that we were leaving it in his hands for the time being. "I've been thinkin' about callin' him up. I'll try to get him over here tonight and see if he remembers anythin'. Sometimes, y'know, when he's off on these benders—"

"What kind of coat was Lem wearing?" Kelt interrupted.

"Todd said it was a white jacket. Musta been the coat Anna bought for him just before she left. She'd gone into some fancy-ass shop down in Victoria when they were on holidays and—" He broke off. Dawning horror washed across his face.

I hadn't heard anything after "white jacket." A cream-colored coat would look white under the stark glare of a streetlight. All too well, I remembered the torn coat that Kelt and I had found in the snow. A cream-colored parka. A parka soaked with Bill Reddecop's blood.

It was late by the time Lem finally made his appearance. When the knock came, we were in the living room, surrounded by Jaime's wooden aviary, talking quietly of movies and our favorite books.

Kelt and I let Jaime answer the door, while we scurried out of sight down the hall and into the kitchen. Safe behind the kitchen door, I peeked around the corner and drew a sharp breath. Lem was focused on taking off his coat so he didn't see me. But I could see him. In fact, I could see him very well. Lem Berman was the strange, thin man I had noticed at Irene's Diner. The one who had jumped when Pete Lenarden had greeted him.

Much as I was loath to give up my suspicions of Gus, everything was clicking into place: Lem's nervousness around Pete, his attitude on the phone which, in retrospect, could be interpreted as suspicious rather than hostile.

As Jaime and Lem settled themselves in the living room, Kelt and I crept back down the hall, determined to hear what Lem had to say for himself. Somehow, I didn't think it would be much. Lem was three sheets to the wind.

"I came assoon as I got yer message," he slurred to Jaime. "You sai' it wassurgent."

"Yeah, yeah Lem, it is urgent. Had a few drinks at the bar tonight, did you?"

"Oh yes, at the bar, yes. I came assoon as I got yer message, though."

"And I appreciate that, Lem. I sure do. But I need to ask you some questions about Bill Reddecop."

Lem paused for a long time. "Bill?" he finally asked weakly. "What d'you wanna know 'bout him?"

"How well were the two of you gettin' along?"

Lem paused again, for even longer this time. When he finally answered Jaime, I realized he was crying. "He fire' me, Jaime," he sobbed. "He up and tol' me I drank too much. Tol' me I had a problem. I don't have a problem. Jus' 'cause I go out for a few drinks with the boys. I work damn hard all day cuttin' them trees. Damn hard! 'S hard work, y'know. Lotsa guys are no good at fallin'. It takes skill, an' I deserve a few beer at the enna the day. Doesn' mean I'm no alcoholic or anythin'."

"I know, Lem, I know." I imagined Jaime patting the other man's shoulder. "When did Bill fire you?"

"S'not my fault. Jus' 'cause I had a coupla drinks before work. I coulda still cut that tree. I coulda cut it with my eyes close'. Wasn' no call to fire me!" Lem sobbed again. "Fi' thing when a man's frien's turn 'gainst him. Fi' thing."

"When did Bill fire you, Lem?" Jaime was insistent.

"Was on Thursday. Said I couldn' operate a saw. I coulda still done it . . . ," Lem mumbled to himself.

"What did you do on Friday then, after Bill fired you?"

"Friday?"

"Yeah, what did you do instead of goin' to work?"

"Oh, I went to work, yes I did," Lem assured Jaime.

"Even after Bill up and fired you?"

The silence stretched out uncomfortably. "Nobody knew nothin'," Lem finally muttered. "I showed up to talk to Bill. But he wasn' aroun' an' nobody knew nothin' 'bout it so I kep' workin'."

"Nobody else knew you'd been fired?"

"Nope, nobody knew nothin' 'bout it."

"What did you do Thursday night, Lem, after Bill fired you? Did you have a few drinks?"

"Oh yes, drinks, yes, I hadda few. It was tha' damn Bill, you know. Had no call to fire me!"

"Did you try to talk to him that night? On Thursday night?"

"I . . . I trie' to talk to him. I was so mad, Jaime. I was gonna poun' him like that 'vironmennal guy did inna bar. Got no call to ruin my life!"

"Did you hit Bill that night?" Jaime sounded tired and disillusioned. "Think, Lem. It's real important!"

"I . . . I doan remember, Jaime. I thin' I mebbe hadda few too many."

"Do you remember the blood, Lem, the blood on your coat?"

Lem began to sob noisily. "I doan know wha' happen'. I doan know how the blood got there. I foun' it the nex' day. It was all over my coat, Jaime, the coat Anna gave me. I doan know wha' happen'."

"You gotta tell Alex," Jaime admonished him.

"Alex?"

"Yeah, you gotta tell him everythin' you remember. What did you do with the coat?"

"I . . . I think I ditch' it."

"Where?"

"I doan remember," Lem wailed.

"Okay," Jaime said soothingly. "Okay, Lem, take it easy now. You gotta go to Alex and tell him everythin'. Somebody saw you that night, Lem. Someone saw you with blood on your coat."

"Someone saw me?" Lem's voice quavered in fear. "But

I doan know wha' happen'. I wouldna done nothin' to Bill. I was jus' gonna talk to him. I jus' wanned to get my job back." Lem broke down again. "I was jus' gonna talk to him."

"C'mon, Lem, you gotta pull yourself together. It's kinda late now, but tomorrow you gotta go to Alex. I can't keep my face folded up about this, Lem, but it'd be a damn sight better if you told him yourself."

Lem sniffled and blew his nose soggily. "Yes, yes, I should tellim mysel'."

"Right. Listen, Lem, I'll give you till tomorrow at noon, and then I'll hafta tell him everythin' I know. This is a murder investigation; you can't keep information to yourself in somethin' like this. Okay?"

Lem sobbed and snuffled a bit longer, but finally agreed with Jaime. "Okay, Jaime, I trus' you. You can' keep information to yoursel' in somethin' like this. I'll go an' tellim mysel' tomorrow mornin'."

I met Kelt's eyes and jerked my head towards our rooms. We crept down the hall, leaving Jaime the task of calming the distressed Lem. Alone in my bedroom, I sat on the bed thoughtfully. So, it seemed one of Bill's workers *had* had a grudge against him. A fairly big one too. Lem Berman was seen covered in blood, he had a motive, and his coat had been found drenched in Bill Reddecop's blood. The evidence against him looked pretty damning. Recalling Inspector Danson's predatory stare, I suspected Lem was in for a difficult morning. I didn't know the half of it.

CHAPTER 26

I got up early the next morning, determined to continue my work—my official, biology-type work, that is. Constable Pete's lecture still smarted, and with Lem's admissions of the night before, it now seemed that Bill Reddecop's untimely death had little to do with illegal clear-cutting or the spotted owl controversy. Although I was still a bit spooked by the whole experience, at least I wouldn't have to keep looking over my shoulder every time I headed out to the forest.

I did wonder how Lem had managed to get a tree spike. I shrugged. Perhaps Bill had found it somewhere. In the bar, Bill had been yelling at Jurgen about the spikes. Maybe he'd discovered a stash, and it certainly wouldn't surprise me to find out that Jurgen had been spiking trees.

I tiptoed down the hall and roused Kelt in the by-now-predictable routine.

What was not routine was the dark pickup truck parked in front of the gas pumps. I didn't pay much attention to it at first, but when we got into my car and I revved the engine, I heard another engine start up. As I eased out of the driveway, I saw the truck's bright head-lights flash on. Odd. I thought field biologists were the only ones unlucky enough to be up at that hour of the morning.

I pulled onto the street, drove for a couple of blocks, and turned right. The truck followed a few car-lengths behind, its lights a bright glare in my rear-view mirror. We were going to survey a section southeast of the town. I had to make another right and then a left onto the logging road that led to the section. When the truck made the turns with me, alarm bells started going off in my head. Maybe they were just going in the same direction. Maybe they were going out to a work site. The truck moved closer. Maybe not.

I pulled onto the gravel logging road, and the truck sped up. I hugged the shoulder, giving him room to pass. Passing wasn't what he had in mind. Instead, he sped up, his front bumper right on my ass.

"Looks like we have some company," I said to Kelt, my voice tight with concern.

He flashed me a startled look and peered behind us.

"He was waiting by the gas pumps," I said tersely.

"We're being *followed?!*"

"Sort of looks that way," I said, glancing again into the mirror. "There's a turnout up ahead; I'm going to turn around. This is giving me the creeps."

I slowed the car to make a U-turn back to town, but before I could swing the wheel around, the truck swung out to the left, picked up speed, and roared past us. It sped by, spraying pebbles and dirt. There were two men in the truck. The passenger turned and stared venomously at me. As I stared back, he mouthed the words "Get out, bitch."

I slammed on the brakes and clung to the wheel as the car fishtailed across the loose gravel. Within seconds the truck had disappeared down the road. I pulled over to the side, my hands shaking badly.

"*Shit!*" I swore. "What the hell's going on here?!"

Kelt had his arm around me comfortingly, but his expression was worried. "It's okay, Robyn," he said. "They're just trying to scare us off. It's okay."

"But I thought Lem was the murderer."

"Nobody's trying to murder anyone." Kelt's voice was calm and reasoned. "This doesn't have anything to do with that. They're just a couple of assholes trying to scare us away from doing the survey. It has nothing to do with the murder. Come on, let's get out of here. We'll do a different section today."

We drove out to another, very distant section, but we might as well have gone back to Jaime's for all the work we got done. I kept looking over my shoulder apprehensively. Stealth—along with my nerves—had gone to hell. If any owls were hanging around in this part of the forest, they must have heard us coming a mile away.

By mid-morning, we gave up and returned to town. If those men had been trying to keep us from completing the survey, they were off to a fine start.

I was walking over to Irene's to meet Ella for our pie date when I caught sight of Bonnie's pale figure across the street.

What with dead owls, a drunken murderer, and a pickup truck of unpleasant, threatening men, I'd almost forgotten about her strange behavior. Understandable perhaps, but inexcusable in light of my investigative aspirations. What did she know? I meant to find out.

I broke into a jog to catch up with her, but just as I was

about to cross the street, she glanced back and let out an audible yelp. I had to wait for a minivan to pass before I could cross. By that time, she'd ducked down an alley and disappeared. Once again I was proving to be a most inept heroine.

I retraced my steps and continued on to Irene's Diner. Ella was already waiting for me.

"Bloody hell!" she exploded as I related the morning's events.

We were ensconced at a corner table. My appetite had apparently deserted me for the day, but Ella had insisted I at least order pie—Marten Valley's universal remedy.

She pursed her lips and frowned. "Between that scare and the poor wee owl on your car, I don't know what this town's coming to. It's a pity nobody tars and feathers anyone anymore!" Ella's Scottish blood was heating up.

I shivered a bit. My own blood could use a little warming.

Ella noticed the shiver and patted my hand. "You can't let it get to you," she advised. "That's what they're after, you know—to get you all riled up so you'll go home. It's stupid really. Even if you did leave, someone else would only come in."

I took a deep breath, trying to drain off the tension. I might as well have tried to drain the Pacific Ocean. "I'm sort of spooked about the whole situation," I confessed to her. "Finding a body, being a murder suspect, and now a dead owl, threatening messages, and people following me. It's not exactly part of my everyday life."

"I'd be spooked too," Ella assured me. "But I wouldn't trouble myself about being a murder suspect. Don't be reading too much into *that*. They're just trying to find out what's going on. I'm sure they don't really suspect you."

I wished I had her confidence. The waitress breezed by, dumping a huge bowl of soup and another basket of crackers in front of Ella. I forgave her brusque service because she also left two enormous wedges of strawberry-rhubarb pie. Perhaps my appetite could be coaxed after all.

"I hear you met Greg Reddecop the other day," Ella remarked, scooping up a spoonful of soup.

"Changing the subject?"

She nodded curtly. "Those idiots aren't worth any more of your time. Take my word on it. And there's no need to discuss their rotten selves while we eat. Let's talk about more pleasant things. Tell me what you thought about Greg."

"It's good to see the Marten Valley hotline is still up and running," I observed wryly.

Ella chuckled. "Oh yes, everybody's talking about how you two were making out like bandits."

"Making out?!" I pretended outrage. "All we did was talk!"

"You know what I mean," she said, catching the twinkle in my eye. "So what did you think of him?"

I grinned at her. "He's nice."

"*Nice?!*" She was incredulous. "Nearly every woman in Marten Valley drools over his very name, and all you can say is 'he's nice'?"

Remembering my own desire to drool, I smiled at Ella knowingly. "Well, okay, very nice."

She rolled her eyes in disgust at my obtuseness before catching my expression again. "Aha!" she exclaimed. "So you're not immune after all!"

I laughed at having managed to tease her. "No, I'm not immune," I assured her. "He's quite yummy. His eyes are amazing! And he talks to you like you're the only person in the world."

Ella laughed at me indulgently.

"And are you one of the droolers?" I asked her.

She laughed again. "Me? No, he's nice enough, I'll grant you, but he's never done anything for me in a romantic sense. I guess I'm just a one-man kind of woman."

"Well, he wants me to take him owling sometime."

Ella was impressed. "Ooh, lucky you! I hope word of that doesn't get around too fast or it'll be the women who try to run you out of town."

"He's popular here, is he?"

"You've no idea." Ella shook her head. "He's handsome and charming, but he doesn't walk around like he's God's gift to women, if you know what I mean. It's part of the reason the women here glom onto him so much—except, of course, for Lori Reddecop. She hasn't got the time of day for him, nor he for her. Rumor has it that Greg hasn't visited much in the last few years because of her."

"Yeah, Jaime mentioned something of the sort. I find it hard to believe. Lori's always been popular with men. Even the perceptive ones."

Ella nodded in agreement. "That's been pretty obvious ever since the day she moved here. She's a nasty piece of work. Flipped her skirt for anything in trousers. Fortunately my Nat could see right through her. He steered well clear. As for Greg Reddecop, they say she made a play for him and he turned her down. On account of his brother, you see. And ever since, he's steered clear himself. But others weren't so lucky."

"And the women put up with it?"

Ella shrugged. "What choice did they have? Most of

them have never lived outside Marten Valley. Married before they were twenty, not much of an education, and now, of course, there're children to think of. Besides, Lori's little flings never seemed to go much past a month or two. Still, there's been a fair amount of trouble over her."

"Why did she bother staying with Bill if she found the rest of the male population so tantalizing?"

Ella frowned. "Now, that's something no one's been able to figure out. She always went back to Bill. Sue Frazer thinks that it's some kind of gratitude thing."

"Gratitude?"

"Yes. You see, Bill went off to Victoria on extended sick leave. He'd pulled his shoulder out or some damned thing. He was gone for a couple of months, and when he came back, he was married. Little Todd came about seven or eight months later. Lori must have got pregnant before the marriage. Sue figures that Lori was grateful he hadn't dumped her like some others would."

"What do you think?" I asked, mumbling around a mouthful of pie.

"Me? Oh, the gratitude theory's possible, I grant you. Bill always did have a sense of what's decent. If he'd gotten Lori pregnant on some vacation fling, he would have married her, I'm certain of it. But staying grateful for near on ten years is a bit much to swallow, don't you think?"

"So why did *he* stick with her? I can't imagine that was pleasant."

Ella shrugged. "No, I don't think it was. But for whatever reason, he never left her. He was an odd man in many ways. Not well liked."

"Didn't *anyone* in this town like him? Jaime and Halmar said he hung around with a few guys but he didn't have any real friends. I can't imagine someone living a life like that."

Ella nodded. "My grandma would say he followed a lonely path. It's true he didn't have many friends, and those he did have, he managed to alienate one way or another. I always felt that he got the short end of the stick, as they say. You know, always being in his brother's shadow. I've had my suspicions that's the real reason why Greg's made himself so scarce."

"A falling-out?"

"It wouldn't surprise me. When popular regard is split so unevenly, I think a falling-out is inevitable. Though in all honesty, I never heard about it if there was one." She paused, absently drawing patterns in the water ring left by her glass. "You know," she continued after a moment, "I used to feel quite sorry for Bill when we were all younger."

"Not any more?"

She lifted one shoulder in a shrug. "I guess not. He'd really become nasty over the years. Not much left to like—or feel sorry for. Not to my mind at any rate. There's been a bit of a rumor going around that he'd been overly close to his secretary, but I don't think anyone's put much stock into it."

I scrunched up my nose. "His secretary? Couldn't the Marten Valley hotline come up with something a little less clichéd?"

"I know what you mean. It's not a serious kind of rumor, though. Jean Hewitt's a sweetheart to everybody, including Bill. And just because she's never married, a few people started looking at it the wrong way just to give their bored selves something to talk about. I'm sure there's nothing to it, but if you're looking to find a friend of his, I'd say Jean's probably the closest thing he had. She hasn't been in to work since he was found. Says she's got a flu bug, but I think she's taken his death pretty hard. She'd been his secretary for years."

Just then, a short, stubby man slammed into the diner. He made his way quickly to the counter and began talking and gesticulating wildly. A small crowd formed around him. Ella looked puzzled.

"That's Joe! What's got him so worked up? Hang on a second, I'll go see." She slipped out of her chair and wormed her way through the crowd. When she came back, her expression was distressed.

"What's wrong?" I exclaimed.

She looked at me, her eyes shocked. "Bad news. They've found another body."

"*What?!*"

She nodded. "Out in the yard, by the logging equipment. The mechanics found him this afternoon when they went to look at the Cat."

"What happened?"

"I don't know," she said softly. "But it was another logger. A faller. His name was Lem."

"Lem Berman?!" I was stunned.

Ella raised her left eyebrow in surprise. "You know him?"

I stared at her in consternation. "Yes ... I .... Did he kill himself?" I blurted out.

Ella's right eyebrow joined the left somewhere in her hairline. "Now why would you think a thing like that?"

"I, uh, I heard that his wife left him."

"Och, that was over a year ago now." She waved it off. "He was unhappy, but I don't think he was the type to suicide. Besides, the men who found him say he was murdered."

Murder again. The word hit me like a well-aimed punch.

"The whole town will be in an uproar," Ella was saying. "Joe says the police have told all those environmentalists to stay in Martin Valley. It's a bad mix; I hope they keep to themselves. Listen, Robyn, do you mind if we cut this short? Joe said they're questioning all the workers, so I guess I'd better get myself down there."

"No, not at all," I assured her. "You go ahead. I'll call you tonight."

She smiled gratefully and dumped some money on the table before whisking off. Our pies were left, unfinished, on the table.

As I ran back to Jaime's, questions descended like migrating geese on a grain field. I'd thought Gus, or someone working for him, had been the killer. That idea had flown out the window with Lem's admissions last night. But now Lem had been murdered too. Why? Was there some rabid environmentalist going around killing loggers? Where had Jurgen been last night? Or had Lem been murdered for another reason? Lem had been part of Bill's crew. Would Lem have known about the illegal clear-cut? Had the boys from Seidlin silenced another rat?

CHAPTER 27

I found Jaime and Kelt sitting silently in the living room. As soon as Jaime looked at me, I knew he'd blamed himself for what had happened. He looked gray and drained, his eyes dull with shock and haunted by guilt.

"I heard," I told him before he could say anything.

He nodded acknowledgment.

"Do they know what happened yet?"

Jaime shook his head, a slow, helpless-looking gesture. "Just that he was murdered. A broken neck."

"It wasn't an accident?" I asked hopefully. "He was pretty drunk. Maybe he fell."

Jaime shook his head again. "No, it'd be kinda hard to fall and break your neck while you're sittin' in a truck."

I sank slowly onto the couch, digesting the information. "Do the police know about last night? About Lem coming here and talking to you?"

"Yeah. I called Alex around noon to ask if Lem had been in. When I found out he never showed up, I had Alex come around. I told him everythin'. He was still sittin' here when the call came in about Lem." He sighed and scrubbed a hand across his tired face. "I should have told him last night. . . ."

Kelt laid a sympathetic hand on his shoulder. "You just wanted to give Lem a chance. It was a kind thing to do."

Jaime shook off Kelt's hand. "Didn't turn out so kindly for Lem, did it?" he snapped.

I stared at him. I hadn't seen Jaime this upset before—not even after Halmar's visit.

Jaime took a deep breath and let it out slowly. "I'm sorry, Kelt," he apologized with a tight smile. "It's not your fault."

"Don't worry about it." Kelt smiled back gently.

Jaime sighed and stared down at his hands. "I figure there's one half-decent thing in all of this," he said.

"Oh? Like what?" I asked.

"Like you're not a suspect anymore, Robyn. Not from the way Alex was talkin'. I guess they figure these murders are connected somehow. Two murders in a week. God, the last murder this town had was about fifteen years ago, and *that* was a drunken fight. I guess they figured you might have been able to poke a spike into Bill, but you sure wouldn't have had the strength to twist Lem's neck around."

A sense of relief washed over me. Being a murder suspect had weighed heavily. But now, if anything, I was more concerned with finding the murderer. The thought of a killer lurking out there left my blood cold. Unbidden, the memory of Gus Nickerson's powerful hands rose up.

Kelt met my gaze and jerked his head towards the kitchen. "How about a cup of tea, Jaime?"

"Whatever," Jaime shrugged.

"I'll give you a hand, Kelt," I volunteered. I squeezed Jaime's shoulder reassuringly and followed Kelt out to the kitchen. "What happened?" I asked in a low voice. "He looks like hell!"

"That Inspector Danson really read him the riot act."

"Danson was here?"

Kelt nodded. "Yeah, he came over with Jaime's pal Alex."

"Were you there when they talked to him?"

"Not really. They wanted some privacy, so I hung out in my room for a while. I could hear a bit of what was going on, though. Inspector Danson has a very penetrating voice. I was surprised that Jaime's skin wasn't blistered by the time he was through with him."

I set mugs and sugar on a tray and got the milk out of the fridge. "I didn't think it was a good idea for Jaime to leave it up to Lem," I said miserably. "But I sure wasn't expecting this."

"None of this makes any sense!" Kelt slammed the countertop in frustration.

"You noticed," I agreed. "If Lem murdered Bill, then who killed Lem? And why?"

"Lem was on Bill's crew. . . ." Kelt's voice trailed off.

"I know, that occurred to me too. But Lem wasn't high up in the company—not like Bill. Lem was just a faller."

"Then Gus . . . "

"Gus Nickerson's in up to his eyeballs with this illegal clear-cut, and he's a big, strong guy, but unless Bill shared his suspicions with Lem, I don't know how Lem would have found out about Seidlin's illegal activities, let alone been murdered over them. And somehow I don't think Bill was the confiding type."

"Which leaves us with some murderous environmentalist lurking about."

"But Lem's murder doesn't make sense in that scenario either. From what we've heard about Bill Reddecop, I could understand *his* murder in that context. He was aggressive and argumentative. But Lem seemed like a quiet soul. According to Jaime, even when he drank, he was a happy drunk."

"Maybe we should try talking to Jurgen," Kelt suggested. "There was definitely something weird there."

"He'd never open up to us," I objected. "But, perhaps Bonnie . . . "

"Bonnie. Jurgen's friend?"

"Yeah, I met her at the gas bar the other day. I tried to talk to her, but as soon as I mentioned the murder, she cut me off and flew out of there. And today I saw her again as I was heading to Irene's, but when I tried to catch up to her, she scooted down an alley. I think she knows something about the murder, and I think it involves Jurgen."

"What about telling the police? I don't think it's a good idea to keep anything to ourselves, especially after what happened to Lem."

"I know," I agreed. "But Bonnie hates the law. She'd clam up. And all I've really got to go on are suspicions."

"Then, once again, I guess it's up to us to find out—"

I sort of liked the sound of that "us" bit, but I cut him off before he could go any further. "You mean *I've* got to find out. Bonnie doesn't know you. I'm sorry, but I don't think she'd talk to you either. I'll try and track her down tomorrow."

Kelt nodded reluctant agreement. "Do you think she'll open up to *you?*"

I took a deep breath. "I can only hope so. With this second murder, she might be feeling a little more talkative. As long as I can get her away from Jurgen."

The kettle began to whistle as Kelt rinsed out the teapot and riffled through Jaime's selection of teas.

"There could be another reason for Lem's death," I said slowly. "Something neither of us has thought of."

Kelt looked at me.

"Maybe he didn't murder Bill, but maybe he saw something that night. Maybe he saw the real murderer."

"But he told Jaime he hadn't remembered anything. It sounded like the truth."

I nodded. "Yeah, but what if the murderer saw him? He or she wouldn't necessarily know that Lem had no memory of it."

Kelt gazed at me doubtfully. "If that's the case, then why wait till now to bump off Lem? Why give him all this time to report it?"

Deflated, I shrugged. And here I'd thought I was having an episode of staggering intuition. "I don't know. It was just an idea."

"Come on." Kelt picked up the tray. "Let's see if we can cheer Jaime up a bit."

"Inspector Danson was that hard on him?"

Kelt widened his eyes. "It was enough to make me swear off a life of crime."

We returned to the living room to find Jaime leafing through old photo albums.

"Look." He directed our attention to a series of snapshots in which the blue sky had faded and yellowed to a pale, alien green. "These here were taken when we were kids. Look! Here's me and Pete."

The two boys in the picture were skinny. All knobby knees and pointed elbows, they had the awkward look of children verging on adolescence. Posed in front of a swimming hole, they stood with their arms slung across each other's shoulders, grins stretching from ear to ear.

The swimming hole looked like a child's dream.

Almost perfectly circular, it was surrounded on one side by a steep, rocky slope topped with a twisted pine straight out of a Tom Thomson painting. A thick rope dangled from one of the tree's gnarled branches, and I could imagine generations of young Tarzans swinging around before letting go and dropping like cannonballs into the cool water.

Somebody had made merry with the camera on that long-ago summer's day. There were two pages of snapshots. Two pages of young, carefree faces, smiling broadly with the knowledge of an endless summer vacation.

The last picture was a group shot. There were quite a few kids in the photo, their faces blurry with distance. But one child seemed to stand apart from the others. A child without a smile. I had a hunch who it was.

"Was this Lem?" I asked Jaime softly.

He nodded. "It's probably one of the few pictures I have of him. One of the few that anybody has."

It struck me to the heart, this image of the outcast child. Forever lonely, never quite fitting in, always on the periphery. Now dead with no one to mourn him.

Kelt shot me a sharp look and I remembered that we were supposed to be the Cheer-Up Squad. "Have you got any pictures of Ella?" I inquired.

We spent the next hour poring over old photos, laughing at Jaime's reminiscences of a happy, if somewhat mischievous, childhood.

The scrapbook's pages marched on in time, showing a remarkably handsome teenaged Jaime; a more serious-looking Jaime dressed for the woods on the first day of his new job at Seidlin Lumber; and a red-faced, laughing Jaime whooping it up at Rusty's Bar with the other loggers. There were quite a few bar photos, all taken on the same night.

"So what was the big occasion?" Kelt asked.

"Oh, that was Bill Reddecop's thirtieth birthday bash," Jaime explained. "God, what a party that was!" He chuckled in remembrance. "Greg was away studyin' at university then. He'd been gone for a couple of years. He came back for the party, and it was a big secret. Him comin' back, I mean. We managed to keep our faces shut about it too." Jaime flipped the page and laughed. "Look! Here's one of Bill at the party, and here's when he laid eyes on Greg. Ha! Look at his face!"

Up until now, I hadn't seen a single picture of Bill Reddecop. The only image I had of him was as a corpse. I pulled the album closer and examined the first picture intently, eager to replace my image with one less horrific.

Even alive, Bill had not been a handsome man. His features were not unattractive, but there was a certain tightness around his eyes, a flat look of selfishness and resentment that ruined any good looks he may have possessed. In the midst of a rollicking party thrown especially for him, Bill Reddecop still managed to look pissed off at the world. I could see why he hadn't been popular. But when I turned my attention to the second photo, I realized that there had been at least one person in his life that Bill Reddecop had cared about.

On the surface, Bill's expression when he saw his brother was comical—eyebrows raised up to his bangs, mouth open in a small O of surprise, blue eyes round and wide. But those eyes held something more than just surprise. They virtually shone with delight at the sight of his long-absent brother.

I had seen Bill's pathetic body lying dead on the moss, and I'd heard stories of his mean spirit. Without even being aware of it, I had built up a picture in my mind of a cruel man, a man lacking in the better qualities of humanity. But as I gazed at those blue eyes, so filled with happy delight, Bill Reddecop suddenly became human for me.

Oblivious to my silence, Kelt and Jaime talked animatedly about the finer bar parties they had attended. I continued to look at the photograph. It was all in the eyes, I reflected. It was amazing what you could learn just by looking into someone's eyes. I bent my head to examine the picture more closely. But there was something about those eyes that bothered me. Something else. Something not quite right. I tried to hold on to the feeling, but the harder I tried to figure it out, the more distant it seemed. Finally I shrugged and turned the page. It would come to me sooner or later.

Kelt was on chef duty again that night, but was missing a few ingredients for his famous grilled prime rib with caramelized onions and herbed potatoes. I volunteered to do a grocery run (who wouldn't?) and set off on foot for Main Street.

I walked with my head down, watching my feet scrunch through the snow. Two people were dead now, and I still had no idea why. Assuming the crimes had nothing to do with Seidlin's clear-cutting (a pretty big assumption which I was by no means ready to embrace), what connection was there between the two men? Both had been murdered. Both had been friendless. But what had Ella said earlier? That Bill had had a friend—or at least the closest thing to a friend. His secretary, Jean Hewitt. There wasn't anyone I could talk to about Lem— Jaime was probably the closest thing *he'd* had to a friend—but perhaps Jean Hewitt would be willing to talk about Bill. Perhaps she could shed some light on the situation. If nothing else, I could express my condolences.

A quick duck into a nearby phone booth and I had her address. It turned out to be a bit of a hike from Main Street, especially after I took a wrong turn, but I found the small house without too much trouble. The lights were off, even the porch lights were dark, but the telltale blue glow from a television set flickered in the living-room window. I rang the bell.

Jean Hewitt was a pleasant but plain-looking woman, somewhere in her late thirties. Her gray eyes were slightly protruding, and her mouth was overly wide, but could probably stretch itself into a lovely smile if she were so inclined. Right at the moment, I couldn't imagine it. She was dressed in an old bathrobe that was spotted and stained with several days' worth of crud. Her eyes were swollen; her hair hung lank and greasy. Jean Hewitt was obviously grieving and, from the sour smell coming off her, just as obviously finding solace in the bottom of a bottle.

"Hello, my name's Robyn Devara," I began a little uncertainly. "I wanted to stop by and talk to you about Bill Reddecop."

She swung the door wider. "Come on in, then," she said grandiosely, and staggered back a step to make room for me in the tiny foyer. "Where's your uniform?"

"My . . ."

"Aren't you with the police?"

"No, I'm afraid not. . . ."

"Well, who are you, then?" she demanded.

"I'm the person who found him."

She stared at me for a second, then looked away. "In the forest?" Her voice was suddenly small and tremulous.

"Yes, that's right. I'm very sorry. I understand you were friends."

Her lip trembled. "Do you want a glass of wine?" she asked softly.

"Uh, sure, that'd be nice."

I divested myself of coat and boots and followed her to the living room. It wasn't a patch on Lori's professionally and expensively decorated living room, but it was infinitely more comfortable, with mismatched furniture and deeply cushioned armchairs.

Jean rummaged around in a tall wooden cabinet and emerged with a second wineglass. The first was already half-empty on the coffee table. She splashed some red wine into the glass and even more on the table, then handed the glass to me.

"Thanks."

"You're welcome."

"I'm really sorry," I said again. "This must be very difficult for you."

She hiccuped. "You know, you're the first person that's said that to me. They all want to talk about who killed him an' how he died. Who cares? He's *dead*, an' nothing anybody says is going to change that."

"It's hard to lose a friend. . . ."

"A friend!?" she cried. "Bill an' I were more than just *friends!* I was more of a wife to him than that little bitch could ever hope to be!"

I nearly choked on my wine. I wasn't expecting this. I looked at her more closely. Her pupils were so enlarged, they threatened to take over her irises. Had she been chomping down Valium as well? It looked like it. She didn't seem to realize what she was saying to me, or even to be fully aware of my presence, for that matter.

"Nobody ever knew," she mumbled. "Seems so obvious, bein' his secretary an' everything. But nobody ever knew. Bill wanted it that way."

"I'm sorry I didn't know. It must be very hard for you."

"Hard? Damn right it's hard! Nobody knew Bill like I did! They all thought he was an asshole, but who wouldn't be an asshole married to that bitch? But he could be fun an' sweet. . . . He was smart too; did you know that?"

I shook my head.

"He was a smart guy, Bill. An' so funny sometimes." She started to cry. "But nobody cared. An' now nobody cares that he's dead except me. Except me."

I squirmed, not knowing what to say. The poor woman had probably been holed up here for the past four or five days, grieving and miserable. Unable, under the circumstances, even to share her grief with a sympathetic friend.

"He was going to leave her, you know. Leave her for me. He only stayed with her because of the boy. But he was going to leave. The bitch! He'd had enough of her."

"Bill was going to leave Lori?"

She nodded miserably, the tears streaming down her face. "He was going to leave her for me."

"Did you tell the police that?"

"What do they care?" she said bitterly. "Alex never liked him either. Always took sides against him. Look at me. Who'd ever believe he'd leave her for me?" Her face crumpled. "But he loved me. He did. He always said so. He used to bring me little presents, you know. . . . He brought me a real silk scarf once . . . with a dove on it . . . just like a wedding cake. . . . He loved me . . . and we

would've been married . . . and maybe had kids and . . . "
Her head fell against the back of the couch.

I put my unfinished wine down and touched her arm.
"Jean?"

She began snoring gently. I withdrew my hand and
watched her sadly for a moment. So this was the other
side to Bill's story. It sounded like his affair with Jean
Hewitt had been a long-standing one. And nobody knew!
Unbelievable in such a gossip-ridden town. Either they'd
been amazingly discreet or the thought of Bill falling for
the plain Jean when he had Lori had been too ludicrous
to contemplate.

I felt a wave of sympathy for Jean. I wondered if it had
been true that Bill was going to leave Lori for her. Or did
that exist only in Jean's hopeful imagination? Either way,
I couldn't see how it would fit in with his murder. Lori
was still too tiny to have killed him, even if Bill *had*
threatened to leave her. I suppose she could have gotten
one of her paramours to carry out the deed, but given the
very married status of her last few flings, how likely was
that? And how did Lem's murder fit in with such a situation? I puffed my cheeks out in frustration. It didn't.
Even with Jean Hewitt's revelations, it looked like my
nickels were still on Gus and his buddies.

I stood up and looked down at Jean's swollen, tear-
streaked face, calmer now in sleep. Her secret was safe
with me. It didn't really matter now, and telling anybody
about Jean and Bill would only bring her more pain. She
had enough of that without me. I covered her with a
blanket I found in a basket by the bookshelf and quietly
let myself out.

Between the news about Lem and my visit with Jean, it had been a long day. It was about to get longer. I got another call from my pal Gus after dinner. He was most definitely unfriendly.

"What the hell do ya think yer doing?" he barked as a greeting.

A wave of fear passed over me. Had he found out about our break-in?

"Gotta call from the Regional Manager," he continued angrily.

I allowed myself to breathe again.

"Asking questions and wanting to see records and files. Don't like that much. No call for it. Someone's been shooting off their mouth. Telling lies."

"I have no idea what you're talking about, Gus—"

"Don't give me that shit," he screamed. "You're here to do a survey. Fine. Do the survey. Tried to give you a hand. Help you out a bit. Now look what you've done."

"Gus, I—"

"No excuse for that. Just back off from now on. Don't come lookin' for any more help from me! Stay out of Seidlin's business!" He slammed the phone down in my ear.

I replaced the receiver in the cradle. Seidlin, I thought, was in sore need of a new PR guy.

CHAPTER 28

It was late and I was weary, but I kept puttering around the house instead of going to bed. Both Jaime and Kelt had long since retired. I suppose I was afraid of what my dreams would bring. The events of the past few days were starting to take their toll.

I'd tried reading a novel, but it turned out to be a murder mystery—appropriate, perhaps, but not exactly what I needed at the moment. I was just about to turn out the living-room light and try my luck with Morpheus when I heard a soft tapping at the door. My heart gave a loud thump. Who could be calling at this hour? Gus?

Cautiously, I poked my head into the hallway. By the porch light I could see Bonnie's pale features looking in. Not Gus after all. I heaved a sigh of relief. Then I realized what Bonnie's presence here meant. I tiptoed down the hall with alacrity and eased the door open.

"Come on in," I whispered.

"I'm sorry I'm here so late," she murmured. "I couldn't get away until now, and then I had trouble finding the house, and . . . "

"That's okay," I assured her. "Let's go to the kitchen, so we don't wake the others."

Under the bright kitchen light, Bonnie looked paler

than ever, but her expression was one I had never seen on her before. Her eyes were wide and flashing; she looked almost emotional. What had happened? I suspected I was about to find out.

"I'm sorry it's so late," she apologized again. "But I didn't know who to talk to."

"What's wrong?" I asked, motioning her to a chair.

She sunk down, her shoulders slumped. "It's Jurgen," she admitted.

Big surprise. "What's the matter with him?"

"I'm not sure," she said, her voice tight with frustration. "He's been acting strangely ever since the murder."

"In what way?"

"Well, he's pretty hyper—more so than usual—and he seems awfully nervous. He won't talk to me about it. Every time I try to bring up the subject, he starts talking about something else. We *need* to talk about this murder—not just because he's a suspect, but because of the way it's affecting our campaign here. Everyone else is feeling the pressure." She laughed nervously. "Nature Defence is never very popular in places like this, but being fingered for murder is unusual even for us. We need to develop some kind of strategy for dealing with it, and he refuses to talk about it!"

"Do you think he had something to do with Bill Reddecop's murder?" I asked carefully.

"No, of course not," she said firmly. A little too firmly? "It's just that . . . well, he's got a record."

"Lots of people have criminal records, Bonnie," I said. "What was it for? Civil disobedience?"

"No, no, you don't understand. He has a record for murder."

"*What?!*" I squeaked.

She nodded. "It was for manslaughter, actually. He was convicted."

"He did time?"

"Yeah, he was eighteen. He was in for five years. When he got out, he started Nature Defence."

"So you think he's somehow connected with what's going on here."

"I never said that!" she exclaimed.

"Well, what's bothering you then?"

"I don't know," she said miserably. "I know he had a fight with that Bill guy and . . . " She dropped her voice to a whisper. "And I know he wasn't with me on Thursday evening."

"You told the police he was."

"Of course," she said scornfully. "They'd haul him away if they knew he didn't have an alibi. I owe so much to Jurgen, I couldn't let that happen."

"But this is *murder*," I said, trying to impress that fact on her. "What do you owe him that could possibly override that?"

"Everything," she said simply. "I don't have any brothers or sisters; my mom died when I was thirteen. When she was gone, my dad couldn't get me out of the house fast enough. I left when I was fourteen and I've never gone back. Jurgen is my family. We built Nature Defence together, and now they're my family too. I couldn't have done any of it myself. You know as well as I do that Jurgen is the driving force behind our group. I can't let that be taken away." Her eyes flashed with uncharacteristic fire.

Remembering my own family troubles, I sympathized with the pain of Bonnie's younger self, and, to some extent, I could understand her feelings now. But murder?

"What about last night?" I asked. "When the other guy was killed. Was Jurgen with you?"

She shook her head slowly. "He didn't come back to the van until eleven-thirty."

"Did he tell you where he'd been?"

"He said he was talking to a few of the guys about our next move. But I saw them coming back earlier, and Jurgen wasn't with them."

I sat silently for a while, sunk in thought. "If you aren't willing to talk to the police about this, why come to me?" I asked finally.

Bonnie turned a trusting look on me. "Because you know us. You know that Jurgen wouldn't do something like this."

I wanted to say that he already had, but I managed to keep my mouth shut. "And?" I prompted.

"And I was hoping you could help us. You seem to be right in the middle of this whole thing and the cops feel sorry for you now because of that dead owl. You could tell them that Jurgen wouldn't hurt a fly."

So, Bonnie wanted a character reference. I shook my head slowly. I wasn't exactly Ms Credibility around here. "You're sadly overestimating my influence, Bonnie. If Jurgen's got a previous conviction, you can bet the cops already know about it. Nothing I can say is going to change that. Quite frankly, I think the best thing you could do is to tell them that he wasn't with you on Thursday night."

"That is not an option," she said icily.

"Look at it from their point of view," I urged her. "If they find out you've been lying, it's going to be hell for you and twice that for Jurgen."

I'd lost her. Her mouth tightened and her eyes grew

hard as quartz. How had I ever thought her to be emotionless?

"You won't talk to them?" she asked.

"It wouldn't do any good," I told her. "As it is, you've put me in a terrible position. I should tell the police what you've just told me. But it would be better if it came from you."

"I'll think about it," she said in a tone that indicated she would do anything but.

After she left, I thought about my advice to Bonnie. The echo from Jaime's words to Lem was pretty deafening. Lem, who had been found murdered.

Under other circumstances, I would have been worried about Bonnie's safety, but I knew something she didn't. Jurgen hadn't killed Lem. Lem had been killed after Jurgen had already returned to their van. I should know: at eleven-thirty Lem had been sitting in Jaime's living room.

Jaime had told me the police were convinced the two murders were related. Presumably they had their reasons. If that was the case, then Jurgen hadn't killed Bill Reddecop either. Which left my old pal, Gus. So where had Jurgen gone on Thursday night? And where had he been last night?

I flicked out the kitchen light and tiptoed down the hall to my bedroom.

Kelt was waiting in my room.

"I heard," he said before my mind had a chance to fantasize about his reasons for being there. "Sorry to eavesdrop, but I got up to go to the bathroom, and I heard voices."

"That's okay," I said. "I was going to tell you about it anyhow. What do you think?"

Kelt folded his arms against his chest. "At the risk of sounding one-note, I think you should tell the police."

"I'm hoping she'll do that herself."

Kelt snorted. "Not likely. She's far too dependent on Jurgen. Besides, Jaime left Lem to talk to the cops himself, and look what happened."

"But that's just it, Kelt; Lem was murdered after Jurgen got back. I don't think he did it."

"What about Bill Reddecop?"

"The police think the two murders are related."

Kelt just gazed at me. "You don't know that for sure."

He was right. "Yeah, okay," I sighed. "Bill Reddecop's funeral is tomorrow. I'll try to pull Constable Pete aside and tell him. The townspeople already hate me, the Seidlin people hate me, the Nature Defence people might as well hate me too. It'll be the one thing everybody agrees on."

CHAPTER 29

I was slogging through wet fields, my legs muddied and scratched. The long, pale grasses were brittle, as sharp as scalpels. They sliced easily through my hands. Blood ran in rivulets down the creases of my palms, falling from my fingertips like thick red tears. As my hands grew slippery with crimson grief, great horned owls began swooping down around me. I looked up at them. Their fiery yellow eyes pulsed from blue to yellow to blue again. They were going to attack! The scent of my fear was in the air; I could almost feel their razor-like talons slicing through the thin material of my shirt. I searched about desperately. There! A stand of trees! If only I could get under cover. I ran and tripped and slid, but the trees seemed to recede farther and farther away. And the whole time, there were those pulsating eyes. . . .

I woke exhausted and clammy with cold sweat. Today Bill Reddecop would be buried.

A hot shower and a large mug of coffee went a long way to dispelling the last vestiges of my dream, but I was left with a vague feeling of heaviness and oppression. Wrapped warmly in my ragged Big Bird robe, I started on a second cup of coffee, greeting first Kelt and then Jaime as they emerged from their rooms. They seemed pale and withdrawn this morning, and I wondered if their sleep had been as haunted as my own. It was all this death. Two murders and a mutilated owl. No wonder I was having bad dreams. Although I loved my job and it had been exciting to find spotted owls, I couldn't wait to shake the dust of Marten Valley off my boots. I looked down at my feet. Or off my orange fuzzy slippers.

The funeral was at ten o'clock. We were all going: under the circumstances, I felt I should pay my respects, and Kelt had volunteered to come with me for moral support. As for Jaime, it was no secret he'd detested Bill Reddecop, but for Todd's sake, he would be at the man's funeral.

I hadn't brought any black clothes—actually I didn't even own any black clothes. With Guido the cat around, there didn't seem to be much point. I finally decided on a pair of hunter-green pants and a matching sweater. It wasn't very dressy, but at least it was understated.

The church was a block away from Colonel Sanders School. It was a smallish, rustic-looking building, with a bright whitewashed exterior and a dark wooden cross perched on top of the steeple. The parking lot was full; latecomers had taken to parking along the street. The whole town had apparently turned out.

Looking around, I spied Lori and Todd. They were standing to the left of the church's entryway; two small figures, Lori draped in black (a harsh color for her pale looks) and Todd looking uncomfortable in dress slacks and a sweater.

As I watched, Greg ducked out of the church and beckoned to them. My heart gave an odd thump at the sight of him, but I was more struck by Lori's reaction. She turned her back decisively on him, seemingly resentful of the summons. When Greg strode over to them, he stopped a few feet away as if he couldn't stand to be closer to her. He spoke, then turned on his heel and went back into the church, Todd trailing after him forlornly. Lori waited a moment, then followed.

It was strange, I thought, and more than a little sad that the two of them couldn't put aside their dislike for each other on this of all days. He had lost a brother, she a husband. You'd think something like that would bring them closer. Or at least make them less antagonistic towards each other. I wondered how Todd was doing and was suddenly glad for his sake that Jaime was here.

It was a closed-casket funeral—a fact for which I was exceedingly grateful. A framed picture of Bill stood by the flowers on top of his coffin. The church was full, its dark wooden pews jammed with townspeople. I recognized Mr. Chase from his photograph. He was seated in the front pew opposite Lori. A tall, stately-looking woman sat to one side of him, with Gus and a few other suits on the other. As I made my way to a vacant seat, one of the men turned and glared at me. I drew in my breath with a gasp. It was the man in the truck!

I poked Kelt in the side, but he'd already seen for himself. His expression grew grim. I would definitely have to talk to Pete Lenarden now—and not just about Bonnie's late-night revelations.

Greg sat beside Lori at the front of the church. You could have driven a logging truck through the space between them. Todd sat on Lori's right, glancing back longingly now and again to where Jaime sat beside me.

There was no sign of Jean Hewitt. I wasn't surprised. Perhaps she'd told people she was still too ill to attend the service. She would keep Bill's death as she kept his life— silently and alone. I wondered if she remembered my visit.

The service was brief but very moving. Greg gave the eulogy, his voice thick with emotion as he remembered his older brother. As he spoke of their childhood together, my thoughts drifted to Jack and Neil, my parents, my friends. I know a number of people who throw the word "love" around far too easily, tacking it on to the end of each salutation, or using it as a reassuring crutch. I love you, do you love me back? It gets worn and tattered, losing its meaning with infinite repetition. But for every person who wears out the word, there are twenty who never speak it. Instead they hide their affection behind a social façade like some dark, shameful secret, letting it slip out in the occasional clap on the shoulder or quick hug. Only when death strikes a loved one do they stop and consider and give voice to the meaning that person brought to their lives. Except by then it's too late.

By the end of the eulogy, Greg was crying openly. I noticed more than a few damp eyes in the congregation—my own included. After the minister spoke a last blessing, we all filed out of the church and into a gray, cloudy morning.

Everyone was going over to the Reddecops' house to express their sympathies and have a bite of lunch. Though Jaime had assured Kelt and me we would be welcome, we had decided to bow out at this point. Despite the friendliness of a few, these weren't our people, and we were both very conscious of being outsiders.

Constable Pete was one of those heading over to the wake. I managed to catch up with him as he was getting into his car.

"Now is not a good time," he told me firmly as I tried to blurt out my story.

"But . . ."

"I've got to go to this wake," he said quietly, his eyes on Sergeant McIntyre. "And then I'm headin' straight for Quesnel. Can't this wait?"

I looked over at McIntyre. He was watching us closely. Right.

"It can wait," I assured Constable Pete with a small smile.

"I'll come around as soon as I get back," he said in a low murmur.

I turned and made my way back to Kelt and Jaime. McIntyre was no longer watching me.

We dropped Jaime off at the Reddecop house and watched as Todd pelted over and into his comforting arms. Kelt turned to me.

"What do you want to do now?" he asked.

"Well, how's your cold?"

Kelt coughed experimentally. "Still there, but feeling better, I think. Why? You want to go look for owls?"

I nodded. "Yeah, I feel like I've been slacking off, and it would probably do both of us a lot of good to get out and clear the cobwebs."

"Okay," Kelt agreed. "Those Neanderthals from Seidlin will all be at the wake for a while. Shall we go back and check on the owls we've already seen, or should we try someplace new?"

"Let's try someplace new first," I suggested. "If we don't find anything after a couple of hours, we'll go back to check on our owl pair."

A two-hour survey of a new block of forest yielded nothing but a pair of horned owls. The female was on the nest, though, which was pretty exciting. At first we could only see her tufts over the mass of branches and twigs. As we drew closer, she raised her head and glared at us. We got the message and retreated, to the relief of her mate, who had fluffed himself out in alarm.

Even more exciting, though, was the sight of our female spotted owl hunkered down in the hole of the huge Douglas fir we had inspected previously.

"Look!" I squeaked. "She's on nest! They're breeding!"

"Oh my god." Kelt grabbed my arm in excitement. "Should we be this close?"

Our presence didn't seem to be bothering the owls, but with birds you can never be too careful. All too often they will abandon their nests if they're disturbed. With some of them, like the bald eagles, the mere glimpse of a human being may be enough to send them off.

"Probably not," I said reluctantly. "Come on, let's head back. I don't know about you, but I'm starving."

Laughing and joking, we headed back into town, stopping to pick up some Kleenex for Kelt. As we drove down Main Street, I caught sight of movement in an alley and leaned forward to get a closer look.

"I see," I said with a sigh.

Kelt looked at me. "You see what?"

I jerked my thumb back towards the alley. "I think I see the reason why Jurgen's been lying about his whereabouts."

Kelt hadn't noticed anything, so I described the scene in the alley for his benefit. Jurgen leaning comfortably against the brick wall. A very pretty, very dark-haired woman beside him. They weren't discussing spotted owls. Technically, given their activity, discussion of any kind would have been difficult.

CHAPTER 30

When we got back, Jaime and Todd were hard at work in the kitchen, surrounded by little curls of wood. Todd's face was drawn but he looked happier than he had been that morning. He seemed completely engrossed in his carving and didn't even look up when Kelt and I trooped in the door.

"Owls! We've got breeding owls!" Kelt crowed in delight.

Jaime's expression could have lit up the city of Vancouver for a whole week. "Are you sure?" he demanded.

"Positive," I assured him. "The female's on nest and her mate is hovering close by."

"The same pair you saw the other day?"

"Yep, the very same."

"That's the best thing I've heard all day." Jaime beamed. "Congratulations!"

"It was hard work, though," Kelt said with a mighty snuffle. "We're starved now!"

"Oh, speakin' of food . . . Greg phoned for you, Robyn," Jaime informed me while I was still divesting myself of coat, binoculars, and maps. "He said somethin' about dinner. I wrote his number on that pad over there. He's stayin' with a cousin."

"Oh . . . um, okay. Thanks." Greg phoning to have dinner with me? I could feel myself starting to blush. Almost guiltily I glanced over at Kelt. He seemed to be taking a long time to hang up his coat, and when he turned around, he didn't meet my eyes. I hesitated for a moment before giving myself a mental shake. What did I have to feel guilty about? It wasn't like I was cheating on anybody.

Nevertheless, I returned Greg's call from the privacy of my bedroom.

"Robyn!" His voice sounded strained. It must have been a difficult day for him.

"Hi, Greg. Jaime told me you called. How are you doing?"

"Oh, as well as can be expected, I guess. I saw you at the funeral today. Thanks for coming; I really appreciated it."

"It was the least I could do," I said uncomfortably.

"Well, there's something else you could do if you'd like."

"Oh?"

"Have dinner with me tonight."

"Tonight?" I was surprised. "Are you sure?"

"What do you mean?"

"Well, I just thought . . . I mean . . . wouldn't you . . . "

"Rather spend time with people who knew my brother?" he finished.

"Well, yes," I said lamely.

"Quite frankly," he said, his voice sounding even more tired, "that's the last thing I want to do right now. How about it? I'll get Irene to cook us something special."

I must admit that I was quite flattered. Of all the people ready and willing to comfort him, Greg had chosen me to keep him company that evening. Who was I to argue with a grieving man?

"I'll be ready by six-thirty," I told him.

"And so after half the office had been incapacitated, we managed to find out from his secretary that it was actually our CEO who had been responsible for everything."

"Seriously?"

"Oh yes, seems the old boy has always had a penchant for pranks. And here we all were quietly drinking from the cooler and carefully not saying a word about it in case he heard and put a stop to it. We got together and confronted him. I've never seen anyone laugh so hard in my life."

All through dinner, Greg had regaled me with stories of the outrageous pranks that had been occurring in his office. All apparently perpetrated by the CEO. The latest one involved filling the water cooler with martinis on a Friday afternoon. I should be so lucky to have a boss like that.

It had been a wonderful dinner—both the company and (surprisingly) the food. Irene was obviously one of Greg's admirers. She had come out and bussed him noisily on the cheek as soon as we'd arrived. Me, she looked at as one might regard an especially large silverfish in the flour. I wondered whether it was due to my environmental leanings or my audacity for going on a date with Greg.

Despite her disapproval of my person, Irene presented us with a truly exquisite meal, quite unlike her usual fare. I'd come with the right person. There was chicken cordon bleu in a delicate white wine sauce, served on a bed of fluffy rice, accompanied by a generous helping of plump green beans and toasted almonds.

Dessert was pie, of course, but a special lemon pie topped with golden swirls of meringue. Apparently a great favorite of Greg's. The pie was exquisite, but quite tart enough to keep you puckered up for a week. Irene must have wrestled long and hard with her conscience over that one. She gave me a hard look when she brought the pie out—no doubt to ensure I would keep my puckered lips to myself.

Greg was an attentive dinner companion, asking me about my work and my family, and telling me about his own life. The man practically exuded warmth and interest, and I found myself talking quite easily to him.

As we started our pies, Greg looked over at me, his coffee-colored eyes twinkling merrily.

"What?" I asked. "Have I got pie on my face?"

He laughed. "No, no, nothing like that. I have something to tell you."

"Oh?"

Like a clumsy spy, he looked dramatically over each shoulder before lowering his voice secretively. "I've found a spotted owl," he whispered.

"You have? Where?"

"Out by the old swimming hole. I went there for a walk yesterday, to do some thinking. While I was there, I looked up and, lo and behold, there was an owl sitting on the tree. I'm pretty sure it was a spotted owl. There were a bunch of those pellet things you were telling me about all around the base of the tree."

"Did it have dark eyes?"

"Yes, and it was brown with white splotches all over it."

"Can you take me there?" I asked.

His eyes glinted. "I was hoping you'd ask. I've got to go back to Victoria on Monday, but I'm free tomorrow if you want to go out."

"Sounds great," I told him, then paused. "You're going back to Victoria so soon?" I was surprised and disappointed.

He shrugged. "I offered to help Lori with things, but I think she'd rather I just left."

"You two don't seem to get along that well," I said delicately.

"No, we don't," he said. "We never have."

He didn't seem to want to discuss it further, so I dropped the subject. I was a little curious about the whole thing, but (call me crazy) I didn't really want to talk about Lori while I was on a date with an attractive man.

Kelt was reading in the living room when Greg dropped me off.

"Hey!" I said with a tentative smile. "Is Jaime still up?"

Kelt's smile seemed reserved, his green eyes guarded. "Hi. No, I think this whole thing with Lem really took a lot out of him. He went to bed an hour ago."

"Did something else happen?"

"Yeah, they found Lem's coat."

I sank down on the couch and stared at him. "I thought we found Lem's coat."

He closed his book and put it on the coffee table. "Seems we were wrong. The police found his jacket buried under a pile of garbage in his back yard."

"But . . . did it have blood on it?"

"Oh yes, apparently it was covered in blood."

"I don't get it. How can there be two bloody coats?"

Kelt shrugged. "I don't get it either, but I tell you one thing, there's still a murderer out there. You should be careful." His voice was tight with concern.

I looked up and lost myself in his sea-green gaze. I couldn't deny my attraction to Greg, but still, there was something special about Kelt. Silently I berated myself for my folly (though at this point, I didn't know which was more foolish—falling for a guy who lives in Victoria or lusting after one who wasn't interested in me). With an effort, I brought my attention back to what Kelt was saying.

"It's a good bet that dead owl and its message were sent by the same guys who were following us yesterday," he told me earnestly.

"Did Pete come by yet?"

He shook his head. "No. Jaime even phoned him. He won't be coming back from Quesnel until tomorrow. Robyn, what if these same guys are murderers too? We *know* they've got a hate on for you."

"You're worried about me," I stated.

He let his breath out in an exasperated sigh. "Damn right I'm worried about you. I'd be a lot happier if you were back safe and sound in Calgary." Unaccountably he blushed.

"This whole situation sucks," he said quickly. "I don't think you should go out alone again. If Gus and his buddies did murder Bill, then they must be getting pretty desperate if they went and killed Lem too. And if something happens to you, Kaye has informed me she'll personally have my balls for bookends."

I grinned at the thought (who wouldn't?) and patted Kelt's hand. "Don't worry," I told him. "Those, uh . . .

portions of your anatomy are safe. I *am* being careful. Believe me, this whole thing scares me as much as it does you."

Kelt made no effort to move his hand so I left mine where it was. We sat for a while, each lost in our own thoughts.

CHAPTER 31

"It's not like I'll be going out by myself. Greg's coming along. He's got to show me where he saw the owl. Don't worry; I'll be fine."

Kelt looked skeptical and he was avoiding my eyes again. I sighed inwardly. "If you guys go to Quesnel, then I can do this. It would be one more spotted owl for our survey. And while you're in Quesnel, you can try to find Pete and tell him what's been going on."

"Okay," Kelt finally agreed. I could tell he wasn't happy about it, though. "But if somebody starts following you again, turn around. Just be careful, okay?"

"Always," I assured him with a jaunty grin.

He didn't smile back.

It was Sunday morning. I'd completely forgotten that Kelt and I had promised to take Jaime to the hospital in Quesnel. Jaime was hoping his sprained ankle had healed enough so that he could ditch the wheelchair. The three of us sat in the kitchen well into our second pot of coffee. I didn't know what to make of Kelt's behavior. Was he jealous or just worried? Jaime seemed to be ignoring it, and I decided to follow suit. If Kelt was jealous, it was his own fault, I thought snippily. He'd had plenty of time to show some interest.

Greg, on the other hand, seemed to have few problems showing *his* interest. He showed up ten minutes early, packing a thermos of coffee, sour-cream-glazed donuts, and a hundred-watt smile especially for me. I love a man who comes prepared. He clapped Jaime on the shoulder and shook Kelt's hand warmly. Before I knew it we were bundled into his truck and waving goodbye to Jaime and a rather forlorn-looking Kelt.

We munched donuts and chatted on the way to the swimming hole. I was a little surprised at how far from the town it was.

"That was nothing to us when we were kids," Greg assured me with a grin. "We just hopped on our bikes and headed down the old logging road. By the time you got to the pond, you were so hot, you didn't care how slimy the water was."

I laughed. "Do kids still go to it?"

"Oh yeah, it's a popular place."

"Strange that a spotted owl would be hanging around. They're pretty shy."

Greg shrugged. "Well, the pond's frozen solid. Nobody will be swimming in it for months yet. He'll probably have flown the coop by then."

We pulled over to the side of the road and Greg indicated a barely visible path into the forest.

"We've got to walk from here. It's through there about half a mile. Sorry, there's no other access."

"Sounds fine." I grinned. "It'll give us a chance to work off those donuts."

It was a bright day, but the temperature had plummeted overnight. I had come prepared with my down parka, and I'd been a bit concerned when I had seen Greg's thin coat. I shouldn't have worried. As soon as we stopped, he reached behind his seat and pulled out a thick wool sweater and matching watch cap.

Greg looked quite different in his hat—almost as if he had hair. Seeing him like that, I felt a strange twinge of recognition.

"You ready?" he asked with a merry wink.

I hesitated for a moment, trying to figure out who he reminded me of. Some actor perhaps? Had Patrick Stewart ever worn a hat? Ah well, it would come to me. "Ready when you are," I told him.

We set out along the path, our boots squeaking on the snow, our breath coming out in frosty puffs. The short hike passed quickly. As we emerged from the forest, I gasped in delight.

The swimming hole was set back in the small clearing. With its ice-covered pond and snow-laden conifers, it looked like a scene from a Hallmark Christmas card. As we stood at the entrance to the clearing, a great horned owl sailed over the pond, pale, wraithlike and beautiful.

"It's lovely," I breathed. "But was that the owl you saw?"

Greg shook his head. "No, it's too pale. Come on, I'll show you where I saw the pellets. They're up on that bluff, where the old tree is."

"Jaime said you guys used to swing from that tree and jump in the pond. Wasn't that a little dangerous?"

"Now it is," Greg said. "The pond is deep enough, but the bluff's unstable. That rope was taken down years ago."

As we drew closer to the pond, I looked up at the old tree perched precariously on the edge of the rocky bluff. It was ancient, its roots twisting out the side of the bluff, its branches a tangled, gnarled mass, dense to the point of impenetrability. After seeing Jaime's yellowed photos, I could tell that quite a bit of the bluff had already succumbed to gravity. The soil was rocky; many of the larger rocks had fallen from their earthy bed to accumulate at the foot of the bluff.

"Look!" I pointed as the horned owl winged over us again before perching on a tall spruce tree by the pond. I raised my binoculars to get a better look, then passed them over to Greg.

I love watching owls, but I also like watching other people watch them, especially if they're not that familiar with them. The look of wonder on their faces always gives me a little thrill.

I looked over at Greg—and stiffened. It wasn't his expression of wonder that arrested me. In order to look through the binoculars, Greg had taken his glasses off, and I suddenly knew why he had seemed familiar in his hat.

Add a mop of curly hair and a neatly trimmed beard, take away the glasses and you had Lori's university boyfriend! The campus Adonis.

I was stunned. Greg!? Greg was Lori's boyfriend from university? What the hell was going on here? Why hadn't he recognized me? I hadn't changed *that* much since school. Not as much as *he* had, anyway.

And then, as if one revelation opened the way for another, it suddenly hit me what was wrong with Bill Reddecop's eyes. Or perhaps I should say what was wrong with his son's eyes.

Both Lori and Bill had blue eyes. Todd's eyes were brown. I, of all people, should have realized what that meant. The alleles that coded for blue eye color were recessive. Technically, it was possible for two blue-eyed parents to have a child with brown eyes, but it was very rare. And when it did occur, the child's eyes were light brown or hazel. Like mine.

Todd's eyes were as dark as coffee beans or chocolate—as dark as Greg's eyes. The same eyes that were now looking at me curiously. My blood turned to icy water in my veins.

"Are you okay?" he asked.

"Of course," I managed to say with a sickly smile. "Wasn't that owl lovely?"

"Beautiful," he agreed. "But the one I saw the other day was even nicer. Let's go up to the bluff."

Everything had fallen into place. Lori's look of fear when I had first bumped into her in the RCMP office. Her exaggerated animosity towards Greg. Lori flirted with every man as if it were second nature to her. It must have been hard for her to rein in her tendencies around Greg. And I had foolishly been relieved—even pleased—when Greg seemed immune to her charms.

There was no doubt in my mind they were continuing a relationship that nobody in this gossipy town knew about. And Todd was Greg's son. I felt dizzy and nauseous. I wasn't sure how Greg and Lori had managed to murder Bill, but I was certain they had.

I knew then that I was in danger. Very real and probably immediate danger. I didn't want to go up on any bluff with Greg. He hadn't forgotten me. He knew exactly who I was—and he knew I was the only person who could blow their story.

"You know, Greg"—my voice sounded strange even to me—"I really don't think it was a spotted owl that you saw. It couldn't have been, not with a horned owl so close by. I don't think there's any point in going up, and it looks sort of unstable."

Greg looked at me, his dark eyes unreadable. "There're pellets and a few feathers up there. Didn't you tell me you could identify an owl based on pellets and feathers? Come on, we should at least have a look. The bluff isn't that bad. I was up there myself the other day, and I weigh a lot more than you do."

I cursed inwardly. For the moment, I couldn't see my way out of this mess. Flight was out of the question. With his long legs, Greg could easily outrun me. And besides, he had the car keys.

As long as I could keep my feelings from showing on my face, I should be okay. After all, I tried to reassure myself, Jaime and Kelt knew I'd come out with Greg, and they knew where we were. Greg could hardly stab *me* with a tree spike. Somehow I didn't feel much better.

We slipped and scrambled up the rocky bluff. I tried not to look at Greg, afraid fear might show in my eyes. When I got to the top, Greg was already hunkered down at the base of the old tree.

"Look; here they are!"

I peered cautiously to where he pointed, careful to stay well away from the bluff's crumbly edge.

Surprisingly, I did see whitewash dripped down the twisted trunk. A lot of whitewash. Some kind of owl was roosting here. "I don't see any pellets," I said, crouching down beside him to look more closely.

Suddenly Greg shot to his feet. "For a field biologist," he snarled, "you sure don't see much."

Out of the corner of my eye, I saw his right arm coming up fast. Very fast. Too late, I tried to fall back, but he caught me off balance and grabbed my arm savagely. I could hear the fabric of my parka tear. Propelled by the vicious shove, I went sailing over the edge of the bluff.

CHAPTER 32

In retrospect, I suppose I should have been thankful I didn't hit my head on a rock. I tried telling that to my right leg. I heard it snap as I hit the ground. Actually I think I heard several snaps. Strangely enough, I felt no pain, but when I managed to lift my head, I could see my leg sticking out at an impossible angle. I closed my eyes and fought down a green wave of nausea.

My eyes flew open as a shower of pebbles and dirt skittered down the incline. Greg! I squinted up at the top of the bluff. The old pine tree's roots twisted out of the ground like the graboids in *Tremors*. I chuckled hysterically at the thought before clamping my mouth shut. No sign of Greg up there. He was on his way down.

Frantic, I tried to move. To somehow get up on my feet. I knew I couldn't outrun him, but maybe I could hide in the bush. I got my hands under my shoulder and tried to prop myself up. Big mistake. Agony lanced up my left arm and I collapsed with a cry. I felt a gush of warmth on my leg, and I twisted around to see my blood slowly staining the snow a deep crimson red.

And then he was there.

I looked up at him, this man I had once found attractive, and wondered how I could have been so blind.

Despite their warm color, his brown eyes were cold and flinty. His expression showed surprise that I was still alive, and then cruel amusement at my pain.

"Why?" I managed to croak.

He snorted. "Surely you can't be *that* stupid?" he drawled, his voice oozing sarcasm. "You finally recognized me though, didn't you? Stupid bitch!" He kicked me viciously in the side and I bit my tongue to keep from crying out. "I couldn't believe it when you showed up here! I saw your car that night, you know."

"My . . . car?"

"Yes, out by the lumber mill sign. On Thursday night. You gave me quite a scare." He aimed another kick at my ribs. "It had been so easy up until then. Getting Bill out in the forest, and then finding those spikes in his truck. Quite a stroke of luck, that."

"Spikes?"

"Oh yes; you see, Bill had found a bag of tree spikes—courtesy of that environmental group, no doubt. Instead of turning them in, he was carrying them around in his truck." Greg shook his head. "Poor old Bill, always spoiling for a fight. I guess he was going to confront the tree-huggers. It was easy enough to palm one of the spikes. I'd brought a knife, but a tree spike was so much more appropriate. Untraceable, except to the environmentalists—and they were already causing problems. If anyone happened to find Bill's body, the blame would be placed squarely on them." His mouth curved up in a self-satisfied smile.

I had to keep Greg talking. It didn't seem like it would be much of a problem. But under my stomach, just beside my right arm, I could feel a rock.

It wasn't a huge rock, but it would fit in my hand and

it had a satisfyingly sharp edge. The only problem was, half of it was stuck in the ice. There was a bit of give; the impact of my fall had probably loosened it.

"But why?" I asked hoarsely. "Why your own *brother?*"

"My brother!" He spat out the words. "My brother who invested his inheritance and made a small fortune. Oh, I invested mine too, but *my* investments went bad while my idiot brother made a killing. Kept bragging about his 'flair for numbers'! I lost everything I owned and then some, and all my dear brother did was lecture me about smart investing. Refused to give me a dime. He said I'd never learn anything if he bailed me out all the time. He loved lording it over me, I could see that. He left me with nothing."

"You killed him over *money?*" I choked.

"Oh no, not just money. He left me with nothing and then he took Lori." Greg's features twisted into ugly fury at the memory. "Lori and I were together the whole time I was in university. But when she got pregnant, she wanted to get married. I didn't have a cent to my name, and I sure wasn't ready to be saddled with a wife and kid. Next thing I knew, Bill had muscled in. He didn't know she was already pregnant. Oh, I didn't blame Lori one bit. She's the kind of woman who needs a man around. No, I didn't blame her, but Bill, he was a *different* matter."

My fingers were growing numb trying to pry the rock from its icy resting place. How deeply was it buried, anyway? I needed more time. Desperately I searched my mind for another question to ask Greg.

"So you kept seeing Lori?"

"Oh no, I stayed well away from Marten Valley. But about a year ago Lori came to see me in Victoria. She was bored with Bill, and bored with Marten Valley. She knew she'd made a mistake in marrying him. Ha! I could have told her that."

"So you took up where you left off," I rasped.

Greg's brow furrowed slightly. "Of course."

"Why not just leave?" I gasped, tears of frustration filling my eyes. This rock wasn't budging for me. "Why bother killing him?"

Greg shrugged disdainfully. "No choice. Turns out he had a little number on the side, and *she'd* been trying to get pregnant. Unknown to him, of course. What an idiot! Couldn't even keep a mistress properly. He found out she hadn't been using birth control and hadn't been getting pregnant either. And it wasn't because anything was wrong with her!"

"Bill was sterile?"

Greg laughed. "Ha! I always thought he was a bit of a mule; I didn't know how right I was. Found out he was completely sterile. No chance of fathering a kid. I guess *that* was a bit of a shock! He had a big blowup with Lori—threatened to leave her and Todd and cut them off without a cent. All those years for nothing? I don't think so. She called me right away. So did he, for that matter."

"So you decided to kill him."

He crouched down beside me and smiled. "Ten points for the lady on the ground! I told Bill I'd be there as soon as possible, and not to do anything drastic before I got there." He snickered. "And when I arrived, I suggested we go for a little walk in the forest to clear our heads."

"But why would Bill listen to anything you said?" I asked. My voice was starting to fade, stretched to the breaking point from shock and strain. "Jaime said you hadn't been close in years."

Greg waved that off. "Blood's thicker than water, you

know. And Bill was under the impression I hated his wife. Who better to discuss the situation with than me?" He laughed unpleasantly. "He was never exactly big on brains."

There! I felt the stone move. It was definitely loose. I just needed a little more time. "What about Lem?" I managed to croak. "Did you kill him too?"

Greg's eyes clouded for a moment. "That was lucky," he mused. "I had no idea Lem had seen anything. It was pure chance I met him outside the bar the other night. He was pissed to the gills, kept muttering on about how 'you just can't keep information to yourself' and how 'Alex needed to know.' I had to do something. It was just lucky I got to him before he had a chance to squeal."

"And . . . me?"

Greg gazed at me and reached out to caress my cheek. I cringed away. "You? Ah, well. I certainly wasn't expecting you. You gave poor Lori quite a turn, showing up like that."

"But I didn't recognize you until now," I said, my ruined voice tight with tension and pain. My left arm was a throbbing mass of agony, but the rock was free now and firmly in my right hand. I just needed Greg to come a little closer.

He shook his head and smiled at me pityingly. "No, you didn't, did you? I might have been tempted to leave you alone if it hadn't been for that newscast the other night."

"Newscast?"

"Yes, the one about the dead owl on your car—I really must find a way to thank whoever did that. You see, I saw your car on the road the night I killed Bill. You drove off just as I was coming out of the forest. Except, of course,

I had no idea who was in the car. At least not until I saw it on the news. I couldn't take the chance. I'm sure you understand."

As he reached out again to touch my cheek, I seized the opening. Rolling over with the sharp rock clenched firmly in my hand, I swung my arm wildly towards his face.

It was a pitiful effort. Shock and blood loss had taken their toll. I was as weak as a newly hatched gosling. Greg fell back, catching only a glancing blow to his temple. His eyes went flat in fury. With a snarl, he grabbed me by my parka and flipped me over. I didn't even see his fist coming. There was a bright flash, then blackness.

The world swam back into focus. I was aware of a bright blue blur that slowly resolved itself into a clear winter sky. I was lying on my back. I could see the tree perched on top of the bluff above me. As I gazed up, I realized that what I had mistaken for a thick tangle of branches was actually a great horned owl's nest. I could see the female peering over the mass of branches and twigs. It was a peaceful view. An owl brooding her eggs on a fine winter's day. My mind twitched sluggishly. There was something wrong about this day, though, something ...

As I struggled to gather my shattered thoughts, Greg's face moved into my field of vision. Greg. Of course.

He was standing on top of the bluff, his hands resting on his hips. "Quite a tragedy," he called down derisively. "An unstable bluff, an overly eager field biologist—I'm sure you can fill in the scenario. Accidents do happen, you know. I will, of course, do my utmost to 'save' you— dragging you to the car, and bringing your battered body back into town. I'll be a goddamn hero. But I'm afraid it will be too late." He shook his head in mock sorrow. "Much too late."

He started to kick at the ground, right beside the old tree's roots. Dirt, snow, and pebbles showered down on me as the bluff began to crumble. I was paralyzed with fear and shock, unable even to raise my hands to protect my face. A few more kicks like that and the big rocks would start falling.

Greg braced himself against the old tree and began kicking in earnest. With each kick, the tree shuddered. I could see the owl clearly now, ear tufts raised in alarm, eyes flashing golden fire. Then from the right, a streak of soft gray shot out. Her mate!

Greg screamed as the owl's razor-sharp talons raked across his unprotected face—a scream that turned into an insane shriek. In horror, I watched blood and fluid spurt out from Greg's right eye. He threw his hands up to protect his face and staggered back from the onslaught—right over the edge of the bluff. He landed to my left with a sickening crunch and lay still.

I watched, unable to move, as his life's blood soaked slowly into the snow.

We lay there together for a while on the ice, three yards and the spark of life separating us. Eventually the owls calmed down, the female hunkering again over her eggs, her mate perched protectively on a nearby branch. I'm not sure how long I lay there before I managed to coax my body into action.

I rolled over slowly, carefully, and began pulling myself across the ice-covered pond. Thankfully I felt no pain. Just an odd sort of detachment. I concentrated on movement. Pushing up with one leg, pulling my body a little further with an arm. My left arm and right leg were dead weight.

Push, pull, push, pull. I was caught in the rhythm of it. Push forward, reach up, pull. Push forward, reach up, pull. I didn't know anymore where I was going. It didn't matter. Push, pull, push, pull.

Kelt found me at the entrance to the clearing.

CHAPTER 33

"I taped Bill's murder!?"

I was lying in a hospital bed in Quesnel. I felt like ten thousand rat turds all rolled into one. My right leg had been so badly broken, they'd had to put five metal pins in it to hold everything in place. I would walk with a limp for the rest of my life.

"But just think, you'll drive them crazy at airport security," the young intern had said with a comforting grin. I thought his bedside manner needed work.

My left arm was in a cast, broken in three different places (no pins needed), I had a hairline fracture on my jaw, and along with assorted bruises and cuts, I sported a shiner that would make a bar brawler proud. Kelt and Jaime sat on either side of me, holding my hands.

"Right where the spotted owl call was supposed to be," Kelt told me. "Jaime and I were talking about owls. He was trying to figure out if he'd ever heard a spotted owl call, so we snagged the tape from the back seat of your car to listen to it on our way to Quesnel. Turned out to be a different tape from the one you and I had been playing. You must've hit record that night instead of play."

"I did!" I remembered now. "When I put the deck

down on the stump. . . . But . . . I taped Bill's murder!?" I still couldn't get my mind around the idea.

Jaime and Kelt exchanged glances.

"Afraid so," Jaime said. "It's kinda faint, but if you jack up the volume you can hear shoutin' and yellin' and then a godawful scream."

"But . . . did you recognize Greg's voice?"

Jaime shook his head. "Nah, not really. Sound's all muffled."

"Then how. . . ?"

Kelt broke in. "At one point in the tape, Bill shouted Greg's name. Then he screamed."

I closed my eyes and sighed. To be betrayed like that, by your own brother. It was still hard to believe. I had spoken to both Jack and Neil on the phone this morning. I'd expected Jack's concern, but Neil's distress surprised and touched me. Perhaps there was hope for us after all. I thought again about Bill and Greg. I would make sure there was hope.

"As soon as we heard the tape, we turned around and broke every speeding limit in the province," Kelt continued. "Jaime told me how to get to the swimming hole, so I left him and the tape at the RCMP station and headed out to find you."

Hovering on the verge of tears, I smiled up at them both. "Thanks, guys. I owe you."

Kelt squeezed my hand. One of my most cherished memories in all this was the sight of Kelt when he'd found me bleeding on the snow. Tears flooding his eyes (I must have looked horrible!) he'd scooped me up as if I were a feather and clutched me tightly to his chest, the whole while berating me for my stupidity. I think I fainted when he lifted me up. I certainly don't remember much of the hike back to the road. Just a pervasive feeling of warmth and security and a gentle hand smoothing my hair away from my battered face.

I cleared my throat noisily.

"How did Greg do it?" I asked. "I mean, how did he get here without anybody knowing? Was he hiding in town?"

"Not likely," Jaime snorted. "Everybody would have known about that. No, I guess he flew Downtown early in the mornin' and drove up in some rental car. He used a false name, of course, but the young gal at the rental place had no trouble identifyin' him from his picture. Guess all that testosterone and charm of his finally caught up with him." Jaime laughed sourly.

"Not only that," Kelt added. "It turns out that Greg wasn't the hotshot architect everybody thought he was. He's been let go from three different firms in the last two years. Word is, he is—or was—technically good, but his design skills were mediocre, and his personality was more appropriate for a prima donna. He wasn't doing well at all. Maybe that's what tipped him over the edge." He stopped, suddenly aware of what he'd said. "Uh, so to speak, that is."

"The funeral's on Wednesday," Jaime said. "I guess they want to get him in the ground as soon as possible. I don't figure many folks'll be at it, but it's hard to say. Greg was real popular before all this. Most people are still kinda shocked."

"And what's happening to Lori?" I asked.

Jaime's eyes darkened in anger. "She's claimin' ignorance. Seems she admits to havin' the affair but says she figured the environmentalists were the ones that killed her husband. Exceptin' what Greg said to you, they really don't have anythin' to nail on her. And you were in shock, of course, so how could you recall anythin' accurately? Accordin' to Lori, you understand."

"Besides, she's got the distraught mother and wife act down perfectly," Kelt said cynically. "She'll get off, you'll see."

So once again, Lori lands on her feet. I sighed bitterly.

"The worst thing about this whole business is Lem," Jaime said in an odd tone.

"How do you mean?"

"You know they found his coat?"

I nodded.

"Well, they went and tested the blood on it. Seems it was his own. Lem musta fallen and given himself one hell of a nosebleed." Jaime dropped his head miserably. "He never had anythin' to do with the murder at all. If it hadn't have been for my damn suspicions, he would never have been talkin' like that in front of Greg. He'd still be alive."

Now it was my turn to hold his hand. "You couldn't have known, Jaime," I told him softly.

He just looked at his hands, his mouth trembling. I didn't know what to say. By trying to help Lem, Jaime had unknowingly sentenced him to death. It would be a long time before he got over his guilt. If he ever did.

"Hey, I bet the Marten Valley hotline is in overdrive," I said with forced cheerfulness.

Jaime nodded slightly, acknowledging my attempt at humor. "Oh yeah," he told me with a crooked smile. "Halmar's coming to see you tomorrow and Ella's waitin' on us downstairs right now. You're only allowed two visitors at a time."

"Ella came all the way here?" I was touched.

"Not only that," Kelt said, his eyes dancing. "She brought you an entire pie, fresh from Irene's oven."

"Pie? I've been trying to choke down hospital food, and she brought pie?"

"Better than owl barf." Kelt nudged me meaningfully.

I poked him back. "Show her in at once," I demanded.

EPILOGUE

We had agonized over what to do with the evidence we'd stolen from Seidlin's filing cabinets. It was now (painfully) clear the company had had nothing to do with murder, but their industry violations were still criminal. On the other hand, so was our method of obtaining the information. It posed something of a dilemma. Surprisingly, it was my lawyer friend Megan who finally suggested a course of action.

The morning we left Marten Valley, Kelt and I were treated once more to Jaime's famous Italian omelet. We ate, slurped down several cups of coffee, and said fond goodbyes to Jaime, Ella, Nat, and Halmar before heading out of town, stopping only once in front of Nature Defence's old VW van.

Bonnie and a few of the ND bunch were standing around beside the vehicle. The dark-haired woman that I'd seen Jurgen with the other day stood off to one side, deep in conversation with a wiry, gray-bearded man. Jurgen trotted towards the car as we pulled up. I'd arranged last night for him to meet us here.

His eyes widened as he took in my appearance. "Holy shit!" he swore. "Are you okay?"

"I'll live."

"Looks like you'll be benched for a while."

I tweaked one corner of my mouth up in a half-smile. "Yeah, the fight's all yours now. Here." I held out the manila envelope. Jurgen reached out to take it, but I didn't release my hold right away.

"You know, Jurgen, Bonnie's a good lady. She deserves the best." Better than you, I thought. I aimed a significant look at the dark-haired woman.

Jurgen followed my stare and swallowed.

"You should take better care of her," I said, turning my gaze back at him and holding his eyes for a long moment.

As the look lengthened, Jurgen flushed. He nodded tightly and I let go my hold on the envelope. It was all I could do.

I hadn't told Jurgen what was in the envelope, but I felt confident he would know what to do with the photocopies and computer printouts. I rather suspected my good pal Gus was in for a bad time.

We arrived back in Calgary the day Seidlin Lumber announced the cessation of all clear-cutting and the establishment of spotted owl reserves in the Marten Valley TSA. It hadn't even gone to court.

I had a hunch their announcement had more to do with recent media attention than any threat by the BCWA, but whatever their reasons may have been, it was the result that was most important. Already other surveys were being planned. In a way, I wished I could help, but with this damn leg, I'd be laid up for a long time.

Now, I felt only relief to be back home in Calgary. I'd talked to Jack last night. He had taken time off work and would be at my apartment now, ready to wait on me hand and foot (left hand and right foot, that is). Megan was planning on coming over as soon as I got in. Jack had also informed me that Guido the cat, irritated at my prolonged absence, had systematically and thoroughly destroyed all my plants. In a twisted sort of way, it was nice to know there were, at least, some constants in my life.

Kelt had been so solicitous in his care of me since my release from the hospital that I had made Kaye promise to leave certain parts of his anatomy intact and off her bookshelves. Even as I hobbled up to my apartment building, he hovered anxiously, ready to lend a helping hand or a supportive shoulder.

Jack flung open the door and enveloped me in a bearhug. "Turd!" he crowed happily. "Thank god you're home!"

"Hey, Jack!" I hugged him in return. Over his shoulder I could see Guido the cat. His ears were flattened back as he stared fixedly at a point just above my head. With a disdainful flick of his stripy tail, he turned his back on me and stalked down the hall. He looked so put out, I would have been concerned if I hadn't caught his brief backward glance making sure I was aware of (and presumably suffering under) his disapproval. With a bit of catnip and some canned tuna, he'd come around in a week or so.

Jack bustled around hanging up my coat and taking my duffel bag and knapsack from Kelt.

"Kelt! It's great to meet you finally. Why don't you come in? I can put some coffee on."

Kelt shook Jack's hand warmly. "Thanks, but it's been a long day. I think I'll just head home." He turned to me and grinned crookedly. "Take care, Robyn."

I smiled back. "I will, Kelt. Thanks for everything."

He hesitated at the door for a moment. "You want to go for coffee sometime?" he asked finally.

I stared at him. We'd been through life and death together, and all I got was a coffee date!? This went beyond owl barf! I looked at his friendly grin, so warm and open. His raven hair was slightly tangled from the wind. Sea-green eyes regarded me, awaiting my answer. Oh well. I returned his smile. At least it was a start.

Polar Circus
D.A. Barry

An edge-of-your-seat thriller featuring bickering environ-mentalists, isolated in the Arctic wilderness, who find themselves surrounded by polar bears—and the bears look hungry . . .
0-88801-253-5/pb $14.95 Cdn./$12.95 U.S.

Sticks and Stones:
A Randy Craig Mystery
Janice MacDonald

The University of Alberta's English Department is caught up in a maelstrom of poison-pen letters, graffiti and misogyny. Miranda Craig seems to be both target and investigator.
0-88801-256-X/pb $14.95 Cdn./$12.95 U.S.

Where Shadows Burn
Catherine Hunter

Kelly, a young costume designer, is struggling to put her life together after the recent suicide of her husband. After a series of disturbing phone calls, as well as more unearthly dangers, she finds herself on the lam with her young nephew, looking over her shoulder and wondering if the danger she faces comes from the living . . . or the dead. 0-88801-231-4/pb $16.95 Cdn./$14.95 U.S.

Dying by Degrees:
An Emily Goodstriker Mystery
Eileen Coughlan

Psychology grad student Emily Goodstriker quickly becomes uneasy with her maniacal professor's experiments. Could a rash of student suicides somehow be connected to the Psych department's extracurricular activity? 0-88801-247-0/pb $14.95 Cdn./$12.95 U.S.

Chronicles of the Lost Years:
A Sherlock Holmes Mystery
Tracy Cooper-Posey

Cooper-Posey picks up where Sir Arthur Conan Doyle left off. *Chronicles of the Lost Years* is the "real" story of Holmes' adventures in the Middle East and Asia during the three years Watson believed him dead—commonly referred to as the Great Hiatus.

0-88801-241-1/pb $16.95 Cdn./$14.95 U.S.

The Case of the Reluctant Agent:
A Sherlock Holmes Mystery
Tracy Cooper-Posey

When Sherlock Holmes' brother, Mycroft, is shot and left for dead, Sherlock is forced to go to Constantinople to uncover the man behind the deed.

0-88801-263-2/pb $14.95 Cdn./$12.95 U.S.

RaveN
STONE

Available at your local bookstore.
www.ravenstonebooks.com

ABOUT THE AUTHOR

Karen Dudley's checkered past includes field biology, production art, photo research, paleo-environmental studies, editing and archeology. Then, a few years ago, she finally realized that what she really wanted to do was ... everything (except maybe game-show hosting). And if you want to do (almost) everything, the best way to do it is to be a writer.

But what to write? She tried to pen a short story, toyed with the idea of science fiction, but ultimately settled on mystery—mostly for the satisfaction of 'bumping off' people who irritate her in real life. Unfailingly cheerful and amiable, she has been known to cackle gleefully while writing.

Karen lives in Winnipeg with her husband and four very nice but occasionally evil-minded cats. She has written three mysteries and a short stack of wildlife biology books, and shows no signs of slowing down. Given the number of irritating personalities in the world, it is safe to say that she will be writing for quite some time.